THE ANGEL

ALSO BY MARK DAWSON

In the Soho Noir Series

Gaslight

The Black Mile

The Imposter

In the John Milton Series

One Thousand Yards

The Cleaner

Saint Death

The Driver

Ghosts

The Sword of God

Salvation Row

In the Beatrix Rose Series

In Cold Blood

Blood Moon Rising

Blood and Roses

Hong Kong Stories Vol. 1

White Devil

Nine Dragons

Dragon Head

Standalone Novels

The Art of Falling Apart

Subpoena Colada

MARK **DAWSON**

THE ANGEL

AN ISABELLA ROSE THRILLER

Published by Thomas & Mercer, Seattle

www.apub.com

ISBN-13: 978-1503947832
ISBN-10: 1503947831

Cover design by Lisa Horton

Printed in the United States of America

To Mrs D, FD, SD and JD

PART ONE

Chapter One

In the year before she died, Beatrix Rose taught her daughter many things. She taught her how to lie and how to tell when someone else was lying. The benefits of meditation and how it was a useful strategy for enduring long stretches of time without sleep or other comforts. How to detect when she was being followed and how to follow someone without being seen.

She taught her other things, too. For example, how important it was to always arrive first for a rendezvous. It was good manners, for one, but – and this was much more important – the person arriving first for an appointment could control how that appointment unfolded. She could choose the environment: a table where it would be difficult to be eavesdropped on, the seat offering the best view of the ways in and out. An agent did not want the seat that put her back to the door. She certainly did not want to be the person arriving last. It was rude, and most important, it decreased your chances of leaving.

Control had contacted her a week ago to propose that they meet. He had suggested that he come to Marrakech, but Isabella had declined. Far better for her to go to him.

She had arrived in London two days before the appointed time and had selected this location yesterday. She had scouted up and down the river until she found a spot she liked. She started at the huge wheel of the London Eye, continued past the twin pedestrian bridges that led across the water to Charing Cross station and headed north into the artistic quarter. There was the National Festival Hall, together with the chain restaurants that had been attracted to the area like parasites to a host. Farther along the promenade was the Queen Elizabeth Hall and the undercroft famed for the skaters and BMXers who gathered there, every spare square inch of wall covered in colourful graffiti. Isabella had walked on, past the painted mime who was entertaining a group of schoolchildren perched atop a box. She had eventually settled on the café that was connected to the National Film Theatre. It offered wide windows with good visibility up and down the river path. There was a double flight of stairs leading up to Waterloo Bridge at the side of the building. If she needed to get away quickly, that would be the route she would choose.

Isabella reached the coffee shop with thirty minutes to spare. It was quiet this morning, and she was able to take a seat at the back of the room. The only luggage that she had brought with her was the leather satchel that she had bought from a trader in the souk. He had looked at her with hungry eyes, no doubt seeing an easy sale at an inflated price. She had disabused him of that notion very quickly. In the end, they had agreed on a fair price. The bag was new, but she had deliberately scuffed it so that it looked older. She didn't want anything at all to attract attention to her.

The doors were wide open, and sounds from the outside drifted in. The café was partially beneath the grey concrete vault of the bridge, and the second-hand booksellers who had gathered here for decades were loudly discussing last night's football as they set up their tables. A busker dressed in a sequinned jacket was serenading the joggers and pedestrians who sauntered past.

It was just after eight-thirty when she saw Control. He stopped at the door, his eyes adjusting to the gloom after the brightness of the morning. He saw her, smiled and crossed the room.

'Hello, Isabella.'

'Captain Pope.'

'It's Michael,' he said. 'Please. No formalities. Would you like something to eat? Breakfast?'

'I'm fine.'

'Coffee?'

'I'm fine, thank you.'

'I'm just going to get myself one. You sure?'

She said that she would have an orange juice. He nodded his satisfaction and went to the bar.

The sight of him brought back memories of the American hospital and the man who had ripped her family apart when she was just a little girl. She had killed him when her mother could not, and Pope had driven her away as the police swarmed into the area. He had promised to get her out of the country, and he had been true to his word. He had driven them west to Charlotte and Douglas International Airport. They had taken a domestic flight to Atlanta and then flown from there, direct, to Paris.

She remembered how Pope had been uncomfortable when she had thanked him for his help and made it obvious that she didn't need any more from him. She could tell that he was reluctant to let her go, but there was little that he could do about it. She had an excellent fake passport, and she had the money to buy a Royal Air Maroc ticket to Marrakech. She knew, too, that he had no idea what he would have done with her if he took her back to London. He had very few options, and eventually, she had persuaded him that the best one was to leave her to get on with her life.

He had compromised, writing his telephone number on the back of a magazine and telling her that if she ever needed him, then all she had to do was call. She had torn the page out, folded it and slipped it into her pocket. She still had it in a drawer in the kitchen at home, but it had never even been unfolded.

And then an email had found its way to her Gmail account. She had no idea how he had found the address. Isabella had treated that as a salutary lesson. She had considered herself well hidden, and the fact that he had discovered her online had pulled her up short. She had determined that she would do better.

Pope returned with a cappuccino and a glass of freshly squeezed juice. He lowered himself into the spare chair and passed the glass across the table to her.

'Thank you for coming.'

She nodded.

'I would have been happy to have gone to you.'

'No, that's all right.'

'Still being careful?'

She gave a little shrug.

'Sitting with your back to the wall, too.'

'I like looking out at the river.'

He smiled. 'Your mother taught you well.'

The mention of her mother made Isabella tense. She still missed her. She missed her every day. She still had nightmares of watching the news bulletin with footage of the burning car, the remains of the bomb that had obliterated her.

Pope could see that she was pensive; he was trying to ease her into the conversation. 'How have you been?'

'I'm all right.'

'What have you been doing?'

She shrugged. She could have told him about her course of self-improvement, about her fluency in Arabic and French. She could have told him about how she was so fit that she had finished the International de Marrakech 10k in forty minutes with another five minutes still in the tank. She could have told him about the weekly mixed martial arts lessons she took in a dojo on the edge of town. She didn't, though. She just shrugged, said, 'This and that,' and then, when he paused, 'How can I help you, Mr Pope?'

'I'm not here because I need your help. I have something for you.'

He reached into his pocket and took out a small envelope. It had been folded over on itself and sealed with a piece of tape. He slid it across the table and withdrew his hand.

'What is it?'

'It's something from your mother.'

She felt a tremble of emotion, and her lip quivered a little before she mastered it. She reached down for the envelope, dabbing her fingertips against it, running her index finger along the edge to the sharp point. She peeled the tape back, unfolded the envelope and then tore it open at one end. She saw a glint of silver and knew, for certain, what it was.

She blinked away tears.

'Isabella—'

'I'm fine,' she said, scowling the tears away.

She tipped the contents of the envelope onto the table. It was a sterling silver locket. The twenty-four-inch-long chain was comprised of alternating circular and rectangular silver links, and the locket itself was of an ornate design, shaped like a heart with a daisy design on the face. Her eyes were damp and her throat felt constricted as she reached down for it. She opened it. There was a picture of her as a baby. She was small and chubby, with ringlets of blonde hair.

She closed the locket and hid it in her fist.

'The Americans found it,' Pope explained. 'Your mother was wearing it when . . . well, when it happened. It was dirty. I had it cleaned.'

'They kept it all this time?'

'It's evidence, Isabella. The police know that others were involved in what happened. They've been trying to put together as much information as they can about your mother. Of course, they don't know that it's you in the locket, but if they did, they would be very interested in talking to you. And it's not just them. There are other people in America who would really like to know who you are. The people your mother went after, for example.'

She collected the chain and dropped it into her fist with the locket.

'I only recently found out that they had it. I have a contact in Washington who was able to get it for me. I thought you'd want to have it.'

She waited a moment until her throat felt less constricted. 'Thank you,' she said. 'I do.'

She stood.

Pope looked as if she had taken him by surprise. He stood, too.

'Are you okay?'

'I'm fine,' she said. 'Thank you for finding this for me. I'm very grateful.'

'Are you staying in London for long?'

'No.'

'You're still in Marrakech?'

'That's right.'

She suddenly realised that she had to leave. She barely managed to choke down a sob, and although she managed it, she knew that it was obvious that she was upset. She hated to show weakness. Her mother had drilled that into her, too. She was barely managing to maintain her composure, and she knew that she needed to get away from him and get outside.

He was standing in her way. 'When are you leaving?'

'Today.'

'Would you like to have something to eat with me later?'

'No,' she said, adding a 'thank you' when she realised that she must have been coming across as a rude and ungrateful brat. 'My flight's already booked. I have to leave for the airport this morning or I'll miss it. I'm sorry.'

He was still standing in her way. He put out a hand and she took it. His grip was firm and his palm was warm. She wondered, just for a moment, whether she could stay a little. There was no reason for her to rush; there was nothing waiting for her at home. And Pope had looked out for her. He had taken a huge risk to save her life in America, and now there was this . . . She wavered, just for a moment, until she remembered her mother's stern words.

'You don't need anyone else. 'The only person you can trust is yourself.'

Her resolution returned. She released his hand and waited for him to step aside.

'It was good to see you, Isabella. Remember what I said before. If you ever need me, you know where I am.'

'Thank you.'

She found a smile and managed to hold the tears back until she was out the door and into the brightness of the morning beyond. She could smell the musty pages of the second-hand books and the freshness of the wind as it whipped in from the water. Her eyes welled up, and then the tears overflowed and spilled across her cheeks. She felt the locket inside her fist, the silver warmed by her skin. She sobbed aloud, turned to the left and then again to the left, and ran up the steps to the bridge above.

Isabella might have been older than she looked, but she was still just fifteen years old. And she wanted to get home.

Chapter Two

The door to Aamir Malik's bedroom had always opened with an annoying creak. It had landed him in trouble before, usually when he returned home after his curfew and tried to sneak into his bedroom, only to find that his parents had been awoken. He had tried to oil it after one particularly annoying grounding so that it wouldn't happen again, but it had never made very much of a difference. The mechanism seemed to soak up the WD-40 that he sprayed onto it, but just kept creaking.

He couldn't afford for it to be a problem today. He pulled it as carefully as he could, managing, for once, to keep the resultant noise to a minimum. He had set his alarm for five, three hours earlier than he would normally have arisen, and he didn't want to disturb anyone else in the house. His parents were in the bedroom to the left, and his two brothers were in the room directly opposite, across the hall. He could hear his father's snoring and the soft breathing of his twin, Aqil. His older brother, Yasin, sometimes got up early to play *World of Warcraft*, but he was asleep today. That was good. There was a loose floorboard on the landing, and he avoided it, stopping in the bathroom to quickly brush his teeth and splash a little cold water on his face.

His mother and father would not usually have awoken for another hour and a half themselves. His mother was an invalid, confined to a wheelchair after the local hospital had botched the birth of Aamir's sister ten years earlier. His mother had suffered serious brain damage. The local boys called her a vegetable, and Aamir's father had quit work so that he could care for her. There had been a large compensation payout, but that wasn't really the point. The money had been exhausted with the modifications they had made to the house, and then there was the ongoing cost of care when his father needed assistance. No, he thought, the money was beside the point. Their lives had been ruined. Aamir had never really gotten over it. None of them had.

He smoothed back his hair, set it with gel and then went back into his room to dress. Hakeem had taken him to Gap and bought him the clothes that he wanted him to wear. He took off his pyjamas and dressed in the black jeans and black T-shirt, liking the smell and the feel of the fresh cotton as he pulled it over his head.

He opened the curtains and looked out of the window onto the street beyond. He lived in Moss Side, a rundown area of Manchester. Before his mother's accident, his father had owned a fish and chip shop and had been a respected figure in the local community. Aamir could see the shop at the corner of the street and, beyond it, the recreation field where he and Aqil played cricket and football in the summer. Beyond that, just visible through the green foliage of the trees, was the dome of the mosque where he had been spending so much time lately. He gazed at these three personal landmarks – from the chip shop to the park, to the mosque – and then at the other terraced houses on the street, all so familiar to him, and he wondered, for the first time today, whether what he was doing was the right thing.

And then he thought of his mother and what the imam had said about that, and he knew that it was.

He was still gazing out of the window when he saw the black BMW roll down the street and pull over next to the front gate. The glass was tinted, but the driver's side window was rolled down, and he saw Hakeem looking out. His friend looked up at him in the window, smiled, then raised his arm and tapped a finger against his watch. Aamir nodded in return, pulled the curtains and looked around his bedroom for the last time. He saw the Playstation 4 he had saved so long to buy, the games scattered across the floor, the posters that he had stuck to the wall with Blu Tack. He felt another moment of reluctance before he remembered that Hakeem was waiting for him, and dismissed it. He had made a promise to him, and he couldn't let him down.

He crept through the door, stepped over the creaking floorboard and made his way down the stairs. Hakeem had said they would get some breakfast on the way. He took his coat from where he had slung it over the banister, unlocked the door and stepped outside. It was a clear day with an icy-blue sky.

The engine of the BMW was still running. 'All right, bruv?' Hakeem said quietly through the open window as Aamir closed the gate and crossed the pavement.

Aamir nodded.

'In you get, then. We're running a little late.'

Aamir opened the rear door and slid inside the car. Bashir was in the passenger seat. He had a black beanie on his head. He turned and smiled as Aamir settled himself in the back. 'All right?' he asked.

Aamir nodded.

It was a cold morning, and Hakeem had the heater running on full blast. He put the car into first gear and pulled away. Aamir couldn't help turning around in his seat and looking through the back window as the house slid out of view. He had never lived anywhere else. Nineteen years. It held a lot of memories for him. Some of them bad, but plenty of them were good. He thought of his mum and dad asleep in their bed. Would they be proud of him? Would they understand?

He hoped so.

Thinking about them made him wistful and sad, so he thought about something else.

'Going to be a nice day,' Hakeem said, looking through the front window at the sky. 'Be warm later, that's what they've been saying.'

'Perfect. Lots of people out.'

Aamir felt a shiver of nerves. 'Have you heard from Mohammed?'

Hakeem made an affirmative noise. 'Going to meet us at the station, like he said. Everything is happening like he said it would. Today's the day, bruv. Big day. Everything we've been working for is going to come to pass, if it pleases Allah.'

Chapter Three

The car was second-hand and had a musty smell to it. They had spent a lot of time inside it over the course of the last few months, just driving around the city. Hakeem had explained that it was the safest place to talk. Phones could be bugged, he'd said. The Internet, too – that wasn't safe. Better to do it all face to face, where they could be sure they wouldn't be overheard. Aamir didn't mind. He liked being with Hakeem and Bashir.

The one time he had met Mohammed had been in the back of the car, too. They had told him it would be like an interview. Mohammed was in charge of the operation, and he wanted to make sure that Aamir's faith was strong enough for him to do what he needed to do. The other man, Asif, had been beaten up by a racist gang in Didsbury two weeks ago. His leg had been broken, and Mohammed had decided that there was no way he would be able to take part. They needed a replacement. Hakeem had suggested that Aamir would be perfect. He had been frightened, at first, but then he listened to what Mohammed said to him, and he realised that he had been given a gift. It was an honour to be chosen. He had said yes.

Hakeem navigated carefully through the suburbs of Manchester. Aamir sat quietly in the back, gazing out of the window at streets that became less and less familiar as they drove on. Had the city really been so bad? School had been all right. He had friends here. There was racism, of course, but that was to be expected. There was racism everywhere, and all the young Muslim boys he hung around with had experienced it.

It came in many different forms. The local white boys with their snarling dogs who chased them out of the park. A taxi driver who, it was said, was a member of the EDF and refused to take 'ethnics' in the back of his car. The police, more likely to stop and search brothers like Hakeem because how was a boy like him driving a car like this if he wasn't involved in drugs? They had all experienced it, and Mohammed had used it as another example of why what they were doing was just. But Aamir couldn't forget the white boys in school who had stuck up for him against racist bullies, the owner of the corner shop who had always put a little extra in his bag of sweets, the lollypop lady who had always given him a cheeky wink as he crossed the road under her watch. Mohammed said it was black and white, no room for ambivalence, but Aamir had never really accepted that.

And then Mohammed had brought up what had happened to his mother, and Aamir had allowed himself to be persuaded.

They followed the M56 to the M6, and then drove south to Rugby. They changed to the M1 at Junction 19. It was 49 miles south to Luton.

'You want some music?' Hakeem said as he settled back and accelerated gently up to seventy.

'Sure,' Aamir said.

Bashir took out his phone and plugged it into the car stereo. He scrolled through the memory and found the track he wanted. Aamir recognised the song immediately. It was 'Dawlat al-Islam Qamat.'

He had listened to it a hundred times on YouTube before Hakeem had told him that he needed to be careful with the sites he was visiting. It was a beautiful song. It started out as an Arabic chant, and the singer's voice was so relaxing that it almost sounded like a lullaby. Aamir had studied history at school, and he thought that the song was something that could have been from a thousand years ago. The melody had a gentle swing, nice and easy, and then the voice was copied and layered, one atop the other, almost sounding like a choir. The song became more strident and impactful.

Hakeem started to sing.

Sound effects dropped in. A sword was unsheathed, then there came the stomp of soldiers' feet and, finally, stuttering gunfire. The name of the song, translated, meant 'My Ummah, Dawn Has Appeared.' It was the most popular song in the Islamic State.

It was, Hakeem argued when he played it for the first time, the world's newest national anthem.

Bashir started to sing, too.

Aamir had written the Arabic down and translated the words himself. 'The Islamic State has arisen by the blood of the righteous,' the song said. 'The Islamic State has arisen by the jihad of the pious.'

Hakeem turned and looked into the back. His face was alight with an infectious smile. 'Come on, bruv! Let's have it!'

Aamir smiled, too, and started to sing. Quietly at first and then, as the song built up to its crescendo, louder and louder until the three of them were singing at the top of their lungs. They raced south at seventy miles an hour, passing signs for Stoke-on-Trent and Leicester and Rugby.

They would be in Luton by eight.

Chapter Four

The Firm had buildings across London. Its headquarters in Whitehall was in the Old War Office building. It had been denied the largesse that had been lavished on those buildings nearby that accommodated other governmental departments. It was in an alleyway off Horse Guards Avenue, a backwater that was easily missed and where the men and women who went to work there could be easily forgotten. Each of the ten floors was low ceilinged and dusty, crammed with steel filing cabinets and ancient furniture. The Firm had taken up residence after the war and had never moved. It was a collection of narrow alleyways and corridors, each as anonymous as the next. Its denizens had dubbed it 'the Warren', and the name had stuck.

The waiting room was on the seventh floor. It had a single small window that looked onto a parapet. Beyond the parapet was a narrow street that accommodated government functionaries insufficiently grand to warrant an office on Whitehall itself. There were faded prints on a wall that was painted the same municipal green found in hospitals and town halls. Another wall was shelved, each shelf bearing a row of leather-bound volumes that filled the room with their dusty scent. There were two doors. One led to the lobby, where an old-fashioned lift wheezed and groaned as it carried people up and down between the floors. The other led to the conference room.

Michael Pope looked around. The waiting room was small, and the three men waiting inside it were large. It felt cramped. The atmosphere was tense. It could have been in a doctor's surgery, or the room where the parents of a misbehaving child are summoned to see the headmaster of an exclusive school. Pope tried to maintain his sense of equilibrium. He got up and went to the window. He looked outside, into a bright blue sky, a warm summer's day. The view was restricted, showing just the cold stone flanks of the building opposite.

He returned to his seat.

He was sitting next to Sergeant Thomas Snow and Sergeant Paddy McNair.

Snow was from the 22nd SAS, but he had served in B Squadron before he was moved to the Revolutionary Warfare Ring, an elite cadre of hand-picked SAS operators tasked with supporting Secret Intelligence Service operations. The RWR carried out special operations as directed by the Foreign Office, including bodyguarding and backup for SIS operatives, extraction of SIS personnel and 'black ops', including fomenting unrest and causing uprisings in foreign countries.

Snow was not doing such a good job of hiding his nerves. That was a reasonable reaction to the prospect of the meeting that they were here to attend. Pope didn't know the precise make-up of the panel that had convened to discuss the events at Liverpool Street station last month, but he knew it would include luminaries from the security services, the police and the politicians to whom they answered.

'You all right?' he asked quietly.

'Bit nervous, Control,' Snow replied.

'Nerves are good. Keep you sharp.'

'So I heard.'

Snow was wearing a suit that looked new, and the caps of his shoes had been polished to a high sheen. *Force of habit,* Pope thought. Ten years in the military did that to a man. The soldier had been in the Group for three months. Pope had selected him personally. He selected all the new recruits to the Group himself. The events in Russia, the conclusion of a series of incidents that had been set in motion by the treachery of his predecessor, had led to the deaths of the agents who had needed to be replaced. Snow had been the latest replacement. He was Number Twelve.

'I'm not going to hang you out to dry. I'm on your side.'

'Appreciate that, sir.'

Paddy McNair, on the other hand, was more relaxed. He was in his early forties and had been in the army for most of his adult life. He had been in Group Fifteen for five years. He looked like a soldier, with a solid build and big, weather-beaten hands. His face, too, had been scoured by the elements until the lines had been etched deeply. He was originally from Liverpool, and his broad accent confirmed his nickname, 'Scouse'. Not much flustered McNair, but as he had confided to Pope as they had shared a drink last night, he wasn't looking forward to the carpeting he knew that they were about to receive.

The operation that had led to them being summoned to this office had been Snow's first in the field. He couldn't have wished for a more inauspicious beginning to his new career. One of the watchwords – *the* watchword – of Group Fifteen was secrecy. Operations were supposed to proceed in such a fashion that the agent carried out his or her task without attracting attention. But this operation had led to Snow's image being plastered over the front pages of all the national newspapers. The Ministry of Defence had issued a D Notice requiring all speculation as to his identity to be curtailed, and they had managed to insist that his face be pixelated. But those undoctored images were out there. They would surface, tomorrow or the next day or sometime in the future. That probably meant that Snow's first mission would be his last. McNair and Pope knew that. Snow did, too. He also knew that it would mean a change of identity and a life spent watching his back.

They made up time on the drive south and pulled into the car park of Luton railway station at a little before eight. It was the height of rush hour, and it was almost full, with just a handful of spaces left. Hakeem drove all the way to the far end of the car park. He slid the BMW into the first of two spaces between a Range Rover and an Audi, and turned off the engine. The music died and the car suddenly felt very different. The atmosphere changed and Aamir felt a twist of apprehension in his stomach.

Hakeem turned. 'Everything all right?'

Bashir nodded.

'Aamir?'

'Yeah,' he said. 'I'm cool.'

Bashir looked at his watch. 'We made good time. He'll be here soon.'

Aamir watched as a train left the station and rumbled along the side of the car park, slowly picking up speed. It was packed. He could see passengers standing in the aisles, some of them looking out of the windows with blank expressions on their faces.

'He's here.'

A Mazda slowed and pulled into the space next to them. Aamir looked over and saw Mohammed behind the wheel. He reached down to switch off the engine and got out. He was tall and slender, with a tanned complexion and a growth of clipped stubble on his chin.

He opened the back door and slid in next to Aamir.

'Good morning, brothers. Is everything all right?'

'Yes, Mohammed,' Bashir said. 'We did everything as you said.'

'Very good. This is a wonderful day.' He turned to Aamir. 'Hello, brother. Are you feeling well?'

'Yes,' he said, unable to hide his nerves.

Mohammed had a cruel mouth with thin lips. He had heavy brows and dark eyes. Aamir remembered what it was like to be pinned in his lizard stare.

'You remember what is next?'

'I remember.'

'And you remember why this is necessary?'

'Yes,' he said quietly.

Aamir knew that Mohammed could see he was nervous. 'We have to do this. You understand that, I know. We can talk and talk and talk, but our words have no impact on them. They will keep ignoring us. We are going to talk to them in a language that they will understand. Remember what Muhammad said. "Our words are dead until we give them life with our blood."'

'I know,' he said. 'I remember.'

Mohammed fixed him in his powerful gaze. 'Thousands of people like us are forsaking everything for what they believe. We are not doing it for worldly things, are we? We do not care about that, about them, about the tangible things that this world has to offer. Our religion is Islam, obedience to the one true God, Allah. We follow in the footsteps of the final prophet and messenger Muhammad.'

'Praise be to God,' Bashir intoned.

'I just . . . I just . . .'

'I can see you are nervous. That is all right. I understand. It is normal. But you need to consider why we are doing what we are doing. This country is not our friend, Aamir. The government perpetuates atrocities against our people, and the people's support of it makes them responsible, just as we are directly responsible for protecting and avenging our Muslim brothers and sisters.'

Aamir nodded his head, mumbling his agreement. Bashir and Hakeem nodded more vociferously.

'We have to take the fight to them. Until we feel security, they must be our target. Until they stop the bombing, gassing, imprisonment and torture of our people, we will not stop this fight. We are at war, Aamir, and we are soldiers. And today, Allah willing, the infidels will taste the reality of this situation. They will feel the edge of our blade. You understand me, Aamir? You must tell me you understand.'

Aamir found himself unable to speak.

'He understands,' Hakeem said for him.

'I need to hear it from him.'

Aamir nodded.

'I need you to say it.'

'I understand.'

Mohammed clasped his shoulder and squeezed. 'Good. When you get to London, there will be no time for second thoughts. You want to stop, you just say so now. You can get on a train and be back in Manchester in time for lunch. But I know you will not do that. I know you are a good soldier. I know, when you feel doubt, you think about your mother and what happened to her. You keep that close to your heart, Aamir. That is where your strength comes from. That is where you will find the certainty when you feel doubt.'

Aamir frowned. He hated it when others suggested that he was weak. He wasn't weak. He was just as strong as Hakeem and Bashir. 'I don't feel doubt,' he said. 'I'm not going home. I'm a soldier. I've got a job to do.'

Hakeem grinned at him and held up his hand. Aamir clasped it.

Mohammed nodded his satisfaction. 'If anything happens during the morning that means you are unable to carry out the operation, you must not go home. It will be too dangerous. You must come to me. There is a safe house in London. I will be there. You must come to me, and I will take care of you.'

They said that they understood. Mohammed gave them an address and made them repeat it to him three times. It was a road in Bethnal Green. They satisfied him that they remembered it, and then he led them in prayer. Aamir closed his eyes and intoned the familiar words. The cadence was almost hypnotic, and he felt himself beginning to calm.

When they were finished, Mohammed opened the door. 'I have the bags,' he said. 'They are in the back of my car.'

They went around to the rear of the Mazda, and Mohammed opened the boot. There were three rucksacks nestled inside. He reached down, lifted the first one out and set it on the ground. It looked heavy. He took the second and third rucksacks and put them on the ground, too. Aamir looked inside the boot and saw a large leather-bound case, the sort of case that a musician might use to carry his instrument. He didn't know what it was, and he didn't feel that he could ask. Mohammed shut and locked the boot, and then stooped to collect one of the rucksacks. He hefted it up and slung the strap over Aamir's shoulder. The rucksack *was* heavy.

'May Allah go with you,' Mohammed said. 'You will be rewarded in Paradise. *Allahu akbar.*'

They repeated it. '*Allahu akbar.*'

He hugged them, one at a time, and then got into the Mazda, backed it out of the parking space and drove it away.

'This is it, boys,' Hakeem said to them both. 'No turning back.'

'I ain't going anywhere,' Bashir replied.

'Me, too.' Aamir said it, and meant it, but his mouth was dry.

'I'm proud of you both. I'll see you in Heaven.'

Hakeem nodded. 'Let's go.'

Chapter Five

Pope went through his report once again.

The shooting had been two weeks ago, but it was still fresh. It had dominated the front pages of the newspapers every day since then and had been the subject of a quickly assembled BBC documentary entitled *Death of an Innocent.* For a man like Pope, required to work in the shadows, the publicity was exquisitely uncomfortable. The establishment could not possibly allow the truth of his unit's involvement to come to light – that was a rabbit hole down which no investigation could ever be allowed to stray – and an extensive cover-up had been put into play. That, too, was embarrassing.

But it was none of his fault.

The Metropolitan Police and MI5 were searching for the members of a terrorist cell suspected of being in the final stages of an attack on the London transport system. A member of the public had found a bag that had been discarded on a common in Wanstead, East London. The dog walker had opened the bag and discovered that it contained a pipe bomb and a detonator.

A large police investigation and manhunt began immediately. An address in Homerton was written on a video rental shop membership card that was found inside the bag. The card was in the name of Ramzi Hassan Omar, and the address was a block of flats designated for those on low incomes. It housed a collection of working-class families. Some were locals who had been driven out of the more affluent streets as property prices were pushed up by the influx of workers from the city. Others were first- and second-generation immigrants from all around the world, the kind of men and women who came to do the jobs that no native Londoners would do.

Fèlix Rubió was a cleaner who lived in one of the flats with his sister, her husband and their children. He worked for a company with a contract to service the offices of a leading London law firm. He was due into the office at 8 p.m., once most of the staff had gone home. He would work for five hours and finish at 1 a.m., when he would then work as the night-shift caretaker in a local hospice. He was, by all accounts, one of the nicest men you could ever hope to meet. Hard-working, honest and good-natured. Not the sort one would expect to have any truck with hard-line jihadist Islam.

The police had the block under heavy surveillance, and at seven-thirty, they saw Rubió emerge from the communal entrance.

The officer on duty had been unable to photograph him as he came out of the building's lobby. Pope had heard that the man had been urinating, but whatever the reason, it was unfortunate for Rubió. The officer was unable to provide an image to Gold Command, the Metropolitan Police operational headquarters that was in charge of the investigation, and it was impossible to compare him to the passport images of the suspects who had been identified.

The commander in charge of Gold Command panicked. He authorised officers to continue pursuit and surveillance, and ordered that Rubió was to be prevented from entering the Underground system.

The officers trailed Rubió as he followed Kingsland Road to a bus stop. He took the No. 242 and headed south. Plainclothes police officers boarded, too, and kept him under close observation. He used his telephone during the trip into the city, and one of the officers thought that she heard the word 'bomb'.

The surveillance officers believed that Rubió's behaviour suggested that he might be one of the suspects and – worse – that he might be on his way to carry out an attack. The pursuing officers contacted Gold Command and reported their suspicions. Based on this information, Gold Command authorised 'code red' tactics and again ordered the surveillance officers to prevent Rubió from entering the public transport system. The commander ordered the surveillance team that Rubió was to be 'detained as soon as possible,' before entering the station.

Gold Command then transferred control of the operation to Group Fifteen. Pope had positioned all ten of his available agents within the boundary of the City of London, and he tasked Numbers Three and Twelve, McNair and Snow, to interdict the suspect. Snow's inexperience within the Group was not ideal, but it was hardly the case that he was green. He was an experienced soldier with five years in the SAS. This kind of interdiction was something he had done many times before.

McNair was held up in traffic and had to sprint the remaining mile. Snow was there before him. In the meantime, confusion over the handover from the police to the Group meant that Rubió was allowed to enter Liverpool Street railway station at about 7.45 p.m., stopping to pick up a free newspaper from a distributor who stood in the lobby. He used his Oyster card to pay the fare, walked through the barriers and descended the escalator to the Central Line. He then ran across the platform to board the newly arrived train.

McNair arrived at street level as Snow was hurrying down the escalator to the platform.

Three surveillance officers followed Rubió onto the train. He had taken a seat with a glass panel to his right, about two seats in. The carriage had a handful of commuters leaving the city to go home. One of the plainclothes officers took a seat on the left, with about two or three passengers between Rubió and himself. When Snow arrived on the platform, a second officer moved to the door, blocked it from closing with his foot and called 'He's here!' to identify Rubió's location.

Snow boarded the train and shot him. The shell casings collected from the floor of the carriage indicated that he had fired eight rounds. Rubió was shot with a classic double tap – once in the chest and then once in the head – and died at the scene.

McNair arrived a minute later.

It took less than five minutes after that to understand that an awful mistake had been made.

McNair and Snow had followed protocol and left the scene at once. A cover story was concocted at short notice and then calibrated overnight. The surveillance officers were anonymised and described as members of the police's elite CO19 firearms division. It was suggested that they had fired the fatal shots. There were witnesses on the train, but pressure was put on them so that they either agreed with the official account or stated that they were (conveniently) looking the other way.

The oak-panelled door to the conference room opened, and a smartly dressed woman stepped out. Pope glanced beyond her and saw a large circular table with a lot of severe-looking men and women sitting around it.

'The committee will see you now,' the woman said curtly.

Snow exhaled.

'Ready?' Pope said.

McNair stood and straightened out his suit. 'Come on. Let's get this over with.'

Snow followed them both inside.

The train was full, with smartly suited commuters heading into London for another day at work. Aamir was in the first carriage. They had split up on the platform. There was nothing to suggest that they would be compromised, but Mohammed had told them that they needed to be careful. Three brown-skinned boys heading into London together with three heavy rucksacks might attract attention.

All the seats were taken, so Aamir stood in the aisle, balancing himself on the headrests of the seats on either side of him. He had the rucksack on the floor between his legs. Several of the other passengers were reading from newspapers, and Aamir was able to look at them over their shoulders. The front page of the popular free sheet was dominated by a messy celebrity divorce, but in a column on the right, there was the beginning of a story that reported that an allied bomb had destroyed a school in Aleppo. Aamir could only read the first three paragraphs, but he didn't need to read the rest to know what the story would say. Children massacred. He could almost hear Mohammed's voice angrily denouncing the 'imperialists' and 'crusaders'. He remembered the words of the clerics who distributed their sermons on CDs so that believers did not have to use the Internet to hear them. It was wrong, Aamir thought. People needed to know that it was wrong. Mohammed had explained it all to him. The only way their message would be heard was to respond in kind. They needed to use the same language.

The train took fifty minutes to reach Kings Cross. Aamir was jostled by other passengers as they surged for the exit, and he wondered whether they would be so brusque and rude if they knew who he was and what he was carrying. What he was here to do. *They don't know yet,* he thought, *but they will. They all will.*

He disembarked and saw the back of Bashir's head as he disappeared down into the tunnel that led to the Underground.

He followed.

Chapter Six

Pope, McNair and Snow took the three empty chairs at the head of the table. The conference room had not been decorated for decades. It was panelled in oak that was warped and cracked. The table was new, but so modern and cheap that it looked out of place here. It was also too big; it was four metres long and one metre wide and would have been able to accommodate fourteen men and women around it. The chairs at each end could barely be pulled out without bumping against the wall.

The passing traffic on Whitehall and Northumberland Avenue was far enough removed to be reduced to a gentle hushing. Pope heard a footfall in the corridor outside, the rustle of pigeons on the parapet outside the window, the whipping of a radio mast in the wind overhead, the gurgle of water in the antiquated central heating system.

It was oppressively stuffy. Pope unbuttoned his jacket and settled in his uncomfortable chair. Snow and McNair sat on either side of him.

This was a meeting of the Intelligence Steering Committee, the body that was putatively responsible for overseeing the secretive work of the MI5/MI6 intelligence operation known within its own walls as 'the Firm'. The organisation was as labyrinthine as the building that accommodated it.

It was divided into fifteen separate Groups. Each was supposed to mesh seamlessly with the others, but in practice, there was as much interdepartmental conflict as one might expect to find in any office of the same size and complexity. Group Three, for example, was responsible for providing intelligence through watching and listening – what the Americans would crassly refer to as IMINT and SIGINT – together with liaising with the electronic dragnet that was GCHQ. Group Five maintained dead-drop 'post boxes' and safe houses for agents in the field, and was also the home Group for the postmen who were tasked with couriering intelligence and equipment around the world. Other Groups were dedicated to research and development, cryptography and cryptanalysis, interpreting and transcription, forgery, vetting, interrogation and research. Service Departments ensured the smooth running of the Old War Office. They occupied themselves with the daily functioning of the building, pay and pensions, the personal problems of agents, the storage of documents and the maintenance of security.

Each Group was led by a man or woman referred to as 'Control'. Pope was responsible for Group Fifteen. His agents were regarded with a measure of fear by the other staff. In the fashion that the operatives of Group Five were known as 'postmen', and those who worked in cryptanalysis were 'crackers', the agents of Group Fifteen were referred to as 'headhunters'. Assassinations and other wet work comprised a large part of their responsibilities, but not all of them. They carried out the Firm's extrajudicial dirty work: burglaries, kidnapping, blackmail. They were responsible for bodyguarding other members of the intelligence community, emissaries of the government or businessmen and women who were important to British interests overseas. They were all well-regarded soldiers before they were selected, but after their year of training at the Manor House, the Group's establishment in Antsy, Wiltshire, they emerged as something else entirely: ethically flexible operators who were adept at submerging themselves within foreign cultures. When so ordered, they became murderers who emerged from cover to eliminate their targets without regret or compunction before disappearing again like shrimps into sand.

The Committee had been imposed on the Firm following the scandals involving John Milton and Beatrix Rose, two Group Fifteen operatives who had gone rogue. The government had installed it as an extra layer of control that would also act as a suppressant to a potentially flammable political situation, should the full details of the organisation's activities ever come to light. The Committee was a mixed inter-ministerial body composed of representatives from Westminster and Whitehall. It brought together senior members of the Cabinet and Whitehall mandarins, and was placed between the intelligence fraternity and the government as a guiding light or, as required, a brake. The staff of the Firm, sceptical to the last, had dubbed it the 'Star Chamber'.

Sir Benjamin Stone, the chief of the Secret Intelligence Service, was on Pope's right. He was in his late fifties, a moderately large man, a shade under six foot tall, with an accumulating gut. His hair was lank and grey, and his smile was as warm as a corpse.

The woman opposite him was Home Secretary Elizabeth Morley, a high-serving member of the cabinet ever since the election. Appointed home secretary three years ago, she was hawkish, aggressively right wing and possessed of an infamously short temper.

The woman to her left was Eliza Cheetham, the director general of the Secret Service. She was in her early sixties and more handsome now than the beauty that he knew she had been when she was younger. She was dressed in simple loose-fitting trousers and a shirt with a jacket over the top.

There was one other man. Pope knew him, too. His name was Vivian Bloom. He was the permanent liaison between the Firm and the Government. He had briefly been the sub-rector of Lincoln College, Oxford, and his previous profession was the reason for the nickname by which he was most commonly referred to within the Firm: The Reverend. Bloom must have been in his late seventies and had held on to his position through dint of the knowledge he had acquired over the course of his long career and, Pope assumed, the secrets he held over those who might otherwise have ushered him into his dotage. He had cut his teeth during the Cold War, and his successful work in recruiting agents at Berlin Station was legendary. Pope wondered how he liked this new world, where the monolithic Soviet enemy had been replaced by a myriad of asymmetric threats.

Bloom was plain and average, very much the archetypal bachelor don, remarkable only for his dreadful dress sense. He dressed like a man with a modest budget but no taste whatsoever. His suit was a little too baggy for him around the shoulders and waist, cinched in with a leather belt. His shirt had been washed too many times, the collar turning inwards and fraying at the tips. His top button was undone, and his tie looked as if it had been knotted by a child. He managed his terrible eyesight with a pair of thickly-lensed spectacles that had the effect of magnifying his pupils. He was pudgy and red cheeked, and his thin hair was cut short to his scalp, as if he couldn't be bothered with anything that would have required more than an occasional wash.

Cheetham cleared her throat. 'Thank you for coming, Captain Pope. And these are Sergeants McNair and Snow?'

'That's right. Agents Three and Twelve.'

'Thank you for coming, gentlemen.'

Snow nodded but didn't speak. McNair grunted.

'We've been briefed by Benjamin,' she said. 'But we wanted to speak to you before we reach a conclusion.'

The atmosphere in the room was tense, and Pope got the feeling that a decision had already been made. This, he worried, was just window dressing. An attempt to give the impression that a thorough enquiry had been undertaken. An exercise to provide the justification for the course of action that would follow.

'Of course, ma'am,' he said.

'Bit of a mess, wasn't it, Captain?'

Chapter Seven

Pope rehashed the events of that day with as much detail as he thought prudent. He was honest and forthcoming, and when he was finished, he answered their questions candidly. The tone in the room was aggressive and did nothing to dissuade Pope from his initial assessment that blame had already been assigned.

'Sergeant Snow,' the home secretary said, 'what can you tell us?'

'Captain Pope has set it all out, ma'am. I agree with everything he has said.'

'Yes, Sergeant,' Stone said. 'Of course, you would say that.'

Pope looked at the chief. He answered to the spook and did not hold him in high regard. His experience suggested that he was a self-serving career civil servant who would not hesitate to throw him under the bus if he thought it was to his advantage to do so. He was, Pope knew, an especially cunning man, and he did not like the way that Chief Stone was regarding Snow.

Stone gestured to include all of them in his next comment. 'The police tell the story very differently. They say that they aborted the operation between the time that you entered the station at ground level and the time you reached the platform. The commander has testified to us that she told you that the target was not a suspect and that you should stand down.'

'That's not true,' Snow said with sudden heat.

'How can you say that, Sergeant?'

'I—'

'When was this communicated?' Pope asked, intervening before Snow could lose his temper.

'The radio log records it at 7.48 p.m. The message transmitted was as follows: "Target is not a suspect. Incorrect ID. Stand down. Repeat, stand down."'

'I didn't receive that message,' Snow protested.

McNair shook his head.

'Neither did I,' Pope said. 'Could I hear the recording, please?'

'I don't know what purpose that would serve. The message is the message.'

'Your radio, perhaps?' Bloom suggested. 'You were underground. Perhaps you didn't receive it.'

'No,' Snow said. 'They work underground.'

'I didn't hear a thing,' McNair reiterated.

Morley took over. 'You understand our problem, Captain Pope?'

'Permission to speak frankly, ma'am?'

'Always.'

'I do *not* understand the problem. What happened is regrettable, but it has nothing to do with Sergeant Snow, Sergeant McNair or Group Fifteen.'

She smiled indulgently, but Pope could see that she was irritated by his candour. 'Who do you think is responsible, Captain?'

'The police. There should have been a firearms team outside the flat to stop and question everyone who left. Instead, they used surveillance officers with no experience in stopping and questioning suspects. They mistook Rubió for Omar, and then they let Rubió board the bus *and* go into Liverpool Street station. All of those mistakes were made before we were involved.'

'That may be true, Control. But the police say they called your agents off.'

'I don't believe them, ma'am.'

'They say that Sergeant Snow determined to kill the suspect the moment he entered the platform.'

'That's not true!' Snow objected loudly.

The room was abruptly quiet, and the tension rose. Pope looked up at them, holding their gazes. He wanted them to see that he was confident.

It was the home secretary who spoke first. 'What happened to Mr Rubió is bitterly unfortunate, and it has brought some misgivings that I have had for some time to the surface.'

Pope realised that the focus of the meeting had now shifted very squarely away from Snow and onto him.

'Go on, Home Secretary.'

'I am uncomfortable that we have had, for many years, a group of soldiers operating in secret around the world. Those agents are granted wide leeway to act autonomously and have often gone beyond the terms of the operation as presented and approved by Oversight. Frankly, I'm uncomfortable with the idea of a state-sanctioned death squad in the first place. This isn't Chile, Captain. I'm not Pinochet, making people disappear.'

Pope let her words settle and then spoke calmly. 'The world is a more complicated place than it was ten years ago. We face a multitude of threats. Asymmetrical warfare can't be defended with conventional methods. An army can't stop one man with a suicide vest. I know I don't need to go through the list of jihadists who have been removed as threats to the public in the last twelve months.'

'Removed,' Morley said. 'A splendidly neutral euphemism, Captain.'

'Use whatever word you prefer, Home Secretary. I try to be thoughtful. I find civilians often have weak stomachs.'

He regretted the slight almost as soon as it had left his lips.

'Thank you, Captain, but I think we can call a spade a spade, don't you?'

'Yes, ma'am.'

'And no, you do not need to remind us. We are aware of the work that your agents have undertaken. And we do not underestimate the need for similar action in the future.'

'Then I don't understand what this is all about.'

'The fact is this, Captain. The Group, as it is presently constructed, is an anachronism. A dinosaur from another time. It's something that Fleming would write about, or le Carré. The unfortunate death of Mr Rubió might be the reminder we need to bring it to an end.'

Chapter Eight

Monarch Catering was a large and well-respected company responsible for a series of contracts throughout London and the South East. Established ten years earlier, it had since that time enjoyed fast growth and numbered several blue chips among its impressive roster of clients. It had secured the main hospitality contract for the Palace of Westminster two years previously and had, by all accounts, performed well enough to suggest that the relationship would be long-lasting.

The warehouse that served the contract was at 19 Crown Road in Edmonton. Ibrahim Yusof parked his car on the street, as was his habit, and walked the short distance to the premises. Ibrahim was wearing a simple pair of jeans and a denim shirt. He wore glasses with wire rims, and his hair was clipped tight to his scalp. He had shaved off his beard months ago, but he still found his fingers darting up to his chin every now and again, as if surprised that his whiskers had been removed. He was of average height and average build. Nothing about him was out of the ordinary. He was the kind of anonymous man who could slip into a crowd and just disappear.

He opened the door and looked at the machine they used to clock in and out. It seemed pointless to go through with that particular rigmarole this morning, but Ibrahim knew that it was important to maintain the appearance of normality, so he took his card from the rack, slid it into the slot so that the time was stamped onto it, and then replaced it. He checked through the other cards. The only other employees present were the two men who stocked the firm's lorries before they went out each morning.

It was as he expected.

The company rented both floors of the warehouse. The first floor was taken up by four small, dingy offices that were only rarely used. Ibrahim jogged up the stairs and moved quickly down the short corridor to make sure they were empty. It wasn't impossible that one of the managers had popped in, and since the manager might not have clocked in, Ibrahim didn't want to be negligent and allow himself to be surprised. The offices were empty. That was good. He went back down and locked the front door.

The open space where they parked the company vehicles dominated the ground floor. The company drove Mercedes Sprinter panel vans, and there was space for three of them in the warehouse. The drivers had backed them inside last night, and the doors stood open as the two warehousemen replenished the supplies carried within.

'Morning,' Ibrahim called out.

The warehousemen were Bill and Dave. They seemed like decent enough types. Ibrahim had worked for Monarch for two months, and the two had never been anything other than pleasant towards him. Bill was in his fifties and celebrated his support of Tottenham Hotspur with a tattoo of the club's crest on his beefy forearm. Dave was younger. He had just become a father, and he regularly complained that he hadn't had a full night's sleep since his son had been born.

'Glad you're here,' Bill said. 'Simon hasn't turned up yet.'

'Really?' Ibrahim said, playing dumb.

'Ten minutes late, he hasn't called – nothing.'

Dave was in the back of one of the trucks. 'Out on the piss again,' he called. 'Not the first time he's bailed after a night out. He'll call in sick when he wakes up – you'll see.'

'Gonna get himself fired if he keeps that up.' Bill indicated one of the Mercedes. 'Your truck's done.'

'Thanks,' Ibrahim said.

'I'm going for a dump,' Bill said.

The bathroom was at the rear of the building. Bill took his copy of the *Sun* from his bag and headed to the back.

'Fuck's sake!' Dave complained. 'I was going to have a piss. No way I'm going in there after you.'

'Up yours!' Bill said as he disappeared from view.

Ibrahim walked around to the back of the van. 'Have you called the office?'

'What for?'

'Simon?'

'Not yet. Was just going to finish loading up, then I was gonna give him a ring. I'd rather give him the chance to get in.'

Very good.

Ibrahim reached into his bag and pulled out the Beretta 92 that he had fitted with a 9mm AAC Ti-Rant suppressor. The detachable box magazine had a fifteen-shot capacity. Ibrahim had thirteen rounds left in the mag after having shot Simon earlier that morning. He had broken in to the man's disgusting flat and found him still sleeping in bed. He had held a pillow over the silencer for added suppression and put two rounds into his head. Ibrahim knew that Simon lived alone. The body wouldn't be discovered for hours. Not until it was much too late.

Dave was stepping down from the back of the van, and there was nowhere for him to go when Ibrahim aimed the gun and fired. The gun barked twice, the suppressor muffling the reports a little but certainly not eliminating them. The man was only five feet away and Ibrahim couldn't miss. The first shot blew a hole in his coveralls to the right of his sternum, and the second punctured his throat. He slumped back into the van, a look of the most exquisite confusion on his face.

Ibrahim turned and walked to the bathroom. It was small, with a handbasin, two urinals and a cubicle. The door was shut, and Ibrahim could hear Bill inside.

'Wait up! I told you, I'm going to be a while.'

Ibrahim fired three shots through the flimsy door. He gave it a kick, shattering the lock, the door jamming up against Bill's spasming body as it slumped forward on the toilet. He fired again, to be sure.

Ibrahim went back into the warehouse.

He made sure that Dave's body was safely inside the back of the first van. He went to the button that opened the main doors and pressed it. The engine whirred and the metal door rolled up, sliding back on well-oiled casters.

Abdul was waiting outside in the beat-up Vauxhall Astra he had bought from an eBay seller two weeks ago. The man had asked for cash, and Abdul had been happy to oblige him. Cash would be much harder to trace. At Ibrahim's signal, he reversed the van into the warehouse, sliding it tight up against the right-hand wall with the Mercedes to the left. Abdul switched off the engine and Ibrahim pressed the button to lower the door again. The door rolled down and gave out a metallic clang as it contacted the concrete floor.

Abdul stepped down. 'Any problems?'

'None,' Ibrahim reported. 'It was easy.'

'Praise Allah.'

'Praise Allah. We must move quickly.'

'The others?'

Ibrahim nodded. 'It is all in hand.'

'You spoke to Mohammed?'

'Yes. As I was walking here. He is confident.'

'The three boys?'

'He said that he met them and that they are on their way.'

'And they will do what needs to be done?'

'Allah willing. It is in his hands.'

The warehouse was brightly lit from the fluorescent lights overhead. Abdul opened the back of the Astra and brought down a selection of large plastic containers. They were branded with the logos of catering supply companies and advertised as holding various ingredients: carrots, broccoli, potatoes and other vegetables. The contents had been poured away and then sharp craft knives had been used to slice from the sides around to the backs. Now the tops of the containers could be pulled forward enough to allow access to the interiors.

'Is everything there?' Ibrahim asked.

'It is. But you should check.'

He did. He carefully split one container so that he could reach inside. His fingers fastened around a metal cylinder. He brought it out: it was the barrel of a Smith & Wesson M&P 9mm. The other containers held a small arsenal of weapons: MP-5 submachine guns that had been broken down so that they could fit into the containers, semi-automatic pistols, magazines, fragmentation grenades.

He clambered into the back of the Sprinter. Racking had been fitted on both sides, and each shelf held two rows of similar containers. He had taken pictures of the cans, and Abdul had matched them at the cash and carry. He cleared the shelf nearest to the front of the compartment, stacked Abdul's containers against the side of the truck and then obscured them behind containers that had not been tampered with. They worked quickly, and when they were done, the weapons were well hidden. Not satisfied with just that cursory check, he jumped down and looked at the interior of the truck from the bumper, the view that the security guards would have if today was one of the days they chose to examine the vehicles passing through their checkpoint.

'Well?' Abdul said.

'Very good,' Ibrahim replied. 'Very good.'

Chapter Nine

Isabella wandered aimlessly all morning. She crossed the river on Waterloo Bridge, walked down the Strand to Trafalgar Square, whiled away an hour in St James's Park and then, finally, ambled along Birdcage Walk to Parliament Square.

She slowed her pace. There was a demonstration, anti-war protestors raging against the suggestion that the British military be put to fresh use against ISIS in Iraq and Syria. She stopped to do up a lace that did not need tying, and used the opportunity to surveil the armed police who were observing the spectacle with wary attention. She looked up to the rooftops: there were officers with video cameras recording the faces of the protestors.

Isabella felt vulnerable, and pulling up her hood, she skirted the crowd. She put on her sunglasses, barely hearing their angry chants in response to the exhortations of the orator, who was addressing them from a raised box with the assistance of a portable amplifier.

Her skin crawled as she walked within range of the cameras. She only regained her equilibrium as she proceeded south down Abingdon Street. She passed Westminster Abbey, and with no real destination in mind, turned into Victoria Park Gardens. The park was adjacent to the south-west corner of the Palace of Westminster and named for the tower that loomed above it. She walked by the statue of Emmeline Pankhurst and Rodin's sculpture of *The Burghers of Calais*, until she was at the stone wall that looked down on the sluggish greeny-grey waters of the river below.

She rested her elbows on the wall and gazed out onto the Thames. A towboat was hauling six barges upstream, and one of the brightly-coloured commuter clippers passed it going in the opposite direction. The sky overhead was blue and clear, latticed with the fluffy contrails of passing jets.

She had been lying to Pope. She didn't have a flight to catch. She hadn't known why he wanted to see her, and so she had left her return open. She had nothing to do and no place to go. There was her continued training, the regimen that she had interrupted to make this visit, and she would pick it up again when she returned to her riad, but apart from that, there was little else to occupy her. She had no friends. No connections. No reason to be anywhere or do anything. Usually, that was something that did not concern her. She preferred a life with no tethers. Today, though, looking down onto the water, she wondered whether she had it all wrong.

She turned her head and looked at the Palace of Westminster. Her mother had dedicated her life to furthering the interests of the government whose decisions were debated within those imposing walls. She had hidden her occupation from her husband – Isabella's father – and it had killed him. She thought about the things that her mother had told her during the short time that they had spent together. Beatrix had explained the betrayal that had inspired her vendetta. She had been unable to complete it before the cancer that had raged through her body had rendered her too weak to follow through with her original plan. She had sacrificed herself in an effort to complete her revenge; when that had failed, Isabella had finished the job. She looked down and found that her fingers had drifted unconsciously up to the sleeve of her shirt, up towards her shoulder.

Her fingers traced over the spot where she wore the tattoo of the rose. It marked that final death, the final addition to the set that her mother had been unable to complete.

She opened her right fist and trailed the fingertips of her left hand across the silver locket.

She was disappointed. She realised that at a dim and distant level, she had been entertaining the prospect that Pope was going to offer her something to do. Something, perhaps, that her mother might have done before her.

She allowed herself a laugh.

That was foolishness. She was fifteen years old. What use could Control possibly have for her?

She unclipped the clasp of the chain, put it around her neck and fastened it again. She slid the locket between her T-shirt and skin and let the warmed silver drop down to her chest.

The blare of the tugboat's horn brought her around again. There was no point in dawdling. She wasn't interested in sightseeing. She reached into her pocket for her phone and called up the map of the Underground. She needed to get to Heathrow. She could take the Jubilee Line at Westminster, change onto the Bakerloo Line at Baker Street and then get the Heathrow Express from Paddington. It would take her an hour to get across the city.

No, she thought. *There is nothing for me here. No reason to stay.*

Time to leave. She would be back in Marrakech by evening.

Ibrahim drove the Mercedes Sprinter carefully. He had driven the route two times before in order to familiarise himself with it, and that familiarity bred confidence. It was twenty miles, and in the heavy morning traffic, he knew it would take between an hour and an hour and a half. That was fine. The itinerary had been designed with that in mind, and it would be flexible enough to be adapted, should that be necessary.

Everything was proceeding as he had planned. Allah was smiling upon them.

Relaxing was out of the question, but as he idled before a red light on the North Circular, he did allow himself a moment to think about the events that had led to this day.

Ibrahim had fought the *peshmerga* in the ultimately futile battle of Kobani, and Abdul had been involved with the foreign hostages in Aleppo and Raqqa. Ibrahim did not have to try very hard to remember what it was like to be pinned down in a defensive position as imperialist jets screamed overhead, dropping their laser-guided bombs and demolishing vehicles and emplacements. He had seen brothers whom he had fought alongside torn to pieces by the bombs. And he had met others, older than he was, who had done battle with the fascists in Afghanistan and Iraq, and others who had fought the Jews in Palestine. He had heard stories of what the enemy had done during the conflicts. He had seen videos of the atrocities at Abu Ghraib, read about the torture at the CIA's black sites and fulminated over the continued injustices at Guantánamo.

The caliph had decreed that retaliation was in order. Ibrahim was honoured to have been chosen to put the plan into effect.

He was a British citizen, born and bred. There were ten of them who had been selected from the ranks of the British fighters who had offered themselves into the service of the Islamic State. Some of them, like himself and Abdul, had seen plenty of fighting in the two or three years that they had been in the Middle East. Others were less experienced, but no less dedicated to the cause.

The government had made it clear that nationals who travelled to Syria and Iraq to fight for the caliphate would be treated as terrorists if they were to return.

Terrorists!

The hypocrisy turned his stomach.

Nevertheless, they could not risk the likelihood that they would be arrested if they returned by air. Mohammed had crafted a detailed and thorough plan that would make that unnecessary and mean that they could travel without fear of detection. They had travelled by sea on a series of cargo ships, trawlers and pleasure craft, transferring from one to the next in the middle of the ocean, far from prying eyes. Muammar Gaddafi had used similar methods to supply the IRA with weapons in the 1970s, and it was just as effective today as it had been then. The final transfer had been in the Atlantic off the coast of southern Ireland. The final trawler had deposited them in a deserted cove close to Kinmel Bay in North East Wales, and they had dispersed into safe houses around the country. They were well funded, with no need to work, and provided with false identities.

The preparation had been perfect. Nothing had gone wrong.

Now they needed to execute the plan.

Chapter Ten

Pope had had just about enough. 'Home Secretary, I'm afraid I'm going to have to speak frankly again. I was reluctant to be Control, as you know. But I have seen things. We live in a world with people in it who are not prepared to observe the usual rules of engagement. They will fly planes into skyscrapers. They will blow up bags of high explosive on Underground trains and buses. They have no compunction in killing themselves if that is what is necessary to achieve their objectives.'

He couldn't hide his anger, and as he spoke, he became angrier still. 'We live by the rule of law. They do not. And because of that, the rule of law has to be a flexible concept. Those men and women are enemies of the state, and they can't be reasoned with. Diplomacy is useless, and intelligence is useful only up until a point. The only way to deal with them is to speak the same language that they do: fight fire with fire. And who is going to do that, ma'am? Are you? Are people at the "highest echelons"?'

He slammed his palm against the table. His wedding ring struck the wood, and the noise was louder than he had intended. His anger had caused stupefaction in the room. They were stunned by his candour. He could see that and knew, clearly, that he was talking himself into a world of trouble, but he couldn't stop.

'I've heard the arguments against the work that I do. But when I hear them, it makes me think about the things I've seen. I know that the only way to prevent these people is to kill them before they kill us. Sometimes it has to be without trial. In secret.'

'Captain Pope—'

He looked around the table. The home secretary was agape at the strength of his denunciation, Stone was shocked and Bloom watched with a mixture of surprise and, Pope thought, amused admiration.

He was talking himself into obsolescence. He knew he should stop. But he couldn't.

'We can agree that Rubió's death was a tragedy. I know Sergeant Snow will never be able to forget what he did. It was a dreadful, horrific error, but if blame is being attributed, it should be attributed correctly. The intelligence was flawed. That is an MI5 issue. The police response was badly flawed. That is an issue for them, and for you, Home Secretary. My agency is a tool. We were given a target; we eliminated the target. You don't blame the tool when it is put to the wrong use.'

'Captain Pope!'

'I'm nearly finished, ma'am. The fact is, you will be put in a position again, very soon, where a similar call will need to be made. Another threat will be identified, at an early stage, and we will have a choice. We either strike pre-emptively and run the risk that the intelligence is incorrect, or gamble and hope that it isn't right. But if you get that wrong, it won't be one jihadi we are mourning. And it won't be a single innocent man who was wrongfully killed. It will be tens or hundreds or thousands of civilians. Yes, Rubió's death was a tragedy. But we have to be strong enough to keep making those decisions because they will save more innocent lives than they cost. And that means that the existence of an agency like Group Fifteen is necessary. You can talk about moderation and proportionate responses and due process all you like, but when it comes down to it, you need the cutting edge we provide. And I think if you are honest with yourselves, you'll admit that's true.'

Pope stood. Snow was pale. McNair was shaking his head, his mouth open and an expression of good-humoured surprise on his face. He was wise enough to have read the same signs as Pope.

Morley was red in the face. 'Is that all?'

'Yes, ma'am.'

'You are suspended, Captain.'

'Yes, ma'am. What shall I tell my agents?'

'That the Group is suspended. Everyone is to stand down. *Everyone.* Anyone in the field is to return home. Everything stops. Effective immediately.'

'Very good, ma'am.'

Snow and McNair stood, and Pope took a quarter turn before he stopped. *In for a penny,* he thought. The writing was on the wall. They were going down. Might as well go out swinging.

'One more thing. With respect, I'm not interested in defending my position to a civilian. I wouldn't expect you to understand. But what I would say is this: if you're serious about suspending the Group, then you should be prepared to explain to the country that your morality is worth more than the blood of the men and women who will die to pay for it. I suspect that will be a difficult speech to write. You should probably ask your aides to start thinking about it now.' He straightened out his suit with two brisk downward brushing movements. 'Good day to you all.'

Chapter Eleven

The van pulled up at the goods in/out entrance on Abingdon Street at five minutes before twelve. A service road led off to the left, passing through a gate and then a checkpoint beyond that. Ibrahim waited patiently as the van was photographed. Software compared the registration with the list of permitted vehicles, and when a match had been found, the gate slid aside. Ibrahim edged ahead, stopping before the metal bar of the checkpoint. Beyond that, a ramp was raised. There was a small office built into the archway through which the road descended, and inside sat two armed policemen. The security was impressive.

Ibrahim had passed through the checkpoint many times before, and he knew the procedure. The detail changed regularly, and he didn't recognise the policeman who came out and approached the van.

'Is this usual?' Abdul asked nervously.

'It is fine,' Ibrahim murmured. 'Just act normal. Relax.'

The policeman came up to Ibrahim's window and indicated that he should wind it down.

'Name, sir?'

'Ibrahim Yusof.'

'Purpose?'

'Food delivery.'

'Your friend?'

'Abdul Mansoor.'

'Wait there, please, gents.'

The man went back into the office and spoke with his colleague. Ibrahim rested his fingers on the wheel and drummed them lightly, presenting as normal a picture as he could. He was nervous, and he could see that Abdul was, too. He knew that he was as well prepared as he could be, but it would only take a moment of inattention on his part or intuition on the part of the guards for the scheme to be compromised. There was a plan B, of course, but that was not the point. Plan A was what he had worked so hard to bring to fruition, and to fail at the final hurdle would be the cruellest of ironies.

Ibrahim had studied the Palace of Westminster for six months. It was simple enough to glean information from online searches, but he had supplemented this with two field trips, posing as a tourist on the official tour and visiting his local MP. It was an impressive building even if he did not agree with its purpose or the decisions that were made there. The Gothic edifice was a vast temple of legislation that covered an area of nearly nine acres. It presented a river frontage of nearly one thousand feet to the east, and there was a centre portion sandwiched by towers, two wings, and wing towers at each end. Inside, there were fourteen halls, galleries, vestibules and other apartments that could accommodate large crowds. Thirty-two river-facing apartments served as committee rooms. There were libraries, waiting rooms, dining rooms and clerks' offices. There were eleven internal courtyards and scores of minor openings that allowed light inside.

He was particularly interested in its security, especially when it had been breached. Everyone knew about the failed gunpowder plot, commemorated every November with the burning in effigy of Guy Fawkes. Spencer Perceval had been shot here in 1812, the only prime minister ever to have been assassinated, and the building had been the target of Fenian bombs in 1885. The Irish Republican Army had struck it twice in the 1970s. In 1974, a twenty-pound bomb exploded in Westminster Hall, rupturing a gas main and causing extensive damage. Five years later, a car bomb claimed the life of Airey Neave, a prominent Conservative politician, while he was driving out of the Commons car park in New Palace Yard. The subsequent threat of jihadist terrorism had upped the ante once again. Today, the palace was guarded by armed officers from the Metropolitan Police's elite SC&O19 unit.

The policeman returned. Ibrahim couldn't help but look at the Heckler & Koch MP5SFA3 semi-automatic carbine that was slung across his chest, his finger resting outside the trigger guard.

'You're on the list, sir, but not your friend.'

'He should be.'

'Says you normally have a Simon Williams?'

He smiled and nodded. 'That's right, we do. He didn't come into work today. He called in sick.'

'I'm afraid I don't have clearance for an Abdul Mansoor. I can't let him in.'

Ibrahim sensed Abdul's tension and spoke quickly before Abdul could say anything stupid. 'Really? He's been with us for as long as I have.'

'Doesn't matter.'

'Call the office. I'm sure they'll be able to clear it up.' He reached forward and took a business card from a holder that had been glued to the dash. He handed the card to the policeman, who still looked dubious. 'I'd really appreciate it if you could clear it up. It's going to take me twice as long to do on my own, and we're already running late.'

'All right.'

The man went back to the gatehouse. Ibrahim saw him take a telephone and put it to his ear.

'There's no one in the warehouse,' Abdul hissed.

'I know.'

'So?'

'The number forwards to Mohammed's phone. He'll sort this out.'

But would he? They had taped the Smith & Wesson 9mm to the underside of his seat, and he allowed his arm to fall down next to the door so that he could feel the cold metal with his fingertips.

The policeman came back.

'I spoke to your boss. Some kind of oversight. I'll let it go for today, but you need to get it fixed. And I'll need to take a look in the back. Could you come around and open up, please?'

'Of course. Not a problem.'

The man drifted to the rear of the van.

'We will be discovered,' Abdul said, his voice tight with tension.

'Relax. Whatever happens is His will. Be calm.'

Ibrahim reached for the keys to switch off the engine, but his hands were trembling and he fumbled them. Damn it. He needed to be calm, too. He managed to kill the engine, extracted the keys from the ignition and stepped out. He glimpsed the second policeman in the doorway of the little office, his carbine similarly held on a strap and angled down to the ground.

He unlocked the rear doors and opened them.

'What have you got in here, sir?'

'Ingredients for the kitchen. Meat, fish, vegetables. That sort of thing.'

The policeman took a half step forward, and for a horrible moment Ibrahim thought he was going to climb inside the van.

Their doctored hiding places would not stand much scrutiny. But he did not. He stepped back and nodded his satisfaction.

'Sorry to bother you, lads. We're being careful.'

Ibrahim knew why that was. The assassination of Fèlix Rubió had caused all manner of consternation in the press and there had been protests and demonstrations afterwards. His funeral last week had ended with a riot that had been put down with brutal efficiency. There was talk of retaliation, of radicalisation, of increased terrorist 'chatter'.

They had *no* idea.

Ibrahim knew that the man's murder would be of benefit to their cause in the long run, but he wasn't interested in that. His focus was on the short term. And the increase in security would make it more difficult to do what he had promised to do.

He got into the van.

'Are we good?'

'We are. Just smile and relax.'

He started the engine again. The policeman gave him a nod of recognition as his colleague raised the barrier and lowered the ramp. Ibrahim put the gearbox into first and pressed down gently on the accelerator. The van bumped over the exposed lip of the ramp and was swallowed by the narrow tunnel.

Chapter Twelve

Isabella bought a ticket to Heathrow from the machine, used it to pass through the gate and joined the queue that was shuffling toward the escalator. It hummed as it carried her down the long shaft to the vestibule below.

Aamir took the Victoria Line to Green Park station and then changed to the southbound Jubilee Line to Westminster. The carriage was full and he had to stand.

The Jubilee Line was newer, and the trains and the stations were all much sleeker and more modern than the others that they had used when they had scouted the capital last month. Westminster, in particular, was an impressive vaulted space, a cavern that had been carved in the earth at the side of the Thames. It was one of the main stations that served the offices of government around the Palace of Westminster and Whitehall. Many of these men and women waiting patiently for the train to carry them to their destinations were puppets of the state, putting into effect the pernicious policies that had led to decades of misery for their brothers and sisters in the Middle East.

Had they seen the effects of those policies, as Aamir had?

Mohammed had told him to watch the YouTube videos of the atrocities that had been carried out in the name of civilisation and democracy, the bombed schools and hospitals.

The dead children.

The families wiped out by drone strikes and five-hundred-pound bombs dropped by cowards from ten thousand feet.

He looked at the men and women around him as they read their newspapers and listened to their music. They were oblivious. They had no idea what he could do to them with just a simple click of the trigger in his pocket.

And yet, as the train rushed through the dark tunnel, the doubts returned. These people were not soldiers. They did not drop the bombs. They had families. They were mothers and fathers, not so different to the brothers and sisters in Iraq and Palestine and Afghanistan and the other Muslim lands.

He closed his eyes and tried to remember what the imam had said to him. The words of the sacred Qur'an.

> *Fight in the cause of Allah those who fight you, but do not transgress limits; for Allah loveth not transgressors. And slay them wherever ye catch them, and turn them out from where they have Turned you out; for tumult and oppression are worse than slaughter; but fight them not at the Sacred Mosque, unless they fight you there; but if they fight you, slay them. Such is the reward of those who suppress faith.*

He could almost hear the cadence of Alam Hussain's deep, sonorous voice. He closed his eyes and let the rhythm of the verse play through his head.

Fight in the cause of Allah those who fight you.
And slay them wherever ye catch them.
Such is the reward of those who suppress faith.

The weight of the rucksack brought him back around. The strap was cutting into his right shoulder, so he carefully transferred it so that it was slung across his left. The bag itself was against his chest. He wrapped his arms around it so that he could cradle it and reduce the downward pressure from the strap. He thought about what was inside the bag and what it would do when he detonated it.

What it would do to him, and all these people.

The train eased into Westminster station. The screen doors on the platform opened first, and then the doors to the train.

This was where he had agreed to detonate the bomb. Right here, in the carriage, catching some as they stepped out and others as they stepped in. His would be the first blow to be struck. The second and third blows would be triggered by his actions, a series of attacks that would amount to a grievous blow against the infidels, deep in the heart of their country, right next to the seat of their democracy.

The scrum of passengers shifted and eddied as people elbowed their way to the carriage's exit. A man told him to move out of the way, and a woman tutted at him, and as he took a pace to the left to allow them the space to squeeze by, he was pushed towards the exit himself. He disembarked, not really thinking, clutching the heavy rucksack to his chest. The tide of commuters carried him towards the opening that led to the main vestibule and the escalators that would take him to the surface.

He thought he saw Bashir.

The tide shifted, people bustling into his line of sight, and he couldn't be sure.

He craned his neck.

'Come on, buddy,' a man said, nudging him.

'Sorry.'

Aamir was bustled onto the escalator. He was breathing quickly, and his pulse was racing.

He looked for Bashir and couldn't see him, even as they ascended. He gazed at the others: the long queue of people going down to the platforms on his left, the others heading up to the surface with him. Men and women and children. A woman staring at the screen of her cell phone. A man reading a book on a Kindle. A couple balancing a child's stroller between them. A pretty blonde girl, not that much younger than him, a leather satchel hung over her shoulder.

No.

He couldn't do it.

He turned back, closed his eyes and waited for the escalator to deliver him to the surface.

Hakeem's train had rolled into the station five minutes before Aamir's. That was what they had planned. He needed time to get into position. The rush hour was long since ended, but this was a busy station. He had seen Bashir get onto the train, but he had lost sight of Aamir in the scrum at Kings Cross. He was a little concerned about the young brother. It had been harder to persuade him that what they were going to do this morning was necessary. Mohammed had worked on Aamir; Hakeem thought that the young recruit could be relied upon, but he wasn't as certain about Aamir as he was about Bashir.

Hakeem looked at the oblivious men and women around him. They were like cattle. They had no idea what was about to happen.

It gave him a wild thrill of excitement.

He walked from the platform into the vestibule that accommodated the escalators. He separated himself from the throng and found a place where he could wait without being too obvious about it. The plan called for him to stay here until Aamir had detonated his bomb. The boy would kill and maim dozens of the infidels in the confined space of the train carriage. His bomb would also cause panic and send hundreds of them dashing headlong to where he, Hakeem, would be waiting for them. He would press himself into the middle of the crush and close his eyes. He would pray to Allah that he would kill as many of them as he could.

He looked at his watch just as he heard the sound of the next train easing into the station.

This must be Aamir.

Not long.

Moments.

He knew this was a martyrdom operation and that he wouldn't live beyond this day. He knew his span on this Earth could be measured in minutes now. Seconds. He was content with that. He was clear-headed and calm, prepared to sacrifice himself to the greater good. His blood would serve the caliphate, and the scripture was clear and unequivocal: he would earn a place in Paradise for his work.

He heard the sound of the train's doors closing.

Now?

The train accelerated.

He looked at his watch.

He waited.

Nothing.

No explosion.

He didn't understand what was happening.

Aamir should have been here by now.

He was trying to think what to do when he saw the boy on the escalator above him. His mouth fell open. Aamir still had his rucksack over his shoulder. He was clutching the bag to his chest as if it was something precious.

He wanted to call out – 'Aamir!' – but he knew that he couldn't draw attention to himself.

Aamir was going to the surface. He had failed. He had lost his nerve and *failed*.

Once again he heard the scripture that Alam Hussain had made him memorise.

> *O Prophet, rouse the believers to fight. If there are twenty among you, patient and persevering, they will vanquish two hundred; if there are a hundred, then they will slaughter a thousand unbelievers, for the infidels are a people devoid of understanding.*

Aamir might fail.

But *he* would not.

He took a step away from the wall and then another, pushing his way into the crowd of people waiting to get onto the escalator. He remembered everything that the imam had said, and everything that Mohammed had said after that. He closed his eyes, ignoring the angry words as he bumped into men and women. He put his hand into his pocket and felt the trigger. He grasped the switch and felt its sharp edge press into the flesh of his thumb.

'Allahu akbar,' he yelled. *'Allahu akbar. Allahu—'*

Chapter Thirteen

'*Allahu akbar. Allahu—*'

Isabella heard the chant as the doors of the carriage closed behind her. She was adjacent to the passageway that led through to the escalators, and she was looking out into it as the train slowly eased into motion. The angle changed and her attention was snagged by a poster for a new film she had been thinking of seeing.

Then came the explosion.

Isabella saw a bright white light that seemed to go on for seconds, and then she heard a dull *crump*. It was loud, but blunt. It was like a thud, a physical sensation that she could feel passing through her body. She saw a gout of smoke punch out of the passageway and onto the platform. At the same time, the glass screen doors shattered and the side of the carriage was peppered with tiny pieces of debris that rang out loudly. A jagged crack appeared in the window, and further down the carriage an entire pane shattered and fell onto the passengers.

The train jerked to a sudden stop.

There was silence for a moment, and then came the sound of screaming from the platform and the vestibule beyond. One of the women in the carriage had been lacerated by the falling glass, and as the other passengers saw the blood that was running down from her scalp, some of them started to scream, too.

The lights on the platform flickered and died.

Smoke drifted in through the smashed window.

The lights in the carriage winked out, too, and in an instant it became completely black.

The smoke was acrid; she heard people retching and coughing.

The carriage lights came on again. A man was stumbling along the platform. Isabella looked at him and saw that he had no face, just a mask of blood and skin that looked like masticated steak.

A male passenger yanked down the handle of the carriage's intercom and tried to speak to the driver.

Other men and women appeared on the platform. Their faces were blackened with soot and dirt and blood, and their clothes were torn and shredded. The whites of their wide eyes stood out against the muck on their skin.

A man tried to wrestle the doors open. He managed to part them a crack and call for help. Two others pushed through the scrum and tried to force them all the way open. She was buffeted to the side, and as she put her weight on her right foot, she felt the crunching of broken glass beneath it.

The lights flickered and died for a second time. A shower of sparks drifted down from the ceiling to the floor of the platform. It was incongruously beautiful.

The screaming got louder.

'Allahu Akbar. Allahu—'

Aamir was at the top of the escalator when he heard Hakeem's strident chant. His call was enveloped by the crashing roar of the bomb as it exploded in the vestibule below him. It was a loud, sudden boom, closely followed by a pressure wave that pulsed up the shaft and flattened everyone in its wake. It lifted Aamir up and tossed him, dropping him on his front, the rucksack beneath him. The rumble was followed by the sound of shrapnel striking against the concrete walls of the shaft and the metal treads of the escalator. The sound was like a whoosh, the noise that a very strong wind might make. It almost felt electrical, and his hair stood up on end.

There came a sudden silence. Aamir heard the sound of his own breathing, in and out, ragged and on the edge of panic, and then came the shrieks and screams. The horror. Smoke coursed out of the mouth of the shaft, black and choking, and Aamir felt it sting his eyes.

Aamir shook the rucksack from his shoulders and left it on the floor as he scrambled to his feet.

He forgot about it and ran.

He crashed into a large man in a London Underground uniform. He was old, his kindly face absorbed with shock and horror. The man was trying to forge a path through the on-rushers so that he could get to the escalators.

Aamir looked up and saw the white of daylight from the station exits.

He had to get outside.

Aamir ran to the gate line, bumped and baulked by the others around him. The gates were all open, and he squeezed through, climbed the steps and emerged into the bright sunlight. He looked up. Big Ben stretched overhead, and behind it, the towers and crenellations of the Palace of Westminster. A single Union Jack flew from a flagpole atop one of the towers. The pennant hung down, rustling in the negligible wind.

Aamir looked across the road and saw Bashir opposite the exit to the station, crossing the road and heading right at him. Bashir looked back at him for a moment, confusion quickly replaced by anger.

'Stop!'

Aamir saw the bulk of his rucksack and knew what was about to happen.

He ran.

Chapter Fourteen

Pope, McNair and Snow stepped out of the office. The street was shaded by the tall shoulders of the buildings on either side, but as they walked on, they passed into the sunshine that shimmered down onto Whitehall.

He had said too much. He had known that he would if they pressed the wrong buttons. He had promised himself that he would be diplomatic, hold his tongue and ignore all the provocation that he knew was coming his way, but he just couldn't. He had no respect for any of those people. They pronounced and opined without any idea of what it was that the men and women under his command did for their country.

He had been an active member of the Group until his predecessor had gone rogue. He had more than his own share of kills, and the price he had paid for each one of them was high. He had always tried to take his own feelings out of the equation. He had been a weapon. Someone else chose the target and aimed the weapon. He simply carried out his orders and then went back to his family and tried to forget about them. That had been his policy, although, of course, it wasn't as simple as that. He had probably handled it better than John Milton, but what did that say about him? Milton had wrestled with his demons for years, tried to drown them in drink, and eventually he had decided that the only way he could deal with them was to take himself as far away from London and his old life as he could. Milton was out, and good luck to him. Pope found that he wished he could join him.

They ambled down Whitehall. Snow was smoking a cigarette, his second, sucking down the tobacco with greedy gulps. He smoked compulsively, especially when he was irritated, and he certainly had grounds for irritation now.

'Fuckers,' McNair said.

'I know,' Pope said.

'They have no idea. Not the first clue.'

'It's not over yet. Someone will see sense.'

He said it, but he didn't really believe it. He knew that there would have to be a scapegoat for what had happened to Fèlix Rubió. A bloodletting was inevitable. It should have been the police and the spooks for the faulty intelligence, but Group Fifteen was an easier target. There would be an inquest to find out what had happened, and far better for the agency to be disbanded and dispersed, to forestall the possibility that a light might be shone on the murky, grubby world in which they operated. Similar steps were taken after Bloody Sunday. The men involved were scattered far and wide to prevent the truth from emerging. The playbook hadn't changed in forty years. It was still the obvious response. It was as craven and short-sighted now as it had been then, but Pope was long enough in the tooth not to be surprised by such things.

He grimaced again and wished, for the second time, that he had held his tongue.

Snow noticed his expression. 'Forget it, sir. You did what you could.'

'At least they know how you feel about it now,' McNair added.

Pope allowed himself a small smile in response.

They passed The Red Lion pub, Derby Gate and then St Stephen's Tavern. Snow finished the cigarette and immediately lit a third. Pope found himself wondering what to do for the rest of the afternoon. He had never been suspended before, and he realised, with a rueful grin, he had no idea what that meant in practical terms. Should he go home? *No*, he thought. There were people with whom he needed to discuss the morning's events. But where should he do that? What did suspension mean? Was he supposed to go back to their building on the river, make his calls and then wait for further orders? Was he supposed to go home?

They joined the scrum of pedestrians at the junction of Bridge Street and Whitehall. He looked up at Elizabeth Tower. It rose up with a stately rhythm, higher and higher, and then there came the iconic clock face, picked out as a giant rose, its petals fringed with gold. There were medieval windows above that and then the dark slate roof, its greyness relieved by delicate windows framed in gold leaf. Finally came a rush of gold to the higher roof that curved gracefully upwards to a fairy-tale spire topped with a crown, flowers and a cross.

It was a minute before midday. The traffic lights changed in their favour just as the minute hand ticked over to an upright position and the famous chimes pealed out. The tune was that of the Cambridge Chimes, based on violin phrases from Handel's *Messiah*.

The Chimes finished, and Pope waited for the first strike of the hour bell.

The detonation came from Bridge Street, in the direction of the river. It was a deep, guttural boom, accompanied by a tremor that passed beneath his feet. Pope knew it was a bomb immediately. The blast had been very slightly muffled. It had come from the direction of the Underground station. He ran toward the entrance, Snow and McNair hard on his heels, just as a huge cloud of dust and smoke poured out and billowed up into the bright afternoon.

He saw the man on the other side of the street. Most people were standing around, confused and befuddled. They were slack-jawed, their eyes black and dazed. But this man was moving. He was dressed in black and carrying, with obvious effort, a rucksack that he wore on his back.

Pope knew how to spot a suicide bomber. He knew the playbook after an attack, too. He had served in theatres where suicide bombings were often a daily occurrence: Iraq, Libya, Afghanistan, Lebanon, Israel. The first blast was often diversionary. Lethal, yes. Deadly. But it was designed to funnel as many targets as possible into a killing zone where they could be attacked by a bigger secondary explosion. The jihadis did it with IEDs, using one to herd soldiers and civilians into a position where the second bomb could do serious damage.

The man with the rucksack wasn't standing still. He wasn't confused. He was walking with a determined stride, right into the middle of the crowd.

'No!' Pope yelled.

The man reached into his pocket.

'Bomb! Run!'

Chapter Fifteen

A bright yellow light, seemingly everywhere, and then Pope was lifted, twisted and flung to the ground. There was the deafening crack of a hideous explosion, and Pope was pummelled by a bolt of boiling air which dented his cheeks and stomach as if they had been made of cardboard. He felt the fierce lashing of debris, hot slugs that scored burning tracks across his cheeks and forehead and the back of his hands. He stayed there on his back, the breath sucked out of his lungs by the retreating pressure. He opened his eyes, blinking hard. The sun seemed to quiver overhead, and then it disappeared in a cloud of black smoke.

There was a moment of unearthly silence, broken only by the music of broken glass, the creaking of metal, the patter of falling debris.

Then the screaming started.

He looked and tried to clear his head. The blast had thrown him fully fifteen feet and deposited him against the side of a black cab that had stopped in the middle of the road. The mass of people who had retreated from the first blast inside the station were not there any longer. He felt something fall on his face, and when he yanked it away, he found it was a piece of yellow fabric, a dress maybe, now soaked in blood. A gory shower of flesh and more bloody clothing fell on him and around him, mingled with fragments of glass and concrete. Last of all came pieces of paper sucked from the offices in the buildings above the station, falling gently to Earth like graceful autumn leaves. There came the unmistakeable smell of roast pork. Once you had experienced it, you could never forget it. It was the smell of burning flesh.

The road was ruined for fifty yards in both directions. There were hundreds of windows in the sand-coloured limestone walls of the Palace, and they had all been blown in. Glass rained down. A man bumped into him and fell to the ground. People were running all around him, screaming and crying. A bus that had been passing had swerved and crashed into the railings. A dump truck had slammed into the back of the bus. The trees that stood between the high railings and the flanks of the building had all been denuded of their leaves and now they stood naked and at crooked angles. The road itself was no more than a smoking crater. There were red smears on the tarmac and the pavements and the walls of the buildings. An inky black cloud mushroomed overhead, obscuring the clock tower and the buildings that faced it. The smell of cordite was everywhere. And it *was* cordite, Pope knew. This wasn't a home-made bomb. This wasn't hydrogen peroxide from boiled-down hair products. It wasn't HMTD from hexamine tablets and citrus acid. This smelled like military-grade explosive.

'Control?'

It was Snow.

'I'm here.'

Number Twelve emerged from the smoke. He was covered in ash and soot. He had been a little closer to the seat of the explosion than Pope, and the blast had ripped his jacket from his back and torn his shirt. He wore his pistol in a shoulder holster, and Pope watched as his hand flicked up to it and yanked it free. It made him think of his own Sig Sauer, and he was grateful as his fingers found that it was still there, too.

'Two explosions,' Pope said, although he knew that Snow would be aware of that. 'First one in the station, second one just outside it.'

'Fucking hell,' Snow said.

'You all right?'

'I'm fine. You?'

'Cuts and bruises.'

'Number Three?'

'I'm here,' McNair said. He was on the ground, ten feet away, carefully pushing to his feet.

'Hurt?'

'Scratches. Nothing. We were lucky.'

Pope looked around, trying to focus. There were dozens of bodies on the ground. Many of them had been torn apart. The bomb had been laced with shrapnel, and the metal debris would have lacerated the flesh of anyone who was within twenty yards. He took in the bloody devastation with as clinical an eye as he could: dismembered limbs, a torso impaled on the railings, the disembodied head of a man, his expression of open-mouthed surprise starting to set as the muscles stiffened.

There were moans and cries for help.

In the distance, there came the sound of sirens.

And then, closer to hand, a sound he recognised immediately.

Gunfire.

It was coming from his four o'clock. Pope spun.

The Palace.

Chapter Sixteen

The man they called Mohammed was waiting inside the empty warehouse. His name was not really Mohammed. He had been given many names, and it had been so long since he had been referred to by the one his mother had given him that he had almost forgotten it. His earliest years had been lived on the streets of the Gaza Strip. He had been wild and unruly then, and the Israeli soldiers had called him *'Arabush'*, or rat. When he arrived in Afghanistan to fight the Soviets, aged just seventeen, the mujahideen had called him 'Kid'. The jihadists in the Sudanese al-Qaeda cell had called him the 'Engineer', because his bombs and martyrdom vests were the most effective that they had ever seen. Now, his brothers in the caliphate called him *'Iblis'*. In Islam, *Iblis* is a jinn born from fire who refused to bow for Adam. The literal translation was 'Devil'.

He had been given the name of Mohammed Shalmalak when he arrived in the United Kingdom. His false passport and driver's licence bore that name, and it was the one he used as he set up a home for himself in the north of the country. It was the name he had used when speaking to the young suicide bombers that the imam, Alam Hussain, had provided. For a man who did not care for names, it was as good as any.

Weeks ago, Mohammed had been provided with the address of this warehouse and a key to open the padlocked front door. He had not questioned its provision, but he had been scrupulous in ensuring that it was vacant. The warehouse had seemed derelict and had obviously been empty for months. There were two offices and a bathroom on the first floor. All had borne the evidence of squatters. There was graffiti on the walls, the radiators had been removed for scrap and what little furniture had been left behind was broken and useless. It had been the same downstairs, too. The small kitchen had been filthy and the large warehouse space was a wreck, with clinker from an unswept chimney gathered in a dirty grate. The only piece of furniture had been a two-seater sofa, the fabric covering ripped so that the yellowed stuffing was poking out.

Mohammed had not concerned himself with the state of the property. It was empty, it could be secured and the windows had been covered by metal sheeting that meant that it was impossible to see inside. It had been the perfect spot to build his bombs.

He was wearing a pair of latex gloves and overshoes and a hairnet. He had dropped his bag on the sofa. He opened it, took out a silenced 9mm Berretta and placed it on the floor. He went back to the bag, took out an iPad, saw that he had a strong 4G signal and opened the BBC's iPlayer app. He navigated to BBC Parliament.

Prime Minister's Questions was held in the main chamber of the House of Commons every Wednesday at midday. It was an unruly bear pit, and tickets in the public gallery were sought after by foreign visitors, who found the occasion both fascinating and appalling. The baying, rude loutishness of it all was so different from proceedings in their own countries. Mohammed found it distasteful, although he admired the adroitness of the combatants. Not many political leaders could cope with quick-fire exchanges that required detailed knowledge of a Barnsley bypass one minute and the finer points of a UN resolution the next.

Attendance was strongly encouraged for MPs of all persuasions, and that usually meant that both the government and opposition benches were full. Most debates in the Commons were dry and dull affairs, with the green benches mostly empty, but Mohammed knew that this would be different. He had watched it on television, and of course he had secured one of those public gallery seats for himself when he conducted his reconnaissance. It was, to borrow a term that the Americans used, 'target rich'. And security, although improved since the day when two protestors had lobbed condoms stuffed with purple flour at Tony Blair, was still unimpressive.

He was confident that they would be able to surmount it.

The ticker along the bottom of the screen announced an item of breaking news.

'REPORTS OF EXPLOSION AT WESTMINSTER UNDERGROUND STATION'

A moment later, Mohammed saw a man in a traditional black suit with knee-length britches and a sword at his side approach the Speaker's Chair and speak quietly into the occupant's ear. The Speaker asked a question, received the answer and then gave a nod that he understood. He called for order.

'Honourable Friends, I have just been informed that there has been an explosion at Westminster Underground station. I'm afraid I have no further details, but the police are requesting that we remain in the chamber until they can confirm that there is no threat to us.'

The camera jerked to the familiar view over the dispatch box, then to the prime minister and the front bench of the government. Another man in a dark suit was leaning over the seated prime minister. The politician rose and followed the man out of shot. Others followed: the leader of the opposition, the front bench.

Mohammed grimaced. They were being taken somewhere else. That was annoying, but it was not unexpected. He had assumed that standard procedure would be to remove the leaders to a panic room, and that appeared to be what was happening. No matter.

The camera pulled back to a wide shot. The parliamentarians were conferring anxiously, a hubbub of noise that provided a backdrop for the sombre tones of the presenter as she explained that sources were now confirming that the explosion had been caused by a bomb.

Mohammed was expecting what would come next, but when it happened, the payoff was better than he could possibly have imagined. The detonation of what he took to be the third bomb was only five hundred feet from the House of Commons. The blast, separated from the House only by the open space of New Palace Yard, was close enough to be audible as a loud detonation, easily picked up by the microphones in the chamber. There were six windows on the east and west sides of the House, each filled with rich stained glass. The pressure wave shattered the westward-facing windows, casting fragments of glass down onto the benches below. The presenter swore, and screams went up from the chamber.

The feed remained live for a moment, men and women standing and hurrying to the aisles, and then it cut to black. When the picture resumed, the feed had been switched to the BBC News Channel. The presenter looked flustered and panicked.

'You join me now as we hear the breaking news that there has been a series of explosions near the Houses of Parliament. Police sources are reporting that an explosion at Westminster Underground station was most likely a bomb. We can only assume that what you are about to see, filmed from inside the House of Commons, is the moment a second bomb exploded . . .'

Chapter Seventeen

Ibrahim Yusof was in the back of the Sprinter. He knew the plan called for three separate blasts. The first was to detonate on the train, and he doubted that he would have heard it occurring one hundred feet below the surface. The muffled crack was the second, in the station. The third, just now, was outside. It was deafening.

It was also their signal to move.

He opened one of the bags of vegetables and took out the small Uzi submachine gun that was hidden inside. He took one of the magazines, pressed it into the pistol grip and switched the three-position selector behind the trigger group to automatic fire. The irony that this was a Jewish weapon was not lost on him. The open-bolt design meant that contamination was more likely than with other weapons he could have chosen, but he had packed the gun carefully, and its compact design meant that it was worth the risk. He took two additional fifty-round magazines and stuffed them into the pockets of his jacket. He wore the machine gun on a bungee cord around his neck and hid it beneath his jacket. Then, he tore back the hinged lid on the empty tin of peas and pulled out two Swiss HG M1985 fragmentation grenades. He put one in his pocket and held the other in his hand. Finally, he opened an empty can of carrots and took out a small bag that could be worn around the waist. He passed the belt around and snapped the clips together.

'Wait here,' he said to Abdul.

'Yes.'

'Get the vests ready. If anyone comes, shoot them.'

He jumped down and hurried out of the loading area. He jogged up the ramp and out into the sunshine. An inky mushroom cloud was unfolding into the blue, already cloaking the walls of the clock tower above him. The sound of sirens was audible, still distant but drawing nearer. He needed to be quick. He ran, knowing that that would not be out of the ordinary given the panic that was erupting around him, sprinting hard along the side of the building until he got to the security booth that served the main exit onto Bridge Street.

The two policemen were out of the booth, standing at the fence and looking east to the seat of the blast. He drew a little closer and saw Faik walking to the gate, fifty feet away. Behind him he saw Nazir, Mo, Bilal and Aneel. The men were in position, just as they were supposed to be.

He slowed to a fast walk.

One of the policemen turned to him. 'Stay back, sir. There's been a bomb.'

'Oh my God,' he said. 'Where?'

'Underground station. Two, I think – one inside and one out. Best stay here. It's not safe out there.'

The policeman turned back to the fence.

Ibrahim pulled the pin of the grenade and rolled it, underarm, into the space between the booth and the fence where the two men were standing.

He pressed himself behind a brick wall strut and held his breath.

Neither policeman saw the grenade. Their attention was distracted. It was equipped with a pre-segmented shell filled with 155 grams of high explosive. The blast turned the steel casing into a storm of razored shrapnel, and it blazed out in all directions. The men were peppered with shards, their backs absorbing most of the damage. They slumped against the fence and then slid down it to the ground, blood pooling on the concrete beneath them.

The door to the booth was ajar. There was a button on the wall that released the lock on the turnstiles, and he pressed it, hearing a satisfying click from outside. The men ran for the gate. Faik pushed through the gate first. He was grinning.

'The weapons are in place,' Ibrahim said as Nazir and Mo followed Faik through the turnstiles.

'Where?'

'Follow the road to the loading area. Abdul is waiting for you.'

He was still inside the booth when he saw the man with the gun.

He was covered in ash and soot, and his clothes were torn, but he did not appear to have been injured. He was walking to the gate, a pistol held out before him in a steady two-handed grip. Ibrahim shouted a warning, but it was too late. Bilal was negotiating the turnstile, his range of movement severely curtailed. The man with the gun adjusted his aim and fired two shots from twenty feet away. They both found their target. Bilal was struck in the leg and the back and fell forward, jamming the gate with his body. Aneel was behind him, and now the turnstile was blocked. Ibrahim watched, helplessly, as the man changed his aim and shot him, too.

Ibrahim tensed, expecting one or both of them to trigger their suicide vests, but they did not. They must have died before they could reach for the triggers. He shouldered his way out of the booth, raised the Uzi and fired a long burst through the railings. The man dropped to the ground and rolled behind the cover of a bus.

He ran. Faik, Nazir and Mo were ahead of him.

'Bilal?' Faik called back to him. He hadn't seen what had happened.

'Shot by the police. And Aneel. Put them out of your mind. There are five of us. That is enough.'

They ran down the ramp back into the building.

'We must be quick. They will start to move the targets.'

Ibrahim took off his jacket and dropped it as he ran, freeing the Uzi. He led the way back to the loading dock, the other men following behind him. As he turned onto the ramp, he saw two members of the resident catering staff coming towards them. He raised the submachine gun and sprayed them with automatic fire. The man and the woman were close, and it would have been difficult to miss them. They were stitched with several rounds each, both of them stumbling, halting and falling to their knees.

Ibrahim ran by them to the van. Abdul was in the back. He opened the door and handed out the hidden weapons. Each man had a submachine gun, a handgun, multiple magazines and three grenades.

Ibrahim turned to the newcomers. 'Do you have your vests?'

He could tell from the bulk that was evident beneath their jackets that they did. Faik unzipped his coat. He was wearing an armless gilet with stitched-on loops into which six pipe bombs had been fitted. Each explosive was surrounded by a fragmentation jacket that was stuffed with nails, screws, nuts, and ball bearings. It was the shrapnel that effectively turned each jacket into a crude, body-worn claymore mine. Mohammed had made them in his workshop and delivered them yesterday.

'Take off your jackets. Let the infidels see them.'

They did.

They had smuggled their own vests into the building inside two paper sacks of potatoes. Abdul had put on one of the vests. He handed Ibrahim the remaining one.

Ibrahim put it on. It was heavy, around forty pounds. But it felt good. It made him feel potent.

He would have liked to pray, but there was no time.

'You know what to do?'

Each man nodded that he did.

There was nothing else to say. Ibrahim took a breath to ready himself and then led the way into the heart of the building.

Pope, Snow and McNair approached the gate, weapons drawn. The first man had fallen onto his face. The second man had tried to force the gate, but it had been blocked by the first man's body. He had taken a step back and had looked as if he was about to run when Pope shot him, too. Snow approached the second man.

'Be careful,' Pope called. 'He could have a vest on.'

Snow fired a shot into his leg from twenty feet away. The limb jerked, but the man did not move. He was dead.

The man lying inside the turnstile was motionless, but Pope was not prepared to take chances with him either. He stayed out of range, aimed and fired a round into his thigh. No movement. He was dead, too. Pope hurried ahead, took the man by the ankles and hauled him out of the way.

'What do we do?' Snow said.

'I'm going in. Paddy – you're with me.'

'And me?' Snow asked.

'Find a policeman, tell him what's happened, then come after us.'

'You see how he fired?' McNair said. 'Close bursts, targeted. He's been trained.'

Pope nodded. He had noticed that, too.

'This is bad.'

McNair dropped to his haunches next to the man beside the gate. He unzipped the man's jacket and swore colourfully. Pope turned to look.

The man was wearing a gilet fitted with pipe bombs.

'It's worse than that,' Pope said. 'Hurry, Snow. Tell the police we've got multiple suicide bombers inside. We're going to need backup.'

Snow sprinted away.

He turned to McNair. 'Ready?'

McNair nodded.

'Come on.'

Pope pushed through the turnstile and ran in the same direction as the attackers.

Chapter Eighteen

Ibrahim led the way. He knew the layout of this part of the building from visiting it every day for the last few weeks. They climbed a flight of stairs out of the basement and emerged in the kitchens. There was a series of dining rooms set out along the oak-panelled corridor that began at the entrance to the kitchen. The staff of the refreshments department were responsible for the food and drink that was served. There were four chefs in the kitchen this afternoon – three men and one woman. They had switched on a radio and were gathered around it as the presenter breathlessly relayed the developing news of the bombing at the Underground station.

Ibrahim raised his Uzi and sprayed them with bullets. Stray rounds sparked off the pots and pans on the metal shelving, but most of them found their marks. The chefs dropped to the floor, one of them sliding off the shining stainless steel counter and bringing a pot of peeled carrots down atop him.

'Eyes open,' Ibrahim called out.

His men advanced in stooped crouches, fanning out, each of them with his weapon drawn and ready to fire. They were well trained and experienced soldiers. Death was not a stranger to them; they had walked with Him for months. Ibrahim knew that they would be ready to kill when the moment presented itself.

He knew that they were ready to die, too.

Ibrahim led the way through the kitchen. There was a window in each of the double doors at the far end, and he glanced through into the corridor beyond. An alarm was sounding. Ibrahim didn't know what it signified, but he guessed that it had been triggered following the blasts outside. He hoped, and suspected, that it would mean that the people inside the building would be held in place until the outside was secured.

Abdul, Faik, Nazir and Mo waited for his instructions.

'You remember the plan?' They nodded, but he repeated it anyway. 'We take the steps to the level up from here. Then we split. Faik – you are with me. We go left and take the long route to the lobby. Abdul, Nazir, Mo – you go right. We meet there. Shoot anyone you see.'

Mohammed had laid out their tactics. They knew that they would, in all likelihood, come across stiff resistance as they headed to the chamber of the Commons. Splitting into two separate teams would increase the odds of at least one of them making it. After all, they only needed one man to get inside.

He checked through the window again. A policeman had entered the corridor. He was walking away from them.

'Ready?'

They nodded.

'Now!'

He eased the door open and stepped through. The policeman turned just as he raised the Uzi and squeezed off a quick fusillade. The man was struck several times, stumbling back until he tripped and fell onto his side. He had collapsed next to the stairs. Ibrahim rushed ahead, put a final round into the man's head and led the way up the flight of stone steps.

Pope saw the Sprinter and the discarded jackets and coats that had been scattered on the ground next to it. There were five of them. He paused quickly and saw the mess of opened tins and packets of produce that had been strewn around. It was easy enough to put together what had happened. The van had brought one or two men inside. Most likely it was two. The weapons for the attack had been hidden inside the opened tins and packets. The bombs were a distraction. One of the men from the van had killed the police guarding the entrance so that he could let the other men inside. The five jackets left on the ground suggested that the plan called for seven men. He had counted four and killed two. The spare jacket must have belonged to the man who had been left to guard the van.

'There's five of them, not four. And they're all armed. Our friend had an Uzi. We better assume they all do.'

They climbed the winding corkscrew stone staircase and emerged on the ground floor, close to the Commons Library, where they split into their separate teams. They split up. Abdul, Nazir and Mo went one way, and Ibrahim and Faik went another. Their paths would converge on the lobby that preceded the entrance to the Commons.

Ibrahim ran, the extra weight of the explosives slowing him down. They passed through the Peers' Lobby and the corridor beyond and reached the Central Lobby. It was a grand octagonal hall that was one of the central hubs of the building. He glanced up at the vaulted tower above them, a full sixty feet in diameter. The stone roof was supported without a central pillar and contained a long series of elaborately carved bosses. It was austere and impressive, obviously designed to cow those who visited. It did not have that effect on Ibrahim.

There were twenty or thirty people there. He saw old men in suits, a few women, and a policeman with his back turned to them. The atmosphere was fraught with tension. They must have heard what was happening outside by now. Ibrahim had trained for precisely this situation and his reaction was instant and ruthless. He released his hold on the Uzi, letting it fall free on the bungee cord, his right hand stabbing down into one of the pouches on his vest and removing one of the grenades.

He pulled the pin, tossed it into the middle of the crowd and slipped behind the cover of a pillar.

The grenade burst apart with a sharp crack. Hundreds of pieces of sharp-edged shrapnel were propelled in all directions. Those near the seat of the explosion were torn to shreds. It exploded on the floor, so those who might otherwise have survived were struck below the waist. They fell to the floor, their hands reaching for the wounds to their buttocks and legs.

Ibrahim and Faik stepped out of cover and fired at the survivors. They both emptied their magazines, then ejected and loaded fresh ones. They fired for ten seconds and then stopped.

Ibrahim paused to get his breath.

He smelled cordite.

Gunpowder.

He heard soft moans.

Faik shouted out.

Ibrahim spun. Another two policemen ran up the steps from St Stephen's Hall. Faik fired first. The policemen hadn't seen them and stood no chance. Ibrahim fired. The policemen collapsed to their knees, clutching their stomachs. Faik approached cautiously and shot both of them again.

'Well done, brother.'

'Allah smiles on us.'

'We're nearly there. We must hurry.'

They left the carnage in the lobby and headed north. The walls of the corridor were covered with grand frescoes. The ostentatiousness was distasteful. He thought of the austerity of the caliph's quarters in Raqqa. The comparison was instructive: the worldly against the spiritual. He knew which he preferred.

He was at the entrance to the Commons Lobby when he heard more gunfire from behind him. He spun around and saw a man crouched low, aiming a pistol. He realised dimly that it was the man who had shot Bilal and Aneel as they had tried to pass through the turnstile outside. There was a second man a few steps behind him. Ibrahim tripped over his feet, just managing to launch himself into a deep recess as the pistol barked again and bullets winged out toward him.

He crashed against the wall.

No hits. Lucky.

'Faik?'

Nothing.

'Faik?'

'He's dead,' a man's voice called out. 'You're next.'

He risked a quick glance back. Faik was laid out on the floor. He had been shot as he had left the Central Lobby. He was on his belly, unmoving, a pool of blood inching out from an open wound in his temple.

A gun fired again. He pressed himself deeper into the recess as a cloud of dust and stone fragments exploded just overhead.

The firing stopped.

'Do not come any closer,' Ibrahim yelled.

'Throw out your weapon.'

'No.'

'You're trapped. Throw it out.'

'I have a suicide vest. My finger is on the trigger. If I see you, I will detonate it. We will both die.'

Ibrahim heard the sudden clatter of gunfire from the other direction. Screams. He turned his head. He was almost at the end of the corridor, ten feet from the entrance to the Commons Lobby. He could see into most of it from where he was. Abdul, Nazir and Mo had entered the lobby from the east. A policeman had been guarding the doors to the Commons, but now he was on his back.

'Abdul!' Ibrahim yelled. 'Help!'

Besides Ibrahim, Abdul had the most battlefield experience of any of them. He knew what to do.

They could see each other, but the angle meant that the men who had shot Faik could not see them. Ibrahim pointed back to the south to Faik's body.

Abdul crept ahead, lowered himself to a crouch and pressed himself against the doorway.

He fastened his eyes on Ibrahim's and counted down on his fingers.

Three.

'Throw out—'

Two.

'—your weapons!'

One.

They both span out of cover, their submachine guns up and firing. He saw a flash of colour against the dun stone and focused his aim on it, fully automatic. Bullets crashed against the wall and a storm of chips was cast out, but the men who had shot Faik were in cover.

Mo and Nazir joined Abdul at the doorway and opened fire.

'Keep firing!' Ibrahim yelled over the sound of the fusillade.

He took one of his grenades, pulled the pin and rolled it underarm toward where he thought the men were sheltering. The fuse was set for five seconds. The grenade detonated with a crash that was amplified by the natural acoustics of the corridor. Shrapnel clanged against the walls, and a cloud of black smoke billowed out.

He took the chance to sprint out from cover, throwing himself into the lobby with the others.

Chapter Nineteen

Pope pressed himself behind the pillar. He had been fortunate. The grenade had gone off ahead of him, and his cover – in a recess, behind a statue of a parliamentarian he did not recognise – had been good enough to protect him from the shrapnel, save for the tracks of scratches that had been scored across his shoulder.

'Con . . . Control.'

It was McNair. His voice was pained and weak. Pope looked across the corridor to where he was sheltering. His left hand was pressed to his gut in a hopeless attempt to staunch the flow of blood that was pouring from the shrapnel wound. His shirt was saturated, and gobbets of blood were soaking through and falling to the floor.

Shit.

McNair shook his head. He knew he was in trouble.

Pope knew there was nothing he could do to help him. There were four attackers left, unless others had breached the building without his knowledge. They all had automatic weapons. They probably all had grenades, too. He and McNair couldn't retreat. If they did, there was no telling what the attackers would do. The terrorists had suicide vests. Pope didn't know what procedure would be in the chamber when the building was under attack. Would they lock it all down? Or would they evacuate? If they did that, there was no telling how long it would take. And if they did, how would they know where the shooters were located? There would have been several hundred MPs, press and members of the public in there. They could be herded into a killing zone.

No. They would defend the doors and lock it down.

But if the attackers could get inside . . .

He shook his head. They couldn't retreat. McNair had to wait. Pope knew he was going to have to deal with them.

McNair coughed. Pope looked over as he spat out a streamer of blood.

'It's a gut shot, Scouse,' Pope said. 'You've got a while to bleed yet. Stay with me.'

'Nah.' McNair shook his head. 'I'm fucked. Feel dizzy. Losing too . . . too much blood. Must've nicked an artery.'

Pope grimaced. Where was Snow? They were badly outgunned.

The attackers had obviously targeted the chamber. Everything else was diversionary. He tried to think. He didn't even know whether the doors could be locked.

He needed help.

'Control,' McNair wheezed.

He looked back.

McNair nodded his head at the body of the dead terrorist. The bomber had fallen between two recesses. McNair was in the first recess, then came the body, then the second.

Pope knew what McNair was suggesting.

'Cover me,' he wheezed.

'Scouse—'

Before Pope could protest, McNair shuffled out of cover and lumbered to the body.

Pope swung out, saw movement in the lobby and laid down suppressing fire. He fired six shots before the gun clicked empty.

McNair grunted with effort. Pope turned and saw him hauling the dead man, face first, around the corner into the Central Lobby.

'Scouse,' he hissed, hoping that his words wouldn't carry to the lobby.

'I'm here.'

'Does he have grenades?'

'No.'

'His Uzi? I'm dry.'

McNair appeared around the edge of the wall and slid the dead man's machine pistol down the corridor. It came to a stop adjacent to Pope's recess. He reached out with his toe, snagged the bungee cord and dragged it to him. He collected it, checked that the magazine was properly engaged and leaned with his back against the recess. They couldn't have very long. Either the attackers would get into the chamber and do what they had come to do, or if they had more grenades, they would roll a couple more toward him, and maybe he wouldn't be so lucky the next time.

'Control?' McNair's voice was weaker.

'I'm here.'

'Ready?'

He tried to compose himself for what he knew McNair was about to do.

'Good luck, Scouse. Been an honour.'

Ibrahim aimed his Uzi at the entrance to the corridor. If anyone was foolish enough to follow him out of it, he would pepper him.

The Commons Lobby was about forty-five feet square, with a door at each side and all four sides formed alike. Each was divided into three equal parts, the central of which contained a deeply recessed doorway, while the remaining parts, which included the corners, were divided into two storeys. Mo was at the double doors that offered access to the main chamber.

'Come on!' Ibrahim shouted.

'The doors—'

Mo took aim at the doors and fired a blast from the Uzi. Chips of wood were thrown into the air, each impact marked by a little explosion of sawdust, but the door was too solid to be disturbed by the small-calibre rounds.

'They've locked themselves inside.'

Ibrahim glanced at the door. He set his Uzi on the ground and unhooked the bag that he wore around his waist. He unzipped the bag and took out two fist-sized portions of military-grade plastique explosive, the fused detonator and the battery.

'Cover me.'

Nazir grinned. He turned on a diagonal so that he could cover the door to his right and the door from which Ibrahim had entered. Mo and Abdul faced in the opposite direction so that they could cover the door to the left and the main door. They couldn't see down into the corridor where Faik had been killed without presenting a target, but if anyone tried to storm the lobby, they would be able to shoot them before they got very far.

Ibrahim took the plastique and tore off the strip of adhesive backing. He had taken two steps towards the door when he heard a loud shout from behind him.

'Hey!'

He turned.

A large white man had staggered out of the corridor.

He was wearing a pair of suit trousers, a bloodstained white shirt and a suicide vest.

Faik's vest.

The trigger was in his hand.

Nazir raised his gun.

'Don't shoot!' Ibrahim screamed. If a bullet struck the vest, it would set off the explosives.

Nazir fired and missed, but it didn't matter.

The man pressed the trigger, closing the circuit and sending an electrical charge to the detonator.

The vest exploded. Ibrahim was picked up by the blast and tossed across the lobby. As he slammed against the wall, he was just vaguely aware of another huge, tearing explosion. The last thought that passed through his mind, obliterating even the promise of heaven and seventy-two virgins, was that it was his own vest.

Chapter Twenty

It had been easy enough for Aamir to get away from the area. The streets around the Houses of Parliament had been chaotic. He had turned onto Whitehall and run all the way to Trafalgar Square. He had made it to the Cenotaph when the first unmarked police car screamed by, its lights flashing and siren wailing. He stopped for breath when he was at the entrance to the square as another three police cars raced south. By the time he had crossed the stalled jam of traffic around the monument, he had counted ten, and overhead the first helicopter was clattering to the scene.

He ran to the entrance of Charing Cross station, but the metal gate had been pulled across. A harassed member of staff was telling people that there had been an incident on the Underground and that the whole network was suspended. He climbed the stairs again, the muscles in his legs burning from the exertion, and looked around. He saw a bus. He didn't notice the number or the destination, but it had its doors open, and it looked as if it was still running. He climbed aboard, stuffed a hand into his pocket and fumbled around until he found a pound coin. He dropped it in the driver's tray and clambered up to the top deck. There was a spare seat a third of the way down, and he slumped down in it.

The woman next to him had her phone out. She was reading a page from the BBC News website. He saw the word 'bomb' before a gout of vomit pulsed up from the roil of his stomach. He fought it back, the harsh acidity burning the back of his throat.

The bus lumbered away into the crush of traffic.

Whitehall was jammed now, too.

He watched through the windows as four armed policemen sprinted south, their weapons cradled before them.

Chapter Twenty-One

Aamir had called the number Mohammed had given him thirty minutes after the bombs had been reported on the news, just as the story was switching to the drama inside the Houses of Parliament. The boy had called on a public phone, as he had been instructed. That was good. He had been frantic. That was not good. Mohammed had spent the first five minutes just calming him down. He had given him the address of the warehouse and then made preparations for his arrival.

Now that he was done, he put on his coat, collected his cell phone and the silenced Beretta M9 and went outside to his van. The warehouse was on Seabright Street. It was a half mile to the west of Bethnal Green Tube station. The entire Tube network was suspended, so he had instructed Aamir to catch a bus that would deposit him on the Old Bethnal Green Road at the stop opposite the Tesco Metro. When he arrived, he was to call him from the public phone box outside the Coral betting shop.

His van was parked fifty yards to the south, nestled between a moped and a dirty white panel van. It was a plain Ford Transit, dented and dirty, and bought for cash. It disappeared into the background, completely unobtrusive. The driving position was raised and offered him an excellent view of the warehouse and the street. The main road was several turnings away, and there were no cameras between it and here.

He had cleared his property from the warehouse that morning, transferring it into the back of the van. He had planned to move on once the operation had concluded. It was unwise to stay in one place for too long. He had a list of safe houses that would accommodate him for as long as he decided to stay in London. The next one was in Leytonstone, to the east.

He sat in the van and waited for the boy to call again, watching the news on his iPad. His mood soured as it became clear that the full, expansive goals of the operation had not been met. He already knew that the first bomb, the one on the train, had not been detonated. Worse, the bulletins eventually confirmed that the six attackers had not been able to get into the chamber of the House of Commons. On that level, it had been a failure.

But it had been encouraging in other ways.

The reporters had switched their attention from the carnage outside the station to the Palace of Westminster as soon as it became clear that the drama unfolding within was pressing and happening in real time. Several reporters covering *PMQs* had been stranded inside the building, and they provided furtive and fearful updates, whispering into their cell phones. There were dispatches from inside the chamber, where gunfire was audible, and then the broadcasters found their money shot. The cameras inside the chamber had been left running, and they had caught the moment when the suicide vests had been detonated in the lobby. The explosion had been enormous. He knew it was more than one vest.

The footage was played back again and again, and the studio experts suggested that three separate blasts could be discerned, each following almost immediately after the other. Mohammed agreed. The doors had been blown into the chamber, and all of the remaining windows had been smashed. There had been a minor stampede as MPs of all persuasions tried to put as much distance as possible between them and the smoke that was pouring into the chamber from the lobby. The police had quickly restored order, and an evacuation had begun. Even now, willing volunteers, no doubt keen to demonstrate their bravery to their constituents, were lining up on Parliament Green to tell their side of the story to the phalanx of reporters.

Yes, he thought, it had not gone quite as well as he had hoped. But it had been a success in the main, most fundamental way. A blow had been struck right to the heart of the country. The caliph had reached out and scratched his fingers down the door that barred the way to the heart of their democracy. They had demonstrated that nowhere was safe. They had proven that they didn't need airliners to cause terror. They could do it with ten men, a handful of weapons and a few pounds of explosives.

His phone rang. It was the boy. Mohammed gave him directions to the warehouse and ended the call.

He navigated to the folder with the martyrdom videos that each man had recorded in the days leading up to today. He would release them at the appropriate time, when the news cycle needed to be given another nudge. That wouldn't be for a few days yet. He doubted that anything else would be talked about.

He saw a slightly built young man cross the junction, pause on the other side and then carry on.

Mohammed leaned forward and concentrated.

The man returned, paused again and then walked toward the warehouse.

Mohammed collected the 9mm Beretta M9 from the glovebox. The gun had been fitted with a suppressor. He put it into his jacket pocket.

The man was closer now. Dusk had fallen and visibility was lessened, but he could see it was Aamir.

He took a pair of latex overshoes and pulled them over his trainers, then pulled on a pair of gloves and a plastic hairnet. He got out of the van, closed the door quietly and crossed over the road.

Aamir was facing the door, half-heartedly pulling the cage.

Mohammed reached into his pocket for the key with his right hand and clasped Aamir around the shoulder with his left. 'Aamir,' he said, 'do not worry. It is me.'

'I'm sorry,' the boy said. He turned and Mohammed saw the tears streaming down his face.

He would have to be quick. He did not want to have a scene on the street; passers-by might remember.

He unlocked the cage, yanked it back, opened the door and pulled Aamir inside.

There was a large space inside. The metal sheets over the windows stopped all the light. The only illumination came through the gaps that edged the door, weak and ineffectual and quickly absorbed by the darkness. The room was damp, and Mohammed could hear the trickling of water from somewhere in the gloom. He had purchased a builder's lamp from a branch of Wickes, and he crouched down to switch it on. The sudden glare created a vivid pool of light, picking out rows of racking that would once have been used for storage. The shelves cast a lattice of deep black shadows against the walls. Aamir looked around uncertainly.

'What is this place?'

'Somewhere we won't be seen. You are safe here, Aamir.'

'I'm sorry . . .' He couldn't finish the sentence.

'What happened?'

The boy's tears came in hungry sobs.

'Tell me.'

'I . . . I . . . couldn't do it.'

'What do you mean?'

'I was there, in the train, but I couldn't. I couldn't . . . there were people there, tourists, I would have killed all of them.'

'It is fine, Aamir. You don't need to worry. I understand.'

The boy looked at him, confusion evident on his face. Mohammed knew why. Aamir must have expected that he would be angry with him for failing to carry out his orders. He knew the effect that he could have on people. He knew that he had a powerful, forceful personality, and a man with his fearsome reputation was not a man that you would want to disappoint. He had relied upon both to fashion his mules as he wished, to inspire them to do his bidding.

But this one had not done as he had been told.

'Did anyone see you come here?'

'I don't think so,' Aamir said.

'You don't think?'

'I was careful,' he whined, 'but I'm confused. This whole thing . . .'

Mohammed spoke with the most reassuring tone that he could manage. 'I'm sure you were careful, brother. You need to be calm. Everything is going to be all right. Where is your rucksack?'

'I left it there.'

'At Westminster?'

'Yes. Inside. I left it there and ran.'

He started to sob again.

Mohammed tried to placate him. 'It doesn't matter. The operation is a success.'

'Bashir and Hakeem?'

He nodded. 'They are with the prophet now.'

'You're sure?'

'Yes. The details are a little confused, but they are reporting that there were two explosions.'

'There were,' Aamir said quickly, trying to please him. 'Definitely. I heard them.'

'Many infidels were killed. It doesn't matter that you did not detonate your bomb. Everything will be fine, Aamir. You need to relax.'

Aamir looked at Mohammed, and a fresh look of confusion came over his face. He pointed. 'Why are you wearing those?'

He meant the overshoes, the gloves and the hairnet. 'I'm very careful,' Mohammed explained. 'I don't leave evidence that I have been in a place.'

'What about me?'

'It's fine. They won't be able to follow you here very easily.'

'So why are you wearing them?'

'We will be leaving soon,' he said, reassuring him. 'You are safe, Aamir.'

He knew that the security forces would identify Aamir soon enough. They would scour the footage from the barrage of CCTV cameras in the station, and it would be a simple enough thing to find the boy with the heavy-looking rucksack that was just the same as the rucksacks carried by the two bombers. They would be able to follow his Underground journey all the way back to Euston, and then they would find him disembarking from the train. They would follow that back to Luton. Mohammed had anticipated that they would, of course. That was why he had proposed the meeting in the car park rather than in the station itself. He had checked very carefully, and he was sure that there were no cameras at the end of the station property. The police would find Bashir's car and be able to trace their journey back to its origin in Manchester. There would be no sign of Mohammed.

And, of course, the police would be able to follow Aamir's footsteps away from Westminster. They would be able to follow him onto the bus. They would know when he disembarked, too. But Mohammed was confident that there would be limited coverage once he left the bus, and none once he turned onto the warren of roads and alleys that eventually led to the warehouse. They would follow him as far as they could and then swamp the area with officers. They would find this place eventually, but it would be much too late by then. He had plenty of time, but he had to deal with the boy.

'They'll follow me here?'

'Some of the way. Not once you left the main road.'

'So why do you need that stuff?'

'I like to be very careful. This is dangerous work, Aamir. I have been doing it for many years. Do you know why I have never been caught?'

'Because you *are* careful.'

'And because I don't leave loose ends.'

He took the gun from his pocket and shot the boy in the gut. The Beretta coughed, the report muffled by the suppressor. Aamir fell to the floor, his hands clasped around his stomach, with the blood already discolouring his shirt. He looked up at Mohammed in shock. He stepped up to him, pressed the end of the silencer against his crown and fired a second time. The force of the round knocked Aamir down onto his side.

Mohammed collected both casings and put them into his pocket.

He took his iPad and opened the BBC's iPlayer app. The usual evening schedule had been cancelled for wall-to-wall coverage of the bombing. There was a helicopter overhead offering an excellent view of the damage that the second bomb had caused. The news anchor was reporting dozens of fatalities and hundreds maimed or wounded. Survivors, many glazed over with shock, were relaying their experiences to the cameras. Senior police officers struggled to answer premature questions about who might be responsible. Politicians, only recently allowed to leave the questionable safety of the Commons chamber, fulminated angrily and promised that the perpetrators would be brought to justice. But the overwhelming impression was one of hopelessness that a powerful blow had been struck in the heart of the capital.

And that was all very, very good.

It would metastasise into fury and the desire for bloody revenge, and that was good, too.

Mohammed took a bottle of water and drank from it. He put his iPad away and made his preparations to leave.

Chapter Twenty-Two

It took an hour before the doors to the carriage were finally opened. The train had moved down the platform a little, and the smashed screen doors did not match up evenly with the doorways. People went through in single file. The emergency lights on the platform were lit. It meant that they could see where they were going. It also meant that they could see the devastation that had been wrought around them.

They went forward as a long snake, each person holding on to the hand of the person ahead of them. A man was in front of Isabella. He was wearing a suit and a polished pair of brown brogues and looked completely out of place. They walked through the passageway and into the vestibule. She heard the man mutter a curse. Up ahead, there was a pile of people. None of them were moving. Some of them were in pieces. They had to climb over and through them.

The woman who was holding Isabella's hand broke out of the line, jostling her, and as she caught her balance, she put her foot down on the leg of one of the bodies. It felt soft, with give to it, and was not what she would have expected at all. The woman stumbled and fell. Isabella kept walking.

A fireman was at the head of their little line. He led them to the escalator and ushered them up. 'Keep going up,' he said as Isabella passed by him. 'The way out is just up ahead. Don't stop.'

The shaft was blackened with soot, and chunks of the plaster had been gouged out by debris. They reached the top, and Isabella saw a woman who was hobbling. She had been in the line ahead of her, and now she was struggling to keep up. She was wearing a trouser suit, and because people were walking in single file, she was holding back the queue. Isabella released the hand of the man in front and went over to her.

'Are you all right?'

'No,' she said, gesturing to her leg.

Isabella looked down. It was horribly bent. She didn't know how she could walk on it at all.

'Can I help?'

'Thank you.'

The woman rested her weight on Isabella's shoulder, and straining with the effort, she helped her walk towards the gate and the daylight beyond.

PART TWO

Chapter Twenty-Three

Isabella Rose idled the engine of her Kawasaki Ninja. The bike had belonged to her mother, and she had taught her how to ride it. It was big and powerful, and riding it was one of Isabella's favourite pleasures.

She waited at the end of the road with the row of industrial units. The little industrial quarter was next to the Route de Safi, four kilometres south of Marrakech. It accommodated dozens of studios that produced made-for-export goods for tourists to take home with them.

She had noticed the workshops as she was riding out to the south. There was a sign staked into the baked ground, advertising cheap space. She had been looking for somewhere more secure than the garage that her mother had left her in the city. That place was in a bad part of town and she was concerned that it wasn't secure. She had visited it one afternoon to find scrapes and gouges around the lock. Someone had tried to get inside. Squatters, maybe, or junkies looking for an easy score. It didn't matter who. They must have been interrupted – she had been fortunate. She had no intention of losing the equipment that she stored there.

A car arrived, passing Isabella and slowing outside the vacant unit. The engine stopped and a man got out. She guessed that it was the *samsar*. Property in Morocco was let in various ways. Some leases were arranged with traditional realtors, whereas others were more ad hoc, employing the services of a *samsar*. They worked in every neighbourhood and knew where all the available property could be found. The landlord and tenant paid a small commission to the *samsar* for his services if the property was rented. *Samsars* tended not to have dedicated offices and advertised their business in tea cafés and convenience stores.

The man was in his late middle age, wearing a cheap suit that was dusty at the ankles, and cheap shoes. It was obvious that his profession did not offer him a particularly lucrative return.

She revved the engine and rolled down the road to him. He checked her out, a quick glance, and then looked right through her.

'Monsieur?'

He looked at her with surprise. He replied, in French, 'Hello?'

Isabella's French was excellent. 'You have an appointment.'

The surprise became mild annoyance. 'Yes, but not with you. With Melody Atika.'

'My mother.'

'And where is she?'

'I'm here on her behalf.'

'And what is your name?'

'Sabrina.'

'I really need to speak to your mother, Sabrina.'

'She would have come, but she has been detained. She sends her apologies, but she thought it was sensible that we keep the appointment.'

'But you . . .' He paused, trying to find the right words to convey his disappointment. He managed a smile. 'But you are just a *girl, mademoiselle*.'

Isabella ignored the man's patronising tone. 'She trusts me to make a decision on her behalf.'

He sucked his teeth. 'I think it would be better to wait, though, don't you?'

'No, I don't. Neither does she. I've come all the way out here. So have you. If the premises are unsuitable, I can tell my mother and save you a second trip. But if they *are* suitable, perhaps you make your commission.' The man still looked uncomfortable, although she could see that she was gradually persuading him. She pointed to the door. 'Open it up. I'll take a look.'

The *samsar* sighed but gave up. 'Fine,' he said, reaching into his pocket for a key that was fastened to a bright red fob. He unlocked the door, bent down to the handle and heaved the door up and over.

Isabella ducked down and passed beneath the half-open door and into the unit. There were no windows, and the only illumination was the daylight that seeped in through the door. The *samsar* pulled a drawstring, and a bulb flickered and caught. She looked around. It was a small space. She could walk from the front to the back with just five paces, and it was the same from left to right.

'It's tiny,' she said.

'The details are all on the website. The dimensions, the—'

'The dimensions are listed as ten by ten. This is – what? Half that?'

'The dimensions—'

'Never mind,' she said. 'How long can it be leased for?'

'As long as your mother would like.'

'How much is it?'

'It is ten thousand dirhams a month.'

She shook her head. 'That's extortionate.'

'I'm afraid that is the price.'

'My mother will pay five.'

'You can negotiate on her behalf?'

'Five.'

He narrowed his eyes. 'Seven.'

'Five and a half. And she'll pay the first year up front.'

'She will agree to that?'

The man was a bumptious oaf, and Isabella had to fight to keep the irritation from her voice. 'Yes, she will. In cash.'

He couldn't disguise the greed that passed across his face.

'Tell her if she can bring the money to the café tomorrow, I'll personally make sure that it is all arranged.'

Isabella said that she would. She took one final look around the space to confirm that it was suitable for her purposes and, satisfied that it was, went back outside to her bike. The *samsar* pulled the drawstring, lowered the door and locked it.

She gunned the engine and rode back to the city.

Isabella followed the main road into the suburbs of the city, then followed a well-worn route to the Rue Kaa El Machraa. It was on the other side of town from the place that she had shared with her mother and was approached through a similar warren of alleyways and passages, each narrower and darker than the last, ancient and mysterious. She turned right and then left, and when it became too narrow to ride safely, she got off and pushed the bike. She skirted two local boys playing games on their phones in the light of a kerosene lamp, and finally reached the thick oak door. The small sign fixed on the wall next to it announced the Riad Farnatchi.

She unlocked it, pushed it all the way back and negotiated the bike inside. The first room was a generous vestibule, and she pushed the bike through it into the open courtyard beyond. Moroccan riads were built around open shafts that typically featured a freezing-cold plunge pool at the bottom. The warm air was drawn down into the shaft, cooled at the bottom and then recirculated so that the rooms arranged around the opening were cooled.

This riad was smaller than the one she had shared with Beatrix, and much less opulent. It had been a wreck when she had purchased it, using some of the bequest that her mother had left to her, but a year of hard work had seen it brought back to life again.

There was still a little work to do, but most of the big jobs had now been completed.

The crumbling bricks had been renewed with fresh courses. The rotting window frames had been taken out and replaced. The décor, which had been so dated, had been brought up to date. The walls had been painted a slate grey, with colourful pieces of local art hung to provide splashes of colour. She had bought second-hand furniture from the souks and then refurbished each piece herself. She had bought carpets from the Berber markets in the mountains. The plunge pool had been retiled in emerald green, and her favourite pastime was to sit beside it in one of her lime-green easy chairs and stare up at the square of sky above.

She climbed the stairs to her bedroom on the second floor, found the false floorboards underneath the Berber rug and lifted them aside. There was a small cavity beneath, with a leather satchel inside. She took it out, opened it and withdrew two bundles of banknotes. She still had a lot of money in a bank in the Caymans, but she always ensured she had enough to manage without needing recourse to it. She had $20,000 in the bag. A rent of 5,500 dirhams a month meant that it would cost 66,000 for the year. That was a touch over $6,500. She counted out $7,000, put the rest back into the satchel and replaced it in its hiding place. She laid the floorboards over it and covered those with the rug.

She returned to the ground floor and made herself a glass of mint tea.

It had been a relief to escape London and return home. The aftermath of the bombing had been chaotic. A triage centre had been established in a nearby branch of Marks & Spencer and the police were insistent that everyone pass through it. The reason, they said, was that they wanted to check that those people who had been in the station had not been injured by the first blast. Isabella had checked herself immediately and was happy that she was unscathed. The police also required that everyone leave their name and contact details. Beatrix had been very clear that she should never leave a record of her presence and so, using the routine that had been taught to her, Isabella provided a fake name and address and then pretended to cry. The policeman who had been talking to her went in search of a box of tissues, and Isabella took the opportunity to make her exit.

It had been difficult to get to the airport. The entire Tube network had been suspended, and there had been no cell phone reception until the early evening. She had walked for two hours before she was able to find an empty taxi. Heathrow had been operating, albeit under the watch of armed soldiers. Anyone who had looked remotely suspicious was stopped. The terminal had been loud with the sound of raised voices and accusations of racism. She had found a space on the floor where she could lean against a wall and watched the looped footage of the atrocities on the twenty-four-hour news channel.

Her plan had been to return to Morocco that day, but she had concluded that it would not have been prudent to fly directly to a Muslim country. Instead, she had taken a British Airways flight to Gibraltar and stayed overnight at the Ibis near to the airport. A ferry crossed the Strait of Gibraltar several times a day, and she had taken a place as a walk-on passenger on the following morning's first crossing. She had caught a coach from Tangier to Marrakech and arrived in the early evening. The diversion had cost her a day's travel, but it was what her mother would have done, and it pleased Isabella to know that she was following her mother's example.

The tranquillity of the riad had been a balm when she finally arrived home. She had stocked up on the things that she thought she might need and intended to stay out of sight for the rest of the week.

She rarely used her television, but she found that she was unable to resist watching the news. That it was a terrorist attack was beyond question, but the authorities were unable to suggest who might have been responsible. Pundits filled the spaces with incessant speculation. Isabella was not interested in international affairs, and she would not have pretended to have the knowledge to qualify her for making her own determination, but even to her eye, it was obvious that the authorities were floundering.

It didn't look as if they had any idea what had happened.

The first footage of the aftermath of the blast was vivid to her. She watched the camera jerk and shudder as the operator struggled to negotiate the debris. She saw the brief suggestions of atrocity caught in the camera's light. The report triggered her own recollection and replayed the things that she had seen. She had nightmares that night. She knew that she was buttressed against shock by the things that she had already seen and done, but that did not mean that the nightmares were any less frightening. She woke up in the middle of the night, wide-eyed with fear and with sweat-drenched sheets wound around her legs.

She went to the roof of the riad and looked out over the sleeping city. There was a breeze blowing in from the desert, and it cooled her. She took a drink, swallowed a sleeping tablet and returned to her bed.

Chapter Twenty-Four

Captain Michael Pope spent the first week of his enforced sabbatical working on his fitness. He had been sitting behind a desk for too long as it was, and he had started to feel lazy and fat. But that wasn't the only reason. He had never felt as frustrated as he did now, and working up a sweat had always been his best way to alleviate stress. He had made it his annual tradition to run a marathon, but he had allowed his resolution to slip since he had been promoted from Number One to Control. He decided that the best way to get back into fighting shape was to run one once again.

Pope was a tall man with close, dark hair. He had the physique of an athlete and the kind of constitution that adapted quickly to an increase in physical activity. He was slender, but muscular. He was also very strong.

He was unfussy and straightforward, and chose his clothes from a simple wardrobe that allowed him to fade into the background without attracting attention. He favoured simple suits in charcoal and black, and when he was out of the office, conservative jeans or chinos and poplin shirts. His only extravagance was his shoes. The years he had spent on his feet as a soldier had incubated a preference for quality, and that was displayed by the two pairs of boots that he owned from Red Wing of San Francisco, each of which had cost him £300.

He was a good-looking man, ageing well. He tended towards the severe in the office, most appropriate for a man with his responsibilities, but when he was on his own time, he had a ready smile and a quick wit that made him popular with his many friends. He looked like a man who could handle himself, a man who would be a better friend than an enemy and a man who could be trusted to do what he said he would do.

He had been born in a village on the outskirts of Salisbury in the south-west of England. It was close to Salisbury Plain, an important army training facility, and the town and its surrounding villages were full of soldiers. He had flunked his way through school, and with no trade to follow, he had enrolled as a boy soldier at sixteen, joining the Royal Green Jackets. There had been time in the sandpit for the First Iraq War, a transfer to the First Battalion when he got back and then the first of several tours of South Armagh. A friend of his brother served in the 23rd SAS Reserves, and he had invited Pope to join him for a weekend's training. Pope excelled and repeated the trip several times after that, attempted Selection and passed it. He joined B Squadron as a medic and spent the next five years carrying out both covert and overt operations around the world. That was until his predecessor as Control picked him out as a man with promise and offered him a transfer to the Firm and, more specifically, to be the new Number Twelve in Group Fifteen.

He had served his country as a Group Fifteen headhunter until his predecessor's treachery had been revealed, and he had been asked to take over. He had accepted reluctantly. He did not consider himself to be a desk man, and he felt that he was young enough and better suited to continue as a field agent. Stone, who had asked him to consider the promotion, had insisted. Pope realised that the choice he was being given was illusory. He was being ordered to take over.

His promotion had come with more generous remuneration, and Pope had moved his family to a thatched cottage in the heart of the Cotswolds. It was a pretty part of the country, known for honey-coloured limestone buildings and the miles of dry stone walls that divided the lush landscape into parcels.

One of the benefits of living here was the number of pleasant roads that he could use in his daily runs. He had gradually increased his distance as he got his legs back beneath him, and this morning, the start of a cold and frosty early autumnal day, he had planned to run the full length of the local amateur marathon. He started in Broadway, climbed Broadway Tower for the views out over the Vale of Evesham, and then crossed to Snowshill and Stanway. He reached the halfway mark in Winchcombe, the walking capital of the Cotswolds, passing Sudeley Castle before attacking the final big hill of the route. Once he had surmounted it, he ran along the escarpment for a few miles before descending again for an easy return on the gently undulating fields, from Stanway back to Broadway again.

Running also enabled him to think. The steady cadence of his steps, the sound of his breathing and the beating of his heart all contributed to an almost meditative state that often allowed him to solve problems that he had not otherwise been able to fix. Today, though, his thoughts were of Paddy McNair.

There had been a low-key funeral the day before yesterday. Scouse had always been a womaniser, and he had no family. His parents had died years ago. The mourners were old friends from the Regiment. There wasn't much left of him to bury, but they had all stood around the grave in the Regimental plot in Hereford and watched as the casket was lowered into the ground. Pope had looked around at all the other graves and seen that the plot was almost full. He had overheard two of the men making the same observation, one of them suggesting that the Regiment would have to buy a new plot or stop going to war.

The former was the most likely solution to that problem, Pope had thought, especially now.

He picked up the pace a little. He could see the village in the distance as a black BMW passed him slowly on his right-hand side. He wondered, for a moment, whether it was just a considerate driver giving him plenty of room, but when the car continued slowly ahead and then indicated to pull over, he started to be concerned. He didn't have a weapon with him, and if he was attacked out here, there would be very little he would be able to do. He scanned left and right, identified a gap in the hawthorn hedge at a spot just ahead of the car and tried to find the energy to sprint, should that be necessary.

It wasn't.

The rear passenger-side window slid down, and as he drew alongside, he saw Vivian Bloom.

He stopped.

'Sorry to surprise you out here, Control.'

He took a moment to fill his lungs and bring his heart rate back under control. 'You couldn't have called to make an appointment?'

'You know better than that, old boy. Do you have fifteen minutes? There's something we need to talk about.'

Pope looked down at Bloom through the open window of the car, scrubbed the sweat from his face and looked away to the road leading back to his home. He didn't know much about The Reverend; almost nothing, in fact, he realised with discomfort. The man was well connected, but difficult to assess. Pope remembered how Bloom had behaved at the meeting when Group Fifteen had been shut down. He had said very little, sitting and observing, an enigmatic expression on his face.

Pope didn't trust very many people, and he didn't trust Bloom.

He exhaled. He couldn't very easily tell the man he didn't want to talk to him and run back home. His country had just been attacked, and Pope was a soldier. He had responsibilities.

He opened the door and slid inside.

'Thank you, Captain,' Bloom said, shaking Pope's hand.

Pope took it gently, like a doctor probing brittle bones, but Bloom surprised him with the firmness of his grip.

'You can probably guess what this is about,' he said.

'Yes, sir. I expect I can.'

'A mess. A bloody mess. But it's been coming, you know. We knew they would have a go eventually. An RPG into Buckingham Palace, Kalashnikovs in Trafalgar Square, a suicide bomber blowing himself up in the Tate. I think it's fair to say that they surprised us with the scale of their ambition and the level of preparation. It was a very well put together operation.'

'The bombs were diversionary?'

He nodded. 'I think that's obvious now. There were supposed to be three of them. The early assessment is that they were going to detonate one on the train, and then the other two as survivors made their way to the surface. It's more sophisticated than we've seen before.'

'It's standard for the sandbox, sir. They draw you in with the first one and then hit you properly.'

'They obviously wanted to do as much damage as they could, but those bombs were designed to concentrate our attention on the station and put the Commons on lockdown. And both of those things happened. It's thanks to you, McNair and Snow that they didn't get into the chamber. Especially McNair. God knows what would have happened if they had managed to get in.'

'It was just good luck we were there.'

'That's as may be. Doesn't change the facts. I want to show you something.'

Bloom opened his briefcase and withdrew an iPad. He tapped an application, and a video player appeared. With a cautious check to ensure that they were still unobserved, he tapped 'Play' and handed the tablet to Pope.

The shot showed a man in a traditional Arabic dishdasha and a chequered scarf around his neck. He was sitting in a blank, anonymous room that would be almost impossible to identify. The black and white flag of ISIS was fixed to the wall behind him. Pope recognised the format immediately: this was a martyrdom video.

The man cleared his throat and spoke in a calm, confident voice.

'What you have witnessed now is only the beginning of a series of attacks that will continue until you pull your forces out of Syria and Iraq and until you stop your financial and military support to America and Israel. I, and thousands like me, am forsaking everything for what I believe. Our driving motivation doesn't come from tangible commodities that this world has to offer. Our religion is Islam – obedience to the one true God, Allah, and following the footsteps of the final prophet and messenger, Muhammad . . . Your democratically elected governments continuously perpetuate atrocities against my people all over the world. And your support of them makes you directly responsible, just as I am directly responsible for protecting and avenging my Muslim brothers and sisters. Until we have security, you will be our targets. And until you stop the bombing, gassing, imprisonment and torture of my people, we will not stop this fight. We are at war, and I am a soldier.'

'This was uploaded to YouTube thirty minutes ago. His name is Ibrahim Yusof.'

'One of the shooters.'

'We have reason to believe that the other men who attacked inside Parliament were Faik Khan, Nazir Begun, Abdul Rashid and

Mo Rafiq. The two men you shot before they could get inside were Bilal Ismail and Aneel Mirza. Until yesterday, we thought they were all in Syria.'

'They certainly knew how to use their weapons.'

'Yes, indeed. Been out there awhile, we think. Training camps, then sent out to the front lines. It appears that they managed to get back into the country without our knowledge. We're obviously looking into that as a matter of the utmost urgency.'

'The bombers?'

He swiped across the screen, and a CCTV picture of three young men appeared. They were on a platform. The sign in the background said Luton. All three were wearing rucksacks on their backs.

'More troubling. Home-grown. The two who triggered their bombs were a little more difficult to identify, for obvious reasons.' He pointed at the two older men of the three. 'This one is Bashir Anwar and this one is Hakeem Mustafa. The bomber who lost his nerve is this man, here. His name is Aamir Malik. These last three are from Manchester.'

'Are you close to finding Aamir?'

'Found him today. His body was found in the Thames. Two bullet wounds: one to the gut, one to the head. We're working on the assumption that he lost his nerve and was killed for it.'

Bloom took the iPad and slid it into his case.

Pope felt a little awkward, sitting in the back of the car dressed as he was, still hot and sweating from his exertions. 'Why are you here, sir?'

'We can't sit back and let this play out the usual way. It's already a bloody mess. The police are all over the place. The forensic people thought it was organic peroxide, home-grown explosives; then they changed their mind to military-grade plastique, and now they're saying the stuff was scraped out of artillery shells. Immigration doesn't know how the shooters got into the country, let alone how they brought artillery shells with them. MI5 is passing off the blame to the local police on the radicalisation of the bombers. No one is standing up to the mark. The investigation is a shambles, Captain. A fucking shambles. And we are taking *everything* our friend Ibrahim said in his little video very seriously. GCHQ says that chatter suggests there's going to be another attack. They are most definitely not done. Remember 7/7?'

'Of course.'

'There would have been 21/7, too, if *those* bombs had gone off, rather than just the detonators. I see nothing to suggest that this isn't the jihadists doing their level best to make sure they do it right this time.'

'So?'

'We need to move in the grey areas to make sure that doesn't happen, and that means you and your headhunters. I need you back in the game.'

'What does the home secretary think about that?'

Bloom's laugh was a dry rasp. 'She doesn't know, Captain.'

'Really?'

'What do you think she would say? The die is cast as far as Group Fifteen is concerned. There will be an enquiry that will reach the conclusion she wants, and then there will be a reorganisation. The Firm itself, probably. Lots of talk about how it's an anachronism, out of place in today's world.'

'That's—'

'I know,' Bloom interrupted. 'It's naïve and dangerous, but she can't very well reverse course now.'

Pope squeezed his hands together in a gesture of discomfort. 'I'll be honest, sir. That makes me rather nervous.'

'It should. What I am proposing is completely illegal, off the books and has severe consequences if it goes wrong.'

'I'm going to speak frankly, sir.'

'Please do,' Bloom said with a chuckle. 'It was quite something the last time.'

'The meeting was clear. No one was in our corner. I'm a little confused.'

'You don't need to be. I'm on your side. I always have been. I don't trust the police. I know it was their mistake that got Rubió killed. I agreed with everything you said at the meeting. It's outrageous that you've been blamed.'

'It might have been nice to hear that on the day, sir.'

'Don't be naïve,' Bloom said with irritation. 'This is a long game. Things have to be done delicately. Changing opinions can be difficult.'

'I can see how someone trying to shoot up *PMQs* might have that effect.'

He smiled at that. 'Between you and me, Control, the irony isn't lost on us that the reason the home secretary wasn't in the chamber for *PMQs* was because she was having her fun bollocking you.'

'It wasn't all bad, then.'

Bloom collected the iPad again and opened another file.

Pope recognised the man in the picture that he called up.

Alam Hussain.

Most people would have known who he was. He was burly, with a bald head and a long beard that reached down to his sternum. He wore a traditional dishdasha and an eyepatch over his right eye. The man had been a hate figure for the right-wing press for months. He was known as the Preacher of Hate and was said to rain down fire and brimstone on the West from the minbar of the Stockdale mosque that he controlled. Much of the media's indignation stemmed from the fact that Hussain had been given asylum when he had fled from Qatar, yet now he railed against the very state that had taken him in. They fulminated that he was happy to take social security handouts and live in a house provided by the local council, yet still he called for the imposition of sharia law. Pope had always made a point of maintaining a strictly apolitical stance when it came to matters such as this. He and the Group had been sent against targets of all political persuasions, and keeping a neutral opinion made things easier.

Saying all that, Alam Hussain was a difficult man to like.

'Seriously, sir? He'd do this?'

'We have very strong intelligence that Hussain was responsible for radicalising the three bombers. We know, for example, that they all attended his mosque. We've had people inside it for weeks. He's been calling for jihad, issuing fatwas against members of the government and military, and distributing propaganda for Da'eash. We need you to go and get him.'

'Dead or alive?'

'Alive. Most definitely alive. I realise that's more difficult.'

'A little. But not a problem.'

'We don't want a big team on this. We were thinking of three or four agents, but I do want you to be one of them. I know I needn't tell you how delicate this is. I need your experience on the ground, not behind a desk. Everything else is completely up to you.'

'Where do you want him delivered?'

'Bit of a drive, I'm afraid. Need you to take him up to Wick. Our American friends have agreed to help us with the interrogation, and they've taken a bit of a liking to Scottish air. Nice and out of the way, minimal chance of anyone seeing them come in and out. They're going to fly him out of the country. Somewhere with more relaxed rules on what can and can't be done during interrogation – you know what I mean, Pope.'

'I do,' he said, not saying what he was thinking.

'I knew you would.'

'Equipment?'

'It'll be minimal, but enough.'

'What else do we know about him?'

'Everything you need. You'll be provided with his address, antecedents and suchlike. Use the usual dead drop. He does have some rudimentary security that you'll have to consider. There have been incidents with the right-wing headbangers up there. Threats and abuse. But it's nothing too sophisticated, just the local police keeping an eye on him. Certainly nothing that will hold you up.'

Pope found he was tapping his fingers against the leather upholstery.

'Well? What do you say?' Bloom said.

'Is this an order, sir? Are you ordering me to arrange this?'

'No. Technically, you and the Group are still suspended.'

'Will there be any backup?'

'None, I'm afraid.'

'And if it goes wrong?'

'I'm sure it won't.'

'But if it did?'

'Then you know how it has to be, Pope. I won't be able to protect you. The story we'll leak to the press writes itself. Your recent experience with the shooters will explain why you have reacted this way. You saw the explosion at first hand. It's PTSD. A dreadful shame, but completely understandable in the circumstances. You'll be looking at a good stretch of jail time, a little less if you can get a good brief who can make an argument about diminished responsibility.'

'You make a very appealing offer, sir.'

'Yes, well, there you are. Sorry about that. What do you say, Control? I need an answer this afternoon.'

Pope remembered the aftermath of the bombs with absolute clarity. He could still smell the burning flesh in his nostrils.

'Of course, sir. I'll start at once.'

Pope ran the rest of the way home, showered, shaved and dressed in a loose-fitting pair of trousers and a sweatshirt.

His wife, Rachel, had come home while he was showering. She was sitting on the sofa in the lounge with her legs curled up beneath her as she read a book.

'How did it go?'

'Good.'

'How long?'

'Four hours.'

'Not bad.'

'Not bad, but I can do better.'

'First time, Michael. Baby steps. You're old and fat now, remember.'

He was unable to keep the anxious smile from his face. She had known him long enough to know what it meant.

'Work?'

'Yes. I'm going to be away for a while.'

'London?'

He nodded.

Rachel knew better than to press him any further than that. He wouldn't have told her, and their married life had always been bracketed by the reality that there would be things that he couldn't share. It had been the same when he had been in the Regiment, and she had learned to accept that he would frequently be out of the country. When he returned, he would often be unable to tell her where he had been. His transfer to Group Fifteen had simply exacerbated that. She didn't ask any more.

'When are you leaving?'

'In an hour.'

'What do you want me to tell the kids?'

Pope's daughter had a football tournament at the weekend. He had promised that he would take her. That wouldn't be possible any more. The children were out with their friends this afternoon. He realised that he wouldn't even be able to say goodbye.

He sighed unhappily. He was committed to his work, but it put a heavy burden on his family life. He was lucky that Rachel was so understanding. 'Can you apologise for me?'

'Of course. How long will you be?'

'I don't know. A few days. I'll call when I can.'

She came over and kissed him. 'Be careful,' she said. She said it every time he went away.

'This isn't anything special. I'll be back soon. Nothing to worry about.'

Chapter Twenty-Five

Isabella arrived at the little workshop at just after seven in the morning. The temperature was cool, and she had enjoyed the sensation of the wind whipping around her body and through the visor of her open helmet as she made the ride south.

She put down the kickstand and got off the bike. She took the key, pulled up the door and looked inside. It was small – smaller than she remembered – and she had a moment of doubt that it might be a little too small for what she had in mind. But as she gauged the space again, she thought that it would just about suffice.

Isabella had visited the *samsar* two days previously and completed the formalities. She had taken the lease home with her the day before that, signing it in the name of Melody Atika and providing a photocopy of her fake passport. The lease had been notarised, and then had come the matter of the rent. Isabella had counted out the money into two piles and put enough for the year's rent inside a manila envelope. She had put the remainder into a second envelope and taken it to the café where the *samsar* was waiting for her. She had given both envelopes to him. He had licked his thumb and made a show of counting it all out. She knew that the fee had been much more than he would normally have expected. She didn't know whether he had bought the story about her mother or not. She was buying his discretion, and the fact that he had accepted it without comment suggested that he had received the message loud and clear.

The sun climbed into the sky and started to warm the chill from the air.

Isabella moved her bike out of the way and got ready. It was going to be a busy day.

The delivery lorry arrived at eight. The driver and his mate opened up the back and muscled the goods down to the ground. Isabella had purchased a series of lockers and safes on the Internet. She had paid extra for installation, and the two workmen hauled the heavy units into place. The units were prepared for wall fixing with pre-drilled holes in the base and fixing bolts that the men implanted into the concrete.

One of the benefits of the workshop was that it was angled so that it was not possible to see into it from the neighbouring units, even when the door was raised. Isabella had noticed this quality at once and, knowing that she was going to be undertaking a considerable amount of fitting out, was pleased that the work would not be immediately visible to prying eyes.

In order to be doubly cautious, she took up a position fifty yards along the road in order to head off anyone who might otherwise wander down to the unit. She had arranged for a locksmith to visit, and she had intercepted him, confirming the work that he would do and directing him to the unit. The man removed the up-and-over door and replaced it with a sturdy new one that was fitted with a chunky lock.

It was midday by the time the work was complete. Isabella thanked the three men, tipped them well enough so that they would not gripe, but not so well that they would remember her, and then waited until they had driven away before she inspected her new premises.

She was pleased.

The lockers were constructed from 5 mm–thick fully welded steel and were secured by two high-security seven-lever key locks with full-length anti-jemmy returns. They would be very difficult to open without the key. There was plenty of space inside them for the equipment she needed to store. The new door was robust and didn't rattle as its predecessor had done. She shut the door, locked it and then tried to force it. It was impossible. If someone wanted to get inside, they would need to fix a tow rope to the handle and use a vehicle to yank it off. The most likely threat to the unit was an opportunistic thief, and the door should be more than enough of a problem to act as a deterrent.

But still she was not done. The last visit of the day was an engineer from an alarm company. Isabella had purchased a system to protect the building. She told him what she had in mind, and he took a ladder from his van so that he could climb up and fix the cameras and the alarm. The equipment was top of the line. Apart from internal and external motion detectors, the alarm came with high-resolution day/night cameras that recorded the feed onto a 250 GB hard drive and broadcast it, in real time, to Isabella's cell phone and tablet.

The man demonstrated what the system could do, showed her how to set a new code and left her alone.

By this time it was six in the evening, and the temperature was dropping again.

She set the alarm, locked the door and climbed back onto her bike. Then, pulling the helmet onto her head, she gunned the engine and headed for the road back into the city.

Chapter Twenty-Six

Group Fifteen was housed in an anonymous office on the banks of the Thames. The building was the putative headquarters of Global Logistics, an import/export company that did enough business to give the Group's agents the scope to travel the world under the cover of their 'employment' with the Firm. Pope knew he couldn't go there. He was, after all, supposed to be suspended. He couldn't very well just waltz inside and plan everything from his desk. Bloom knew that, too, and he had planned alternative accommodation for him. Bloom had told him that all the information he would need would be left in the Epping Forest dead drop that Group Fifteen had often used before.

Pope drove north, left his own car in the long-term parking at Heathrow and picked up a hire car from Avis. He followed the clockwise M25, came off at exit 26 and took the A121 the rest of the way. The increased security was evident as he approached the capital. The news reported that nearly twenty thousand troops had been deployed around the country to ward against the follow-up attacks that the intelligence was suggesting were likely. Pope saw a troop transport rumble by, the olive-green lorry melting into the gloomy undergrowth that fringed the road. Five minutes later he heard and then saw a pair of Tornado GR5s curving through the air, much lower than would normally be allowed in civilian airspace, the unmistakeable sight of missiles loaded onto the underwing hard points.

It felt as if the country was under siege.

The sky was darkening as he parked at the visitor centre near Chingford. He locked the car and followed the path into the trees. It was unusual to fall back on old-fashioned tradecraft. These days, information tended to be buried on little-known forums or as draft emails on shared Gmail or Hotmail accounts. The recipient gathered the information and then deleted the relevant message. Pope felt like an anachronism as he stalked through the thickening wood, remembering the wooden seat with the chalk mark on the slats that had indicated that there was something for him to collect. The dead drop itself was an oak tree, particularly old, with a useful natural niche six feet above the mulch of the forest floor. He checked to ensure that he was not being watched and, satisfied that he was alone, reached up to the niche and jammed his fingers inside. It contained an envelope.

He took it back to the car and, under the illumination of the courtesy light, slit it open. A key for a Yale lock dropped into his hand, together with an address in Hackney, an eight-digit code and a USB stick.

Pope pressed the ignition, reversed out of the car park and followed the A104 south towards East London.

The safe house was on Valentine Road, between Homerton and Hackney. It was a terraced street with a pub to the west and a row of shops to the east. Pope drove past the address and then parked five minutes up the road. He walked back, taking a different route, and allowed himself to adjust to the location. He tuned in to the cadences and rhythms of the place. Valentine Road was busy with traffic, the houses a little more flyblown than those on the quieter streets that fed into it. It was close to a social housing block, and the shiftless youths who gathered around the off-licences and convenience stores regarded him with sour hostility as he made his way along the road past them.

He approached the house, climbed the steps from the street and put the key into the lock. He turned it, the door opened and he went inside. He closed the door and slid the anchor of the security chain into the receiver. He drew his pistol and stood in the dark for a minute, concentrating on acclimatising himself to his new surroundings. He heard the ticking of a pipe somewhere towards the rear of the property, a distant car alarm and a police siren. Nothing else. The place had the dusty smell of somewhere that had lain empty for a while. It felt like he was alone, but he wasn't in the business of making assumptions. Assumptions got you killed. He had to be sure.

The house was set on three storeys. He moved to the stairs and descended, careful to put his weight on the outside of the treads so as to reduce the risk of noise from a squeaking board. The basement accommodated the kitchen, bathroom and one bedroom. He checked each room, opening the door and then going inside with his gun up and ready. The kitchen looked as if it had been recently installed, with stickers and labels fastened to the units and appliances. The fridge was stocked with milk and a supply of ready meals for the microwave. The bathroom was long and narrow, with a bath that had a shower attachment over the taps and a toilet that still had the label from the builders' merchant affixed to the inside of the lid. The sash windows were all secured by sturdy locks, and the rear door that opened onto the back garden was locked and bolted.

Clear.

The ground floor had two reception rooms. He walked from one to the other through a set of open double doors, his weapon primed. The rooms were furnished with IKEA sofas, a low table and nothing else.

Clear.

The first floor had a further two bedrooms, one with an en suite, and another tiny bathroom had been crammed at the top of a steep staircase that led up into the roof space. The bedrooms had flat-pack beds and wardrobes.

Clear.

He opened the hatch to the loft and hauled himself up. There was a badly fitted hatch to the roof, and a breeze pushed through the gaps. He activated the torch on his phone, found a light switch and switched it on. He saw the large metal crate laid out across the unboarded joists. There was a digital lock on the crate, and when he tapped in the code that had been written on the envelope, he was rewarded with a glowing green light and the sound of a metallic click as the lock stems were withdrawn. He opened the crate. Inside was a small cache of arms: three Sig Sauer P226 pistols, together with silencers for each of them, and a dozen boxes of 9mm ammunition. A combat shotgun that had been fitted with an EOTech sight for day or night use, a fixed iron sight and a telescopic buttstock. Cartridges of solid shot and buckshot for the shotgun. Four H4855 Personal Role Radios and the UHF transmitter-receiver issued to the British Armed Forces, together with small notebooks that contained call signs and frequencies. There was also a pick gun. It was a breaching tool that could be used to force mechanical pin tumbler locks.

Not bad, Pope thought.

He closed the crate, the lock automatically clicking back into place, and descended to the ground floor. The rear reception room was spacious enough for four or five people, and when the double doors that separated the large room into two halves were closed, it would be impossible to see in from the street. He opened his bag and took out the printouts he had made before he left the Cotswolds and the large-scale Ordnance Survey maps of Manchester that he had purchased. He had also bought a pack of Blu Tack and a container of drawing pins, and working quickly and efficiently, he stuck all of the material onto the walls, adjusting the order until it made sense to him. He spent an hour looking at it and making notes in a spiral-bound notebook that he would burn when he was finished. When he finally checked his watch, it was nine, and he was happy that he had the basis of a workable plan.

He slipped on his coat, locked the front door behind him, jogged down the steps and set off for the car. The others were due to arrive at Kings Cross, Euston and Liverpool Street, over the course of the next two hours. He needed to pick them up.

There was a lot to do.

Chapter Twenty-Seven

Bloom had given Pope a free hand as to the composition of the team. Each of the twelve men and women who made up the operational strength of Group Fifteen would have been more than capable of carrying out the mission objectives. The infiltration of the mosque was little more than a simple Breaking & Entering job, and the kidnapping of Hussain, though more challenging, was nothing when compared to the tasks that they would more normally have been given to do. Group Fifteen's current complement was a team of ten men and two women. The men were typically drawn from the ranks of British Special Forces: the Special Air Service, the Special Boat Service and 18 (UKSF) Signals Regiment. The women were both from the Special Forces Reconnaissance Regiment.

He had chosen four agents, plus himself. Group Fifteen operations were usually solo, but teams of two were deployed for more sensitive or difficult operations. These were not difficult jobs, but there was absolutely no room for error. Bloom had made that very clear. Pope was not prepared to take the risk that they would deploy below strength, but the five of them should be plenty to achieve their aims.

He had collected them earlier that evening. Hamish Munro, Number Four, had travelled down from Edinburgh. He had served in 22 SAS, A Squadron, for six years before Pope's predecessor had selected him. He was a proud Scot, cantankerous to a fault, and one of the toughest soldiers that Pope had ever served alongside.

Number Twelve was Thomas Snow. Pope felt obligated to include him. He was already involved.

Next to Snow was Victor Stokes, Number Seven. He was in his early thirties and had been selected from the Z Squadron, SBS. He had been a Royal Marine commando before his special forces posting and had made his name during the evacuation of Western oil workers from remote Libyan desert facilities.

The final member of Pope's team was Hannah Kelleher. She was Number Nine and the youngest of the four, having recently celebrated her thirty-second birthday. She had served with the Special Reconnaissance Unit in Iraq in the recent hunt for the British jihadis responsible for the murder of Western hostages. She was implacable and focused, rarely smiled and was a dead shot. Pope would not have wanted to be on her bad side.

There was a brew kit in the kitchen, and Pope had made tea for all of them. They were sitting in the rear reception room now. Munro and Snow were on the sofa, their feet on the low coffee table that stood between it and the fireplace. Kelleher was on the floor, her back propped up against the wall. Stokes, who was constitutionally cautious, was at the rear window, gazing into the dark garden below.

Pope took a sip of his tea and rested the cup on the mantelpiece. 'Thanks for coming on short notice.'

'This is unexpected,' Stokes said. 'I thought we were stood down.'

'Officially, we are.'

'Unofficially?'

'Not so much.'

Pope went through the details of his conversation with Bloom yesterday. They had all seen Ibrahim Yusof's martyrdom video and the subsequent ones that had been posted on behalf of Bilal Ismail and Aneel Mirza. Backlash was beginning to hit the security services, anger that they had been allowed to plot without challenge.

Pope explained that the imam of the Stockdale Mosque, Alam Hussain, was strongly suspected by MI5 of involvement in the operation.

'How good is the intel this time?' Munro asked. 'I only ask, because, you know, it wasn't great the last time we were in the field. Twelve got it in the neck.'

Snow sighed at the reference to Fèlix Rubió and looked away.

'I'm just saying – '

'We have orders. We have to assume it's accurate.'

'What do they want us to do?'

'Two tasks. First, we get Hussain off the street for questioning. Second, we break in to the mosque and conduct a search for useful evidence or intel.'

'Security on the target?' Hannah Kelleher asked.

'Some. More since Westminster. You've read the news the same as I have – there have already been retaliatory attacks. Everyone knows that those boys went to his mosque. Hussain has a reputation, and there are plenty of knuckle draggers out there who won't believe he didn't know anything about it.'

'They might be knuckle draggers,' she said, 'but it sounds like they might be right.'

'Whether he's involved or not isn't our problem. We need to get him and anything useful we can find.'

'What's the plan?'

'Two teams.' He pointed to Munro and Stokes. 'Four and Seven – you get the mosque.'

'Delightful,' Munro said.

Pope directed their attention to the walls. He had arranged the intelligence that Vivian Bloom had provided. There were photographs and diagrams. There was a map of Central Manchester that he had ringed in red ink with the location of the mosque. It was standing on substantial grounds between Anson Road and Conyngham Road.

'Here it is,' he said. He pointed to the photographs around the map. 'It's a new building, purpose built, and they put it up at a time when they knew that making it as secure as they could was probably a decent idea. It's surrounded on each side by a six-foot-tall brick wall, and there are railings on top of the walls. The main gates are the same height and covered by at least three CCTV cameras. Going in the front way isn't going to work.'

'And the back?' Munro prompted.

Pope pointed to another of the photographs. It showed a five-foot gap in the wall that had been blocked with temporary fencing. 'Turns out a car smashed into the wall last week, and they haven't had it rebuilt yet. This is how you get into the grounds. There's at least one camera with coverage, but take that out and you should be in and out without being seen.'

'Easy enough.'

'I think so too.' He had enlarged the architect's plans of the mosque, and it was to these that he turned next. 'Two floors once you're inside. The ground floor is the worship space. Ignore that. Take these stairs to the first floor. There are offices and classrooms up there. You're looking for hard drives, documents – anything you think might be worth a second look.'

'Alarms?'

'Yes, and probably good ones. If you can't find them and they get tripped, Bloom thinks you'll have five minutes before the police arrive. I wouldn't plan on staying any longer than that in any event, but the detail of how you structure things is down to you once you've had a look at the target.'

Munro and Stokes shared a glance and then turned back to Pope, nodding their agreement. 'Piece of cake.'

Pope agreed with that. A simple breaking and entering, even against a well-secured building, offered no particular problems to operatives as well trained as Four and Seven. The second part of their orders was more challenging. He pointed to Hannah Kelleher and Thomas Snow. 'Nine, Twelve and I will go and get Hussain.'

He took a quarter turn and nodded across to the other maps and photographs. Alam Hussain lived in Moss Side, a neighbourhood of Manchester that had earned the unfortunate sobriquet of 'Gunchester' over the course of thirty years of gang violence. Hussain's address was a mid-terrace house on Roseberry Street, a road that ran horizontally from east to west among a tight grid of similar streets. The houses were dilapidated, plenty of them sealed with metal sheeting to keep squatters out. The doors opened straight onto the street. Each house had a ground-floor window next to the door, and there were two narrow windows on the first floor. Every house was disfigured by a satellite dish, a few of them of the larger variety that were powerful enough to pick up transmissions from Eastern Europe. There was a park opposite, including a children's fenced-in play area, with a slide, swings and a roundabout. There were no trees, it was enclosed and there were no obvious spots for surveillance.

'Lovely spot,' Kelleher said with a wry smile.

An alleyway ran north to south, splitting the terrace in the middle, and Hussain's house backed onto it. The narrow space was obstructed by bin bags that had been torn open by scavenging dogs and the remains of wheelie bins that had been set on fire. The alleys were known as ginnels by the locals, and, Pope thought, this one could be very useful.

'Our man lives here,' he said. 'There's what you could charitably call a park to the south. You've got vehicular access to the east and west, but the locals park on both sides of the road, so there's only likely to be enough space for one car. We'll need to plan for that. Once we have him, we'll head for Princess Road, then the A57, M603, M61 and M6 up to Wick.'

Snow leaned back in his picnic chair and shook his head. 'Wick? As in Wick in Scotland?'

'We're going to be handing him over to the CIA. They've been itching to speak to him. Now's their chance. I'm allowing eight hours to get up there.'

'Why can't they do things like normal people?' Munro grumbled. 'Find me a lock-up. Give me a day alone with him, and I'll have him saying whatever they want him to say.'

'I'm happy to leave that to the CIA,' Pope said. 'We're in it deep enough as it is.'

'When do we go?'

'We need to get up there and get eyes on. We don't know anywhere near enough about him yet. I've got a hire car, and we'll get another. We'll go up tonight and get a better idea of the lay of the land. If we think we can get him tonight, we go tonight. If not, we'll wait. We hit the mosque simultaneously.'

The five of them stood.

'Let's get to work,' Munro said.

Chapter Twenty-Eight

They stopped to hire a second car. Munro and Stokes were in the first, a Renault Megane, and Snow, Kelleher and Pope were in Pope's Volkswagen Passat. Snow was driving, and Kelleher and Pope were in the back. He spent the four hours it took to drive north to Manchester reviewing the information on Alam Hussain that had been provided on the USB stick.

Hussain had been born in Bethlehem in the West Bank in 1960, which at that time was under Jordan's control. That gave him Jordanian nationality. In 1989, it was reported that he travelled to Peshawar in Pakistan, where he served as a professor of sharia sciences. There were unconfirmed reports that he had met Osama Bin Laden while in Peshawar. After the first Gulf War in 1991, Hussain was expelled from Kuwait, along with many other Palestinians. He returned to Jordan, but in September 1993 he fled with his wife and five children to the United Kingdom, using a forged UAE passport. He requested asylum on grounds of religious persecution, claiming he had been tortured in Jordan, and asylum was granted in June 1994. He had been in the country ever since.

Although Hussain publicly distanced himself from al-Qaeda, his MI5 file remarked that he was known to have extensive contacts with al-Qaeda operatives in Afghanistan. The analyst noted that Hussain had 'impeccable traditional and modern Salafist credentials and has acted as the in-house *alim* to radical groups, particularly in Algeria, from his base in Manchester since 1994.'

According to the indictment of the Madrid al-Qaeda cell responsible for the bombing of a train in 2004, Hussain was 'considered the spiritual leader' of al-Qaeda in Europe and other groups, including the Armed Islamic Group, the Salafist Group for Preaching and Combat, and the Tunisian Combat Group. He was considered to be a preacher or advisor to al-Qaeda terrorists Zacarias Moussaoui and Richard Reid. Videos of his sermons were found in the Hamburg apartment of Mohamed Atta when it was searched after the 11 September 2001 attacks. When questioned in the UK in February 2001, Hussain was in possession of £170,000 cash and £805 in an envelope labelled 'for the Mujahedin in Chechnya.'

'What's the bottom line?' Kelleher asked him.

Pope put the papers down. 'He's a bad man.'

It didn't really matter what Pope thought, since he would have carried out his orders whatever conclusion he had formed, but he was quite clear about that. Hussain *was* a bad man.

And he was about to have a very bad night.

He read on. Hussain had been attacked by members of the English Defence League after one of his sermons had been posted on YouTube. His nose had been broken, and his wife's burqa had been torn away. The police had provided him with protection, and the report noted that his detail had been strengthened in the light of threats to his life in the aftermath of the Westminster bombing.

That was going to make things a little more difficult.

Moss side was just as bad as advertised. The houses were typically in poor condition, many of them empty. The group drove along one street where all but one had been deserted, the remainder boarded up or secured behind bright orange anti-squatter panels and painted with red crosses to signify that they were to be demolished. A group of boys, their hoodies pulled up over their heads, walked by a house that had been allowed to collapse in on itself. Another pair of boys endlessly kicked a football against the wall of another blighted property. Rubbish blew on the gentle nocturnal breeze.

Pope was driving. Snow and Kelleher were in the back.

'What a dump,' Snow said.

Pope followed the satnav to the junction of Greame Street and Rosebery Street and then peeled it off the windscreen and dropped it into the footwell. This area was hardly a destination that anyone would want to find, and he did not want the glow of the unit to draw attention. He turned onto Rosebery Street and maintained a steady twenty miles per hour. He would allow a single pass of the address. He rolled west to east and passed ten feet from the red front door of number thirty. The others were quiet, both of them absorbing as much of the surrounding detail as they could.

The park to their right was small and unlit, and the pinpricks of red light before the faces of the three kids on the swings gave away the cigarettes that they were smoking. Cars were parked on both sides of the road, and there was only space for a single car at any one time. Pope was unhappy about that. It would make exfiltration more difficult.

Pope reached Claremont Road and parked in the empty courtyard in front of Mr McFresh Bakery. He turned and nodded at Kelleher. 'We'll go and take a look at it on foot. Snow – take the car, meet us at the junction of Rosebery Street and Great Western Street.'

They got out of the car, Snow going forward and sliding into the driver's seat. He pulled away, leaving Pope and Kelleher behind.

'Take the alley at the back of the house,' he said to Kelleher.

She nodded, waited for a pair of cars to pass, crossed Claremont Street and then set off along Cowesby Street, the road that ran adjacent to Rosebery Street.

Pope waited for her to reach the corner. 'Comms check,' he said into the tiny microphone that was attached to his lapel.

'All fine,' Kelleher responded, her voice audible in his earpiece.

She turned the corner and passed out of view.

'Loud and clear,' Snow reported.

Pope crossed the road and walked north along Rosebery Street.

He paid much closer attention to the house this time. It had a plain red door, the paint peeling away at the bottom. The single ground-floor window and the two windows on the first floor were obscured with patterned net curtains. There was a burglar alarm fixed to the wall above the door and two satellite dishes – one bigger than the other – fixed above that. A batten that would at one time have supported an estate agency sign was still screwed into the bricks. The house was unremarkable and similar to all the others on the terrace. He stopped when he was almost upon it, ducking down behind a parked car to pretend to tie his shoelace.

'There's an alarm,' he said into the mic. 'We'll need to disable it. There's a junction box on the other side of the street. Shouldn't be too hard to cut the power. Might not be a bad idea to put the lights out, too.'

'Are they in?'

Pope waited as long as he dared, but he saw no sign of life inside the house. 'Doesn't look like it.' He kept on. 'Surveillance is going to be bloody difficult if we need to do it. There's nowhere to park, and I can't see any buildings that would work.'

Pope finished with the lace, got up and walked on another ten feet. The alleyway that bisected Rosebery Street had an exit here, and as he strolled slowly by the opening, he saw Kelleher walking down it from the other end.

'There's a paved back garden, maybe thirty feet by ten feet. The one next door has a dog, so there might be noise. There's a gate at the back to get into the alley. It's unlocked. You've got two wheelie bins, then a stretch of concrete, then maybe ten feet with a couple of bikes and an old washing machine before you reach some kind of lean-to attached to the back of the house. There's a door and a window. There's a light above the door.'

'What do you think?'

'That's the way to get in.'

'Can you get a look at the lock?'

'I think so.'

Pope saw the glare of headlights jerking up and down as a car negotiated the speed bumps in the road in the direction from which he had just arrived. He took a quarter turn so that he could look back and made to fumble with his lace again. The car was a Volvo Estate. Stone's intelligence suggested that Hussain drove a green Volvo Estate. It was too dark to make out the colour, and the car was too far away to read the plate, but as Pope watched, it slowed and drew up outside number 30.

'Target might be coming home,' he said.

'I'm coming out.'

'Stay on your side of the street. I'll meet you.'

Kelleher tapped the pressel switch on her radio two times: universal code for 'copy that.'

'Control to Twelve. Bring the car back to the house.'

'We're doing it now?'

'Maybe. Eyes open.'

'Copy that.'

Pope stood and crossed, joining Kelleher as she emerged from the mouth of the alley. He took her hand and walked back to the house as if they were a couple.

The Volvo had reversed into a space outside the house.

They were twenty feet away when the car's lights were extinguished. Pope reached his spare hand into the pocket of his jacket and felt the fibres of his woollen balaclava.

They were fifteen feet away when both front doors opened, and two people stepped out. He could feel the bulge of his Sig in its shoulder holster beneath his left shoulder.

The passenger was a woman, her identity hidden beneath her dark burqa. The man, though, was instantly recognisable. He was burly, with a bald head and a long beard that reached down to his sternum. He wore a traditional dishdasha, had an eyepatch over his right eye, and he walked with a pronounced limp. Hussain had given two conflicting explanations for the injuries. In one interview, he said that he had lost his eye and his leg while working on a humanitarian demining project in Jalalabad, Pakistan. In another, he said it happened while he was preparing explosives for the Pakistani military in Lahore.

They had a positive ID.

Ten feet. Kelleher squeezed his hand. He readied himself. They would both draw down on the targets, Pope would get in close and shove the barrel of the Sig against Hussain's head and then he would hustle him off the street and into the back of the car. He would get in next to him, Kelleher would ride up front. Fifteen seconds, maximum.

It was going to be easier than he had expected.

Hussain limped across the pavement to the front door, the key in his hand. His wife waited behind him.

Pope felt the buzz of adrenaline, the expectation of sudden violent action.

Snow's voice crackled in his ear. *'There's another car coming.'*

Pope saw it, too. Lights bumped up and down as the car negotiated the speed bumps that had been laid to deter joyriders using the grid of streets as a racetrack. The street lamps were defective at that part of the street, but as the car drew nearer, moonlight fell across it, and he saw that it bore the markings of the local police.

He gripped Kelleher's hand tighter, and the two of them stepped around Hussain and his wife and continued on.

He clicked the pressel three times: 'Abort.'

The police car slowed right down. There were two officers inside it, and Pope glanced across as the driver looked back at them.

'I'm going around,' Snow said. *'I'll meet you where I dropped you off.'*

Chapter Twenty-Nine

Aqil Malik stood at the open graveside as his brother's body was taken out of the casket and lowered into the ground, arranged on his right-hand side in such a fashion that his head was facing Mecca. It was important that this be done correctly. They had already had the anguish of not being able to bury Aamir quickly, as ordained by the scripture. The authorities had not released the body, probing and prodding it, until they had all the evidence they needed. It was an abomination. They had no respect. No understanding. Aamir had had nothing to do with what had happened, but they had not listened.

The male members of the family stood around, grim faced. The women were waiting for them at home. It was a dank afternoon, and rain pattered against the umbrella that Aqil's elder brother, Yasin, held over both of their heads.

The imam finished his short prayer. 'Indeed to Allah we belong, and to Him we will return.'

He stood back, and Aqil's father dropped the first three fistfuls of wet earth over his son's body. He recited the Surah: '"*We created you from it, and return you into it, and from it we will raise you a second time.*"'

Aqil felt his throat tightening, and a tear began to roll down his cheek, mixing with the rain.

Yasin stepped forward, stooped down to collect the mud, and scattered it over the body while reciting the same verse.

The mosque had taken care of all the necessary requirements. Aamir's body had been washed and bathed and draped in the plain white *kafan* sheets as a part of the *takfeen*. They had taken him home for an afternoon, laying his casket out in the living room so that family members could pay their respects.

Their mother had wanted to close the lid. The bullet that had killed him had been fired at close range, the muzzle of the gun pressed against his crown so that a little circle of hair had been charred away. The exit wound was just above his jawline, below his left cheek. It was a purple bruise with a blackened hole in the centre. Their father had insisted that the casket be left open. He wanted people to see what the security services had done to his boy.

Not many people had come.

Even fewer had come to the *Janazah* prayer at the mosque.

Aqil had overheard his father and mother talking about it. Their friends had apologised, saying that it was too dangerous to come to the house. They had been given a police guard after the windows had been put in for the second time, and now their mail was being checked after white powder – later found to be flour – had been posted to them. And then there was the dog shit through the letterbox, the vitriol and the threats.

Aqil had closed his Twitter and Facebook accounts after the trolls had found them. They had threatened to kill him and his brother and rape his sister and his mother. One had even set up a fake account in Aamir's name, complete with a head and shoulders shot that had been copied from one of his social media accounts. The fake Aamir had posted that there was no Paradise, that he was in Hell, and that Aqil would be next.

The community didn't want to bring any of that down on themselves.

It was his turn now. He stepped forward to the lip of the grave, sank his hands into the wet muck and brought out a small pile in his cupped hands.

"'We created you from it, and return you into it, and from it we will raise you a second time.'"

His twin had been a simple boy. There was a suggestion that Aqil had taken more from their mother when they were in the womb together, more nutrition or something, and that Aamir had suffered because of it. Aqil didn't know how much of that was true, but it had been something that he had hated to be told. As they grew older, the evidence mounted. He was the bigger of the two. He was brighter, did better at school, had more friends. Aamir was more vulnerable, easily led, impressionable. Aqil had been concerned when Yasin had started taking him to the mosque more and more often. Yasin had never tried to persuade *him* to come, which made him suspicious, but Aamir was eighteen and could do whatever he wanted. Neither Yasin nor Aamir had ever brought his increasing piety up in front of their parents, and if the latter had noticed, they had said nothing.

Aqil knew the mosque was rotten. He had stopped going. He knew, too, that Yasin had grown close to Alam Hussain. Their father would have objected if he had known. The imam was persuasive and full of poison. His view of Islam was radical and more aggressive than the peaceful teachings of the man he had replaced. Aqil wished that he had said something. Perhaps it would have been different. He could have stopped it.

He had been furious when Yasin had explained what had happened. Yasin swore that he didn't know about the planned attack, but he had refused to condemn it. Aqil didn't believe it. Yasin wasn't telling him everything. Aqil's first reaction had been fury. He had struck his brother and would have struck him again if their father had not pulled them apart. He had been very close to telling the police officers who interviewed them what his brother had told him, and what he suspected.

But then the abuse had started. The dog shit had been pushed through the letter box. The bricks had been thrown through the windows. His mother had been assaulted in the street. The threatening phone calls came all through the night. The abuse had flooded his inbox. It was a tide, an avalanche, and it was getting worse and worse and *worse*.

Yasin had begged him to be quiet, and he had. What would have happened if he had spoken out? Yasin would have been arrested. The opprobrium wouldn't have stopped.

'Come on, bruv,' Yasin said.

Aqil turned and followed Yasin away from the graveside. The protestors had been gathered at the gates of the graveyard for an hour before they had arrived. There had been twenty of them then, but as they walked through the drizzle back to their cars, he could see that there were more now. The path led down a slope to the ornate iron gates. Beyond them, and behind a cordon of police in their fluorescent yellow hi-vis jackets, an angry scrum of perhaps a hundred men and women had gathered. There were skinheads there, right at the front, shouting out that they were terrorists and they should all be sent home. But, behind them, there were ordinary-looking men and women with angry red faces, joining in the chants and bellowing their indignation.

'Bastards,' Yasin swore under his breath.

'Ignore them,' their father commanded sternly. 'They want us to react. Don't give them the satisfaction.'

The funeral director had provided a black BMW for the immediate family. They got inside. The driver was pale faced, but as the cortege moved off, he put the car into gear and joined the slow-moving queue. The police opened the gates, and the cordon split into two halves, each holding back the protestors so that they could drive out onto the road beyond. The noise rose as they approached, a furious baying that was barely muffled inside the car. Aqil stared ahead, his jaw clenched tightly, his fists bunched up in his lap. He heard the abuse, the racism, saw the spit as it slid down the windows and then, as the cordon broke, saw the two skinheads surge forward and pound their fists against the glass.

The driver swore, his hands shaking as he pressed down on the accelerator and raced clear.

The mourning, or *hidaad*, would last for three days. The family had gathered in the hall of the only community centre that would take their booking. Several had turned them down when they realised what the booking was for, so their father had pretended that this was to be a birthday party. The caretaker would have realised that he had been lied to as soon as the cars with their police escort drew into the car park, but by then it was too late.

Aqil stood at the edge of the room and watched. There were very few mourners, and those who had attended looked lost in the space of the hall. His brother did not deserve this. He did not deserve to be shunned. He did not deserve to be *dead*.

Yasin saw him and came across. He took him to one side.

'You all right?' he asked.

'What do you think?'

'I know. Me too.'

'Where is everyone? All the others?'

'Scared,' Yasin said.

'It's not fair.'

'No,' his brother said. His voice was as hard and as cold as iron. He took out his phone and opened the app for Twitter. 'Seen this?'

'No . . .'

'Look at it.'

Yasin handed it over. Aqil had seen something similar on his own feed; he didn't need to see it again. There had been hundreds of updates, each tagging his account so that he could see what had been said about him and his family. There were obscene photographs – a mocked-up picture of Aamir's body seemed to have gone viral – together with dozens of death threats against him and the promise that his mother and sister would be raped.

'I know you don't agree with what Aamir did,' Yasin said carefully, 'but when you see this, it becomes easier to understand. You know what I mean?'

There was a short while of silence.

'Have you thought about it?'

Aqil looked down. 'I've been thinking.'

'And?'

Aqil tried to compose himself. He had been tortured by it all morning. Yasin had been on at him ever since the abuse had started.

They would be blamed.

It was their fault.

What had they done?

His efforts built to a head last night. They had no choice, he said.

They had to do it.

They had to go.

What Yasin was suggesting was frightening. The first time he had brought it up, Aqil had told him that he was crazy and that there was no way he would ever agree to it. He didn't hate his country. He was born here. He had friends here. People he had grown up with. He had school, college, the prospect of a job, the chance to make money, something to look forward to. A stake in the future.

But then the abuse had increased, and he thought about what his brother was proposing some more. He thought about the Twitter messages, the threats and the hatred, and he started to think that maybe Yasin was right, after all.

How would he get a job with the stain on his family name?

Who would employ the twin brother of a terrorist?

He had no friends. They had deserted him. Where were they now, when he needed them most? They were gone.

He thought about the newspaper reporters who had slept in their cars outside the house. They had raked through his past, running pictures of both of them, accusing them of things that they hadn't done, accusing them of thinking things that they didn't think. They'd discovered their father's affair from twenty years ago, suggested his business was a front, said their mother was a benefits cheat, that she hadn't been as badly damaged by the hospital's negligence as they had said.

They wrote in twenty-point type, on a million tabloid newspapers, that the Maliks were traitors who hated their country.

And so he allowed himself to be browbeaten. He'd finally said yes when they spoke last night, but he had woken up this morning to find himself unsure again. He had looked at the streets as the convoy had driven to the cemetery, all the familiar places, and he had been buffeted by doubt. This was his home. Even the insipid Mancunian rain was a trigger for his memories. He had decided to tell Yasin that he had changed his mind, but then there was the funeral and the protestors with their yells and their fists hammering on the roof and the loathing that burned in their eyes.

Aqil angled himself so that he was facing Yasin and spoke quietly. 'When do we do it?'

Yasin looked at him, and when he spoke, Aqil thought he could hear a little fear in his voice. 'Sure?'

'I'm sure.'

He almost seemed angry. Aqil knew why: he was suggesting something that would take him away from the family, and although Yasin believed it to be the right thing to do, he hated himself for the pain he was going to cause. 'Don't just say yes because you're upset. This isn't a joke. This is serious. We won't be able to come home.'

'I know that!'

'Easy,' Yasin said, his palm upraised. 'Keep your voice down.'

Akil hissed, 'I'm not stupid. I'm sure.' He meant it.

Yasin nodded his head. 'I'll need your passport. I'm going to get the tickets this afternoon.'

'When will we leave?'

'Soon. The next few days. I don't see any point in waiting, do you?'

Chapter Thirty

They reconvened in the car, and Snow drove them to an arcade of shops half a mile away. They parked outside the Zuhayp Café.

'We're not going to be able to put in any surveillance,' Pope said. 'There's nowhere obvious on the street, and if those police patrols are any good, they'll see us if we try and watch from the car.'

'So we go tonight?'

'We'll wait until one.' He looked at his watch. 'Thirty minutes.'

'Breeching where?'

'The back. Nine?'

Kelleher took out her phone. She had taken a close-up picture of the lock on the door at the back of the house. She rested the phone on her knee and unzipped the bag of kit that was on the back seat between her and Pope. She took out the pick gun, selected the correct bit and slotted it into place.

'Getting in won't be difficult,' she said, hefting the gun. 'What about the layout inside?'

'My guess is that you'll have a room off the hallway at the front of the house, and the kitchen behind it. Flight of stairs up to the first floor, two bedrooms. It's most likely that Hussain will be upstairs, but he has a bad leg. I wouldn't rule out the chance that he has a bedroom on the ground floor.'

'Options?'

'Twelve – you stay in the car. Park on Greame Street, and be ready to move on my signal. If you see the patrol car, I want to know about it.'

'Roger that.'

'Nine – you breach the door. I'll go in first; you come in after me. Standard clearing after that. Ground floor, then up the stairs. We keep the lights off, and keep both of them quiet.' He reached into the bag for a roll of gaffer tape. 'We'll tape their mouths shut before we get him out. Back through the garden, into the alley, Twelve meets us on Cowesby Street, we get away and head straight for Scotland. Any questions?'

There were none.

Snow switched on the radio and tuned it to the BBC's news channel. There was a discussion going on between the presenter and a security analyst. The presenter was complaining that recent events had left the public with no confidence in the police or the intelligence community. First had been the catalogue of errors that had led to the unlawful killing of Fèlix Rubió. And then, trumping even that disaster, had been the bombing of Westminster Tube station and the assault on the Houses of Parliament. How could anyone feel confident that they were protected when things like that were allowed to happen? What was being done to make sure that there was no repeat?

Pope knew the analyst. He rode a desk for a trendy Whitehall think tank. The man had no operational experience and had bluffed his way into a lucrative career as a talking head on news shows thanks to a series of guesses and speculation that occasionally proved to be correct. Pope had no respect for him.

He started a monologue about how he understood the public's frustration, that his 'sources' were frustrated, too, and that there would need to be progress soon.

'What a twat,' Snow growled.

'Turn it off,' Pope said.

Snow did as he asked. Pope reached into his jacket, withdrew his pistol and, keeping it below the line of the windows, checked the magazine and pushed it back into its housing with a click.

Ten minutes.

Two miles away, Munro and Stokes were readying themselves to break in to the mosque. They had skirted the perimeter of the building, confirming Pope's intelligence. It was well covered by CCTV cameras and would not be easy to infiltrate without leaving evidence that they had been there.

The wall that had been damaged by the car had not been fixed, and it had been a simple thing to move aside the temporary wire fence and slip through the broken teeth of the opening. They pulled on their balaclavas and gloves and hurried into the grounds. They saw the CCTV camera and knew that they would be seen on the footage. But that wouldn't matter. It would be impossible to identify them.

There was a secondary entrance on this side of the building. It was secured behind a wire cage, but Munro was able to pick the lock so that it could be pulled aside. The door itself was flimsy, and the lock had been shattered with a single firm kick. The two agents raised their torches and went into the dark interior beyond.

Snow dropped Pope on Hartington Street and Kelleher on Greame Street. They had been spotted together once, and it would risk suspicion if they were seen together again. This was hardly the street for a late-night romantic promenade. Hartington Street ran north–south, two streets to the west of Rosebery Street. He was carrying a small shoulder bag with the kit that he thought he might need. He turned onto Alison Street and walked east, crossing Beresford Street and then Rosebery Street. Street lamps flickered on and off, and the moon was obscured by a slow-moving stack of silvery cloud. Visibility was more limited than before. That was helpful.

He saw Kelleher at the mouth of the alley. She stepped around an overturned bin and pulled on her balaclava. Pope reached the alley and did the same. She pointed to the first gate and, on his signal, opened it and slipped inside. Pope saw the back garden just as she had described it: a concreted-over space, junk discarded across it, a short distance to the dilapidated lean-to. There were no lights visible on either the ground or first floors of the house. He heard a low growl from the next garden across and glimpsed a powerful-looking pit bull chained to a fence post. Pope reached for the silenced Sig. The dog growled again, but it didn't bark. Lucky dog.

Kelleher hurried to the rear door. Pope came up behind her and glanced in through the single window. The pane was covered by a patterned net curtain, and nothing was visible.

Pope reached into his bag and pulled out a pair of latex gloves and overshoes, putting them on over his hands and feet. He made sure that the elasticated openings were snug over the cuffs of his shirt and his trousers so that the chances of anything being left behind were minimised. Kelleher did the same. It was imperative that they left nothing that could be traced to them. The medical and dental records belonging to agents of Group Fifteen were routinely scrubbed, but the last thing they wanted to do was leave a DNA trace that might be tied back to them at some point in the future.

Number Nine inserted the pick gun into the lock, squeezed the trigger three times and worked the tension rod until the pins of the lock were lined up correctly. The breaching was quiet, but it was not silent. The gun exhaled little bursts of compressed air, and the pins rattled as they were forced into the open position. The door opened, and Kelleher stepped aside.

Pope stepped up, held up his pistol in his right hand and counted down from three with the fingers of his left.

Three.

Two.

One.

He gently pushed the door and went inside.

Kelleher followed, closing the door behind her.

They were in the kitchen. A little moonlight filtered through the net curtain. He saw battered kitchen units on the wall, one missing its door, and a freestanding cooker and refrigerator. There was a linoleum floor, peeling back from the wall at the edges, sticky in parts where liquid had been spilt. There was a pile of dirty dishes in the sink. He smelled the residual odour of curry. The room was empty.

Kelleher split off behind him and checked the door to what Pope guessed was a downstairs toilet. She nodded that the room was clear.

He circled his finger in the air to indicate they should proceed and then pointed at the open door that led to the hall, light filtering inside from the frosted glass panel in the front door.

There was a door to the right, halfway between the kitchen and the front door, and to the left, he saw the start of the stairs. He continued down the hallway and took up position at the foot of the stairs. Kelleher paused at the door, listened for a moment and then gently opened it with her foot. It swung back with a groan that sounded unnaturally loud, and she went inside.

Pope concentrated on inhaling and exhaling normally, fighting the urge to hold his breath. He glanced up the stairs and saw the deeper darkness of the landing above. Nothing was visible. A floorboard creaked from the front room. Pope gripped the butt of his cocked pistol tighter. Kelleher emerged again, shaking her head.

Pope pointed up the stairs. He took a thin Maglite from his bag and shone it down as he climbed the stairs, his feet on the outside of the treads. Kelleher followed behind him. He reached the landing and cast the light around him. There was a laundry basket directly ahead, stuffed full of dirty clothes. He reached the top and turned to the left. There was a chest pressed up against the wall and, atop it, another pile of dirty clothes.

Two doors up ahead of him. One was opposite his position, the other immediately to the left.

Pope paused, listening hard. He could hear the sound of low breathing, but he couldn't discern from which direction it was coming.

Number Twelve's voice crackled low in his earbud. *'The police car is coming back.'*

He clicked the pressel twice to acknowledge the message and turned back to Kelleher, who gave a nod. She had received it, too.

Pope edged ahead. The door to the left would lead to the room at the front of the house. He pressed his fingers against it and gently exerted enough pressure to push it open.

He went inside, his silenced weapon up and ready to shoot.

It seemed to be an office of sorts. He took the three paces necessary to reach the window to the street below, and pressed up hard to the side of it, he risked a quick glance through the net curtain. The police car rolled slowly down the street, slowed to a stop outside the front door, and then rolled on again.

Snow: *'It's moving on.'*

Two clicks.

There was a desk on the other side of the window with a PC and a monitor atop it. He noted that, so he wouldn't forget it later, and crept back to the landing. He motioned that the room was empty and pointed to the remaining door. He had suspected that this was the room where they would find Hussain and his wife. The layout of the house suggested that it was the bigger of the two.

The door was halfway ajar, and he looked in. There was a wardrobe ahead and, to the right, a bed on which he could make out the shape of two recumbent bodies. He pushed the door open enough to step inside, his teeth set on edge by the low groan of badly lubricated hinges, raising his pistol and aiming it down at the bodies in the event that they awoke.

They did not.

There was a bedside table to each side of the bed. Each table held an identical lamp. Hussain was on the right. He was on his back, and Pope could see the fuzzy grey mess of his beard. There was a copy of the Qur'an on his table.

Pope took four steps until he was alongside him.

Kelleher moved around the bed to stand over the woman.

Pope counted down from three, and on one, they both moved with fluid, practised efficiency. They put their left hands over the mouths of the couple and pressed the guns hard against their heads.

Hussain bucked in sudden alarm, but Pope pushed down and anchored him to the mattress. He tried to scream, the noise muffled by Pope's palm. He bucked again, trying to free his arms from beneath the duvet. Pope took the butt of the Sig and cracked it down hard against his forehead. It was a strong blow, and the sharp edge of the butt cut the skin and drew a little furrow of blood. Hussain moaned, the noise smothered once again.

Pope looked across the bed to Mrs Hussain. She was lying still, her eyes wide and eloquent with fear above Number Nine's restraining hand.

Pope switched his grip on the pistol so that he could put his index finger to his lips. 'I'm going to take my hand away,' he said in a quiet, firm voice. 'If you make any noise, my colleague will shoot your wife and then I'll shoot you. Blink if you understand.'

Hussain's wife might have been frightened, but he was angry. He stared unblinkingly up at Pope.

'Last chance.'

He pressed down hard with the Sig.

Hussain blinked. His good eye was full of fury.

He drew back with the gun, the end of the silencer leaving a circular red tracing on the cleric's forehead.

Pope pulled his left hand away, putting his finger to his lips again to remind the man to lie still and quiet. He reached into his bag and took out a roll of gaffer tape.

'Lift your head.'

Hussain did as he was ordered, and Pope unrolled the tape, wrapping it all the way around his head two times. When he was done, the bottom half of the cleric's head was covered with it. There was just enough space for him to breathe through his nose.

'Now you do your wife.'

His eye shone hatred at him, but again he did as he was told. He did a thorough job, winding it twice around her head, tearing it off and handing the roll back to Pope.

Pope switched the pistol to his left hand, and using his right, he dragged him out of bed. He told him to put his arms behind his back, and he wrapped another length of tape around his wrists, fastening them together. Finally, he took the tape and wound another length around his eyes, fashioning a makeshift blindfold.

He tossed the roll of tape to Kelleher and spoke as she bound the woman's wrists together. 'We need to speak to your husband. We're just going to take him downstairs. If you make a sound or try to come after us, we'll shoot you both. Nod if you understand.'

She nodded vigorously.

'Very good. If you do as we say, you won't be hurt. Stay here. Don't come out, and definitely do not come downstairs. Understand?'

She nodded again.

Pope stood, hooked his right hand between Hussain's pinioned arms and dragged him to his feet. Kelleher backed away, her Sig held in a steady aim at the woman's head.

'Get the hard drive,' he said to Kelleher, and then, when she had hurried into the other room, he spoke quietly into the mic on his lapel. 'Twelve, Control. Move.'

'Copy that.'

He moved the cleric to the head of the stairs and jabbed the pistol between his shoulder blades. The man took the stairs carefully, each foot probing for the next tread, Pope up close behind him. He reached the bottom, and Pope grabbed him by the shoulder and yanked him into the corridor, bumping him off the walls as he shoved him into the kitchen. He heard Kelleher following them down the stairs.

Snow reported. *'I'm here.'*

Pope opened the back door and pushed Hussain into the back garden. After his earlier restraint, the pit bull next door started to bark. It didn't matter so much now. They were nearly done. Pope pushed the cleric against the gate, opened it for him, then shoved him into the alleyway. The Passat was waiting at the mouth of the alley, the passenger-side front and rear doors open. Hussain stumbled over the overturned bin and fell flat on his face. Pope hauled him to his feet, put a hand on his head, pushed down and then propelled him into the back, immediately getting in next to him. Number Nine leapt into the front, the doors were slammed shut and Snow drove.

Pope and Kelleher took off their balaclavas, latex gloves and overshoes.

'All okay?' Number Twelve asked.

Pope looked at the cleric beside him, his head mummified in gaffer tape. 'No problems.'

Chapter Thirty-One

It would take them nine hours to drive from Manchester to Wick. They had stopped as soon as it was safe, just outside Manchester, to transfer Hussain to the boot. Now, several hours later, they had left the motorway to stop a second time, giving their prisoner a chance to relieve himself.

As Pope raised the lid of the boot, the courtesy light casting a subtle amber glow over Hussain, he could see that the cleric had brought his knees up to his chest so that he fitted snugly.

'We're going to drive for another hour,' Pope said to him. 'If you're a good boy, and there's no noise or trouble, you can stretch your legs for five minutes. Understand?'

The cleric nodded. Pope hauled him up, dragged him out of the boot and stood him on the side of the road. Pope saw that the man wanted to speak. He tore the tape away from his mouth.

'Why are you doing this?' he said plaintively.

'You know why, Mr Hussain.'

'Those boys. Hakeem and Bashir and Aamir?'

'That's right.'

'I do not approve of what they did.'

'Save it for later. I'm just in charge of delivery.'

'You're not listening to me, sir. I had nothing to do with what happened.'

Pope took him by the shoulder. 'You need to relieve yourself?'

Hussain ignored him. 'They listened to my sermons, perhaps they shared my view of things, but I would never have approved of what they did.'

'You're wasting your breath. Go now if you need to; we're not stopping again.'

He ignored him again. 'None of this is necessary, sir. Please – let me go, I have nothing to do with any of it.'

'I'll take that as a no.'

Pope took the gaffer tape.

'Please!' Hussain said.

He wrapped the tape around his head again, pushed him back into the boot and shut the lid.

'You believe any of that?' Kelleher asked him as he got into the car.

'Irrelevant what I think. Not up to us to decide, is it? Come on. Sooner we get back on the road, sooner we can drop him off and get back to civilisation.'

There was an unmarked Gulfstream V Turbo waiting on the edge of the taxiway. Pope guessed that the plane would be registered to a Delaware corporation that would front ownership for the CIA. They would pass it around different front companies every few months, change the tail number and otherwise make it more difficult to trace out the truth. An investigation by a liberal British newspaper had made things a little more difficult last year. They were able to chart the to-ing and fro-ing of a particular jet through the observations of plane spotters posted on the web. Its flight plans always began at an airstrip in Smithfield, North Carolina, and ended in some of the world's hot spots. It was owned by Premier Executive Transport Services, incorporated in Delaware, a brass plaque company with nonexistent directors, and had been hired by American agents to revive an old CIA tactic from the 1970s. Agency men kidnapped South American criminals and flew them back to their own countries to face trial so that justice could be rendered. Pope had delivered a suspect for rendition before, to an aeroplane very much like this one. Paddy McNair had called it the Guantánamo Bay Express.

Pope was able to park right alongside the aircraft, which was being refuelled by a mobile bowser. A man and a woman in bland business dress were sheltering under the cover of a wide golfing umbrella next to the open door. Pope checked left and right before he got out of the car. They were in an isolated part of the airport, and there was no suggestion that they were overlooked. He opened the door, went around to the back and opened the trunk. Hussain was inside, curled into a foetal ball. Kelleher and Snow got out, their weapons drawn, and then, working together, they hauled the cleric out of the boot and dumped him on the tarmac.

Hussain was on his knees in the sheeting rain. His head hung down low between his shoulder blades and there was a low murmur of discomfort that was muffled by the tape around his mouth.

'Alam Hussain,' Pope said. 'As requested.'

The woman nodded. She didn't say anything. Pope would have been surprised if she knew who he was, and besides, there was very little to discuss. This was a simple transaction. A handover, an exchange that had been repeated many times previously. He knew that Hussain's immediate future was bleak. It promised pain and discomfort. Then he would be buried deep in the CIA's penal system, and Pope doubted if the cleric would see the light of day for years. He didn't feel uncomfortable about it. Hussain might have information that could save the lives of hundreds of innocent civilians. He might not, of course, but that was a risk that Pope was happy to countenance. Simple calculus. The needs of the many outweighed the needs of the few.

The male agent reached down and helped Hussain to his feet. He guided him to the fuselage and helped him place his feet on the stairs that led inside.

'Thank you,' the woman said as she turned on her heel and followed her colleague into the jet. The pilot came out to retract the steps and close the door. The bowser detached its hose and drove back in the direction of the terminal building.

They were left alone. They got into the car. Kelleher offered to drive. Pope was tired and didn't demur. As she turned the Passat around and accelerated away to the gate, Pope heard the Gulfstream's engine fire up and watched as the plane slowly began to roll towards the runway.

'Back to London?' Number Nine asked.

'Yes.'

They had another long drive ahead of them. As they started south, he looked through the wire-mesh fence and out onto the runway. The jet streaked towards them, launched itself into the air and roared overhead at two hundred feet. It banked steeply to port and disappeared away to the south.

'Poor bugger,' Snow offered.

PART THREE

Chapter Thirty-Two

Isabella killed the engine of her Kawasaki and rested it on its side stand. She unlocked the brand new door and pulled it up, then went into the dark space and disabled the alarm. The place felt secure now. She was pleased with the work that she had arranged and ran her fingers across the cold steel lockers.

Today was a big day.

The delivery was arranged for the afternoon. The ancient white Vauxhall Astravan turned off the Route de Safi and bounced across the uneven approach road to the row of industrial units. The driver drew to a halt and got out with a clipboard in his hand.

'Sabrina Atika?'

'That's right,' Isabella said.

'You need to sign here.'

She took the clipboard and signed where he indicated.

'What?' he said when she held on to the clipboard.

'Can you move them inside, please?'

'You have to. I don't do that.'

'I'll give you an extra three hundred dirham if you do.'

The man grunted his assent and went to the back of the van. He opened the doors. The space was crammed to the roof with wooden packing crates of various sizes. The man took one of the larger ones and hauled it out. It slid off the back of the van and crashed onto the ground.

'Careful!' she said.

He cursed under his breath. 'What do you have in there?' he asked.

'Equipment.'

'*Heavy* equipment.'

'Stop moaning,' she said. 'You want your money—or don't you?'

They moved the crates from the van into the unit. Isabella paid the driver his extra money and watched him get into his van and drive away.

It was just past dusk, and she paused outside the unit for a minute, just letting a sense of the place sink in. The neighbouring properties were empty. Some of them were vacant, as advertised by the signs of the realtors that were fixed to the doors or the walls. Those that had been busy earlier were empty now, their occupants packed up and returned to the city. The occasional car hummed along the Route de Safi, headlights snapping on as the desert approached, but there was nothing else.

She pulled the drawstring to turn on the light, shut and locked the door, and set to work.

Isabella had packed the equipment from the garage into the crates, protecting it with balled-up newspaper and old blankets. The crates came in several different sizes. There were those that were long and thin and others that were square. She had sealed them carefully, driving nails through the lids so that they could only be opened with deliberate effort and not accidentally.

She had a claw hammer on the floor, and using the end, she pried off the lid of the nearest box and stood it against the wall. The inside was stuffed to the top with newspaper; she cleared it out to reveal an M-15 ArmaLite flat-carbine. She pulled it out. It had the M4 collapsible buttstock and forged lower receiver, the mid-length hand guard and gas system, a chrome-lined sixteen-inch heavy barrel, a rail front gas block and a flash hider. The chamber had elongated M4-style feed ramps for more reliable feeding with heavier bullet weights. It was an excellent weapon. Beatrix had shown her how to use it.

Her mother had left her an impressive armoury of weapons. She pried open the lids of the other crates and started to sort through the contents. There were semi-automatic pistols, rifles, submachine guns, shotguns. She took out a TAR-21 bullpup assault rifle and an MK249 with ten one-hundred-round soft-pack ammo bags. There was a Mossberg 500 shotgun and an M110 sniper rifle with bipod. Flashbangs. Knives, frag grenades, night-vision goggles, a radio set, and boxes upon boxes of ammunition of all different calibres.

She arranged them carefully in the lockers: the rifles went into one locker, the revolvers and semi-automatics in another, the shotguns in a third. She matched the various calibre ammo with the relevant firearms. She opened a box of 9mm rounds, and they glittered in the light.

She intended to break each firearm down so that it could be cleaned and maintained, but it was late by the time that she had unpacked, and she decided that she would start that task another day. She was pleased with what she had done. She felt good about the weapons. They were safer here. She didn't know how she could make them much safer.

She opened the door, switched off the light and stepped outside. It was cold now. She put on her leather riding jacket, pulled down and locked the door, got onto her Kawasaki and rode back to Marrakech.

Chapter Thirty-Three

Pope visited the dead drop every day for the next three days. On the third day, the chalk mark on the seat indicated that there was something waiting for him. He walked on to the tree, waited until the path was clear and then retrieved the small slip of paper that had been left inside the nook. It gave a code that he knew referred to a motorway service station on the M25, a date and a time. The location was correct, but Pope deducted a day and an hour from the time to find the correct details for the rendezvous.

It was today's date. He had three hours to get there.

He drove to Junction 9 of the motorway and came off at Cobham services. There was a branch of Costa Coffee, with a number of tables arranged outside. Vivian Bloom was sitting at one of them. He was wearing a knitted waistcoat under his tweed jacket, despite the warmth in the air. His tie was knotted loosely and bore a stain just before it disappeared into the waistcoat. He looked particularly ecclesiastical today, Pope thought. Tweedy and donnish.

Pope sat down next to him, and the spook shook his hand.

'Good afternoon, Control. Can I get you a coffee?'

'No, sir. I'm fine.'

A man passed them. Bloom waited until he was gone and then leaned forward. 'Well done.'

'No problems?'

'None,' he replied. 'It was very well done.'

Bloom was thinner than Pope remembered him. There was a lilt in his voice, a sibilance to his consonants that gave him an effeminate aspect that Pope did not remember from before. He did remember the bookishness, the way he steepled his fingers when he was thinking, the sense that he was being assessed when Bloom fixed his rheumy gaze on him. He remembered the thin lips that whitened when he smiled, the mousiness, the same apologetic loyalty to decisions that he professed to find ridiculous. He remembered, too, the obvious sharpness of his wit and counselled himself to keep that in mind. Bloom had been a player in the intelligence community for many years. Pope was reminded of an old joke that had attached itself to the man during the Cold War. In the case of nuclear attack, it was said, the only things that would survive were cockroaches and Vivian Bloom.

'Where's Hussain now?'

Bloom chuckled. 'You know better than to ask that, old boy.'

Pope knew enough to have a pretty good guess. The CIA had black sites on the territory of several compliant states, and given the limited range of the Gulfstream that had taken off with Hussain, he would have put money on Vilnius in Lithuania or Ain Aouda in Morocco. The location was irrelevant. He would have been taken to an anonymous cell in an anonymous building. As far as Hussain was concerned, he could have been anywhere. But Pope doubted whether it would have been something that would have had much of his attention. The treatment he would have been receiving would have been the main thing on his mind.

'Did you get anything useful?'

Bloom took a pipe and a packet of tobacco from his pocket. He reached into the packet with his thumb and forefinger and drew out a wad of tobacco. 'He has been very cooperative,' he said as he pressed the tobacco into the bowl. 'He's confirmed that he was responsible for radicalising the three boys. His mosque ran a conference last year and flew in a handful of jihadi clerics. Two of them have been banned from Britain since then. Shouldn't have been let in at all, you ask me, but there you go. The other one's on the US no-fly list. Hussain admitted that he met Bashir and Hakeem at the conference, and that Bashir introduced him to Aamir. He spent the next six months grooming them.' He put a match to the bowl and puffed until the tobacco was alight.

'What about the others? The shooters?'

'He says they had nothing to do with him. He says he just supplied the bombers. He says there's another man.'

'You believe him, sir?'

'Our CIA friends believe him. They seem confident that he wouldn't be inclined to lie to them. You know how *thorough* they are, Control. I think we can rely on their assurances.'

'The organiser – does Hussain know who he is?'

'Unfortunately, no. Only that he's still in the country and that there will be follow-up attacks. The word he chose was that there would be a "wave" of them.'

'That's not very helpful.'

'No,' Bloom said, puffing on the pipe. 'But it does get a little better.'

He laid the pipe on the table and took a printout from his briefcase. He gave it to Pope. It was a photograph of a man and looked like some sort of promotional shot. The man was wearing a pristine white dishdasha topped with a red-and-white keffiyeh. He was handsome, with a well-trimmed beard and clear, laughing eyes. He looked confident. He looked like money.

'His name is Salim Hasan Mafuz Muslim al-Khawari. Bit of a mouthful, I know. Prominent Sunni cleric, naturalised Lebanese, partly resident in the UK until last year, lived in a big place in Mayfair. His family made their money in oil, he inherited it and now he's as rich as Croesus. Hussain says al-Khawari is the financier behind the attack.'

A family of four, laughing and joking, strolled past. Pope waited until they were out of earshot.

'Were we watching him?'

'Of course we were, but we didn't have a clue he was anything other than an Arab playboy who comes over here to get the things he can't get back home: booze, whores – you know. Hussain says he's heavily involved with the Kuwait Clerics Union, which we know has channelled tens of millions of dollars to ISIS and other jihadi groups in Iraq and Syria. He's made a big PR play about a big collective fundraising trust he set up for Syria involving a host of Kuwaiti charities. But Hussain says that's all bollocks. The money's been sent to fund the caliphate, and a million of it was earmarked to help those boys blow up the House of Commons.'

'You think it's credible?'

'There's always a financier. The Qatari who provided 'financial support' for Khalid Sheikh Mohammed before 9/11. The Saudi prince who paid for training and equipment for 7/7. I don't think it's beyond the pale at all.'

'Where is he now?'

'Switzerland. His European businesses are headquartered there. He's not usually in the same place for long. Tends to live in hotels. But his family is there. His wife – one of them, anyway – and his children.'

Bloom put the stem of the pipe back into his mouth and inhaled. Pope felt that he was being assessed.

'Sir?'

'How close were you to the third bomber?'

'Very close.'

'What happened to McNair? You saw it, didn't you?'

'I was very close to that, too.'

'How do you feel about that afternoon?'

It was a strange question. 'If you're asking if I'm all right, I am. I've seen a lot of death in my time.'

'But not like the bomb? The civilians?'

'Are you asking whether I feel angry? I do.'

'Surely more than anger, Control?'

Pope found the questions irritating, and he spoke with sudden heat. 'Are you asking if I want to be involved in making sure it doesn't happen again? Yes, sir. I do.'

'You've said it yourself, Captain. You've seen a lot of death. And in my experience, most men have a tolerance for that which cannot be exceeded without consequences. Episodes. Breakdowns. Your friend Captain Milton is a perfect example of what can happen if a careful watch is not kept on these things.' He smiled benignly. 'I suppose what I'm saying, Captain Pope, is that I want to be quite sure, if we are to continue with this, that you have the mental capacity to carry out my instructions. What comes next has the potential to be rather more difficult than abducting a one-legged, one-eyed man from his bed.'

Pope found his watery gaze discomfiting, but he held it. He saw the street outside Westminster station, the man with the rucksack on his back, the certainty in his stride as he walked into the middle of the crowd of shocked onlookers; he saw the flash as he scrubbed himself from existence; he saw the flayed skin and the blood; he smelled the cooked flesh. He put firmness into his answer. 'Let's stop with this charade, sir. I haven't reached my tolerance yet. You don't need to worry about that.'

'You are happy to continue?'

'I am.'

Bloom nodded at his conviction. 'I believed that would be your answer, but you'll understand why I need to be sure. We are already in choppy waters. Conditions will get worse before they get better.'

For God's sake, thought Pope, *I've told you that I'm in. Get on with it.* 'You want me to have a word with him?'

'I'd like that very much, but I'm afraid al-Khawari will be rather more difficult. It isn't Moss Side. His security is rather more effective than a couple of sleepy bobbies. The direct approach is unlikely to be successful.'

Pope had the impression that he was being very mildly belittled. 'So?'

'We need evidence of his involvement. Interrogating him would be best, but we think that will be too much to ask. There's the problem with him being on neutral territory, of course. You *know* how the Swiss would play it if we took him. That prized neutrality.' He shook his hand as if waving away an unpleasant smell. 'We need to go about things more quietly. We need to get into his computer.'

Pope frowned. 'So give it to Group Three?'

'Yes, of course, we've tried that already. Our friend is very particular with what our specialists describe as 'network hygiene.' Very particular, and lavish with the funds he spends on it. I'm told access is possible but that it needs to be done in situ.' Bloom smoked his pipe for a while and then said, 'You're familiar with Cottonmouth?'

'Yes. I've used it.'

Group Six had perfected a wide range of devices that could be used to bug the IT equipment belonging to persons of interest. Cottonmouth was a particularly neat piece of kit that they had invented. It was a USB plug bugging device and was disguised either as a keyboard's USB plug or as a type of USB extension cord that could be connected unnoticed between a peripheral and the computer itself. It could send and receive radio signals and made it possible not only to monitor the bugged computer and its compromised network but also to send commands to both. They were small and so discreet as to be almost undetectable unless you knew to look.

'Wonderfully clever piece of kit,' Bloom said, 'but we need someone to go in and fit the device. And that isn't going to be easy to do. I'm open to ideas.'

Pope felt himself being sucked deeper and deeper into the rabbit hole, but he was committed now. He knew he wouldn't be able to pull back. He wasn't sure that he wanted to. There was no guarantee that the Firm would be able to find the jihadist who had promised Hussain that there would be additional operations. More would be killed. This might be the best chance they had to track him down.

Bloom looked down at his pipe for a while. Pope puckered his lips for a moment before settling on a recommendation. 'Surveillance first. Let's see what we can find out. Everyone has a blind spot. You just have to know where to find it.'

'The same parameters apply. We've never spoken about any of this.'

'I know, sir.'

'And if you get into a sticky situation, you'll be on your own.'

A driver wandered a little too close to their table.

Pope waited until he was gone. 'I'll need to communicate with you online.'

'Visit the dead drop before you go. I'll leave instructions.'

Bloom stood. There were no goodbyes. He turned and set off into the car park.

Pope waited for him to leave. A police van sped along the motorway, its lights flashing and siren wailing. A helicopter buzzed overhead, a mile to the west. There were two armed soldiers at the entrance to the services. Again he noticed that London felt as if it was under siege. Pope watched as Bloom's sleek, expensive car pulled out into the sluggish traffic and headed onto the slip road.

He put on his sunglasses and started the walk back to his car.

Chapter Thirty-Four

Pope decided that he would conduct the surveillance himself. But since a target like al-Khawari would be difficult to track alone, he pegged Number Nine and Number Twelve to assist. It wasn't just a question of numbers. Hannah Kelleher was from the Special Reconnaissance Regiment and was the best undercover surveillance operative that he had; it made sense for her to be included. Snow, on the other hand, needed confidence. Number Twelve had tried to brush off the mauling that he had received at the hands of the steering committee, but Pope had seen through it. It was not surprising that he felt bruised. Add that to the guilt he would be feeling over the death of Fèlix Rubió, and it was important that the soldier got back on the job as quickly as possible.

They flew to Geneva on separate flights, using false diplomatic passports. They took rooms at the Ibis Geneva right next to the airport. They had arrived late, and Pope decided it made more sense to get a full night's sleep so that they could start early the following day. It was a bland, anonymous hotel. Beige walls, beige carpet, identical layouts. They could have been anywhere in the world. They ate room service in Pope's room, discussed what they would do tomorrow, and then went to their own rooms for sleep.

Pope showered, undressed and lay on the bed for thirty minutes with the BBC News channel playing on the flat-screen TV. It was a week after the attack, and there was still practically nothing else that made the bulletin. New CCTV footage had just been released of the shooters trying to force their way into the Commons. Pope saw the men and remembered their professionalism, their familiarity with their weapons and the ingenuity of their plan. They had been lucky that the casualties inside the House were so minor compared to what might have happened. They had McNair to thank for that.

The news anchor cut away to an interview with the prime minister. Pope reached for the remote and turned up the volume. The report began with the moment, preserved forever on the cameras inside the chamber that had been recording *PMQs*, when the boom of the first explosion in the Underground station had interrupted the childish squabbling between the PM and the leader of the opposition. A particularly effective riposte had seen the MPs on the government benches waving their motion papers at their rivals across the chamber. Their boorish laughter had been interrupted by the muffled crump of the blast. The PM's coup de grace died on his lips. The chamber was quiet when the second bomb detonated. This one was in the open, nearer the palace, and deafeningly loud. The windows nearest the blast were blown in by the pressure wave. There were screams and shouts of panic.

The footage cut away to a head-and-shoulders shot of the PM. He was dressed in black. There were the usual questions about what had happened in the chamber when they had heard the bombs, and then the reaction when the Serjeant at Arms had sprinted past the Bar of the House to the Speaker's Chair, and then the instruction from the Speaker, his ragged panic barely suppressed, that they were under attack and should begin an orderly evacuation. The anchor led the PM through some set questions so that he could deliver the sound bites that his scriptwriters had prepared for him. Pope shook his head at the dull predictability of it. The terrorists were cowards. The nation grieved. A debt of gratitude was owed to the men and women of the Metropolitan police.

He was about to switch off the screen when the interviewer posed her final question.

'Prime Minister, do you have a message for those responsible?'

'Yes,' he said. 'I do.' He paused for a moment, as if composing himself, and then he turned from the quarter shot and looked directly into the camera. 'We are under threat because we are a country of freedoms, and because we are a country of freedoms, we will neutralise threats and punish aggressors. No one should think that he can act in the United Kingdom in a way that is contrary to the principles of the United Kingdom, and attack the very spirit of this country: the idea of democracy itself. My thoughts today are with the victims. More than two hundred people have died, and many others are hovering between life and death. That is where we stand right now. We are committed to finding those responsible. They will be hunted down by our police and intelligence services. There will be nowhere for them to hide. And when they have been found, they should be in no doubt that we shall exact the full measure of justice. Thank you.'

Pope killed the screen.

The full measure of justice.

That was as near as he had ever heard to a politician making it plain that those guilty of the attack would never make it to court.

Vivian Bloom had provided him with a dossier of information on Salim Hasan Mafuz Muslim al-Khawari. His property in Switzerland was a sprawling mansion that had cost him £50 million when he had purchased it last year. It was in the small village of Genthod, on the outskirts north of the city. They hired two cars and set off, Pope in the lead car, with Snow and Kelleher in the car behind him. They drove north-east, the airport to their left, and followed the E25 to Chemin des Rousses in Bellevue.

Snow's voice came over the radio. *'How do you want to play this?'*

'We'll take a look today. If we can get eyes on him, so much the better, but we're going to have to be careful. If he is our man, he's going to be on edge. And he can afford very good security.'

They reached Genthod and followed the picturesque streets down to the roads that overlooked the hugeness of Lake Geneva. As they drove to the north, the properties became fewer and farther between, set in vast grounds and secured by tall walls and wire-tipped fences.

'Exclusive neighbourhood,' Kelleher said.

'Keep driving,' Pope said. 'You keep going. I'm going to have a quick look.'

'Copy that.'

Pope slowed as he approached the gates, saw that there were security cameras there and pulled away again. He drove on for half a mile, took a turning that led him to a quiet country lane and parked the car out of sight.

He was able to stay off the main road, following a cycle path to the south-east. The terrain was hilly, rising up to a height of fifty feet to his right and then sloping down to the shore of the lake to his left. He turned off the path so that he could climb, forcing his way through the undergrowth until he reached the crown of the hill. There was a small clearing there, and as he turned and assessed the landscape to the east, he had his first good look at the property he was interested in.

It was a big house, four storeys tall. It was surrounded by enormous grounds and enjoyed perhaps half a mile of prime frontage onto the lake.

'Control, Nine, Twelve. Report.'

'We've stopped,' Kelleher said. *'Lay-by on the Route de Malagny. What's your location?'*

'South of you. I've found a good spot for a look at the house. Hold your position.'

Pope rested the holdall on the ground, unzipped it and took out the binoculars he had brought with him. He raised them to his eyes and gazed out onto the mansion. He estimated that he was three kilometres away from the property. As he adjusted the focus, it came into clear view.

He could see why it had been so expensive to purchase. It was enormous, for a start, with three separate wings that had been constructed in a distinctly modernist style. There was a huge amount of glass, with generous picture windows to every aspect. The east-facing side of the building was just twenty feet from the start of the lake, suggesting that there would be stupendous views from inside. A path cut down the gentle slope to a boathouse and a jetty. There was a pool to one side, a pair of tennis courts to the other, and a separate complex that looked like it housed the staff. Pope scanned across and saw a car showroom to the left of the house. He watched a Bentley Continental GT and a Land Rover Discovery being washed and polished by two members of staff.

The place would be very, very difficult to breach. He saw security cameras around the estate, and he would have been surprised if it wasn't protected by laser tripwires and motion detectors. He saw guards. They would probably be armed. There would be a direct line to the local constabulary. It would be difficult to get in even with a large, well-equipped team. As it was, there were three of them, and they had very little in the way of kit.

He could see no easy way to infiltrate.

He was getting ready to put the binoculars away when he saw activity from the front of the house. A large door had opened, and two figures emerged. Two men. Business suits. One was much bigger than the other. The big man had a shaved head. The other had his back turned, perhaps talking to someone still inside the property.

'Control, Nine, Twelve. Come in.'

'Nine, Control,' Kelleher responded. *'Copy that.'*

'Turn around and start coming back. There's activity at the house.'

'Copy. The target?'

'I'm just waiting for him to turn around so I can get a look at him.' The man was gesticulating angrily. His irritation continued for thirty seconds, the gestures becoming angrier and more impatient, and then a third figure came out of the property. It was a teenage boy. Brown skin and long dark hair. He was wearing a T-shirt and jeans. He lolled and when the other man stabbed a finger in his face and then pointed away to the cars, he set off with an insolent slouch.

'Twelve, Control. We're half a mile away. What do you want us to do?'

'Hold and wait for instructions.'

Pope squinted into the rangefinder, gently adjusting the focus, and then the third figure turned around. He tilted his head, and for a moment it looked as if the man was staring right into the binoculars. It was al-Khawari. The man was impossible to mistake. He looked like Omar Sharif, slight and dapper, his white hair standing out against the dark-tinted window that was behind him. Al-Khawari didn't move, his eyes aimed right at him, and Pope wondered uneasily if he had betrayed himself. He dismissed that as foolish. The sun was behind him and it was impossible that he could be visible to the naked eye from there. The man turned to watch the teenager, and finally he set off in the same direction.

Pope panned right.

The big man was joined by another two who had been waiting in a small outbuilding. It was obvious now that these three were al-Khawari's personal security detail. Pope saw that one of the newcomers had a long gun, although he was too far away to identify it. The man with the rifle got into the Land Rover. The big man got into the driver's seat of the Bentley. The third man disappeared into the garage and drove out again in a second Land Rover. The three cars lined up in convoy, with the Land Rovers bracketing the Bentley, and set off up the sloping driveway to the gate and the road beyond.

'Control, Nine, Twelve. They're coming out. Our man is in a Bentley, and he's between two Land Rover Discoveries. Three men in a security detail.'

'What are our orders?'

'Follow.'

'And engage?'

'No,' he said firmly. 'Do *not* engage. There's an unidentified teenage male in the car. Could be his son.'

'Copy that.'

'I need to get back to my car. We'll run surveillance as a team. Update me on their location, and I'll catch up.'

He put the binoculars into his bag and moved as quickly as he could through the undergrowth on the flanks of the hill until he was back down on the cycle path. He ran as hard as he could and reached the car in three minutes. He got into the car, turned it around and set off back to the main road.

'Position?'

'Heading north-east. Just going through Crans-près-Céligny.'

Pope looked at the satnav stuck to the inside of the windscreen. The convoy was three miles further up the road. He needed to get there as quickly as he could. He was driving fast, nudging the car up to eighty as he tried to catch up with them. The limit was seventy-five, and he knew that the road was usually heavily policed, but he couldn't dawdle. If al-Khawari's men were good, and he had reason to believe that they were, they would be skilled in counter-surveillance. It was very easy to identify a single pursuer. If they made Kelleher and Snow, all they would need to do would be to peel off onto a quieter road and see whether they followed. If they did, they would be suspicious. Another turn onto another quiet road would confirm their speculation. A two-car surveillance, though not optimal, would increase their chances of staying undetected. In an ideal world, Pope would have operated a 'floating box,' with multiple cars that could merge into and drift out of the pursuit. But this was not a perfect world, and they would have to make do with what they had.

He saw them half a mile ahead and started to slow down so that he was travelling just a little faster than they were.

'I've got a visual on you,' he said into his mic.

'Want us to drop off?'

He looked at the satnav again. 'There's a turning two hundred yards ahead on your right.'

'I see it.'

'It'll pick up this road again in a mile.'

'Copy.'

Pope watched as Kelleher and Snow decelerated, indicated and turned off.

He edged closer to the Land Rover at the rear of the convoy. He could see nothing through the darkened windows, but they were driving carefully, observing the speed limit. He marshalled the gap between them, getting a clearer view of the other two cars as they followed a gentle bend in the road. There was a uniform twenty feet between each car and the next.

They were on the E62. It was the main thoroughfare along the northern shore of the lake, and it would have appeared natural for Pope to have been behind the convoy. The roads coming off it were minor ones, not ones that it would be unusual to keep missing. Kelleher reported that she and Snow were back on the E62, and Pope told them to keep their distance in case he needed them, but as they travelled on, he grew more comfortable. They hadn't been made yet, and he saw no reason why that would change.

He saw a sign for Rolle, and the lead Discovery indicated that it was going to come off the main route and follow the turn.

'They're coming off,' Pope radioed. 'I'll go ahead and come around. You follow.'

'Copy.'

Pope drove on for half a mile and then took the next left-hand turn off the E62, coming back on himself and entering the village from the north. He passed the Chateau de Rolle and the Île de la Harpe in the lake, an artificial island with an obelisk poking from between the trunks of a clutch of trees. Kelleher radioed their location and Pope navigated to the north-west, taking the Route de Gilly and then the Avenue du Jura until he saw the signs for the Institut Le Rosey and realised where the convoy must be going.

'It's a school,' he radioed.

'There's a long driveway. They've turned onto it. We're going on.'

'I'll go past for a look. Stop in Rolle. I'll radio in fifteen minutes.'

Pope parked the car for a second time and followed the narrow road back to the south, retracing his route. The property to the east was demarked by a tall stone wall. He continued until he came to a pair of impressive stone pillars with 'CHATEAU DU ROSEY' engraved into each of them. There was a pair of security cameras on tall posts set just behind the pillars, so he continued onwards, following the lazy curve of the wall until he was far enough away from the cameras to be confident that he would not be seen. A young oak grew out of the verge between the road and the start of the wall, and after checking that the road was clear, Pope clambered up it.

He pulled himself onto the top of the wall and brought out his binoculars again.

The road wound its way through picturesque grounds until it straightened out into an avenue lined by elms. The road stopped at a collection of buildings that were half a kilometre away from his position. Pope's eye was drawn to a chateau and, set around it, a campus comprised of a series of impressive buildings. He found the two Land Rovers and the Bentley. They had parked alongside a two-storey building painted a mellow yellow, with red tiles on the sharply sloping roof. He watched as al-Khawari and the boy he now assumed to be his son got out of the car. One of the heavies brought a suitcase down from his Discovery and hauled it to the entrance of the building that they were nearest to.

'Nine, Control. What's going on?'

'That was the school run,' he said quietly. 'Ask around town. See what you can find out about this place.'

'Will do.'

Pope watched the buildings a little longer. He saw a group of teenagers exiting one of the buildings, milling around near to the Bentley. Al-Khawari was talking to the boy, but as they noticed the newcomers, something was said, and they shared an awkward embrace. The boy turned and went to join the other pupils.

Pope had an idea.

Chapter Thirty-Five

Michael Pope was at the same motorway services as before. It was raining heavily and he had taken shelter inside. The building was arranged as a large atrium with fast-food outlets and coffee shops around its edges. The space in the middle was given over to seating and tables. It was busy, noisy and hot. Pope sipped at his cup of coffee and kept a cautious watch of the people around him: families struggling with children, businessmen and women stopping to use the facilities before heading off to wherever it was that they were needed. There was a big LCD screen on the other side of the room, and Pope glanced at it occasionally. It was showing the first pictures from inside the damaged ticket hall at Westminster. He had watched the footage in his hotel room when it had been released last night, but the broadcasters kept returning to it again and again. Pope found it all a little salacious. He had switched channels to try to find something else, but it seemed that every programme had some connection with the attack.

He saw Vivian Bloom at the entrance, gave a slight tilt of his head and waited for him to come over.

'Bloody weather.'

Bloom was wet. He took off his dripping overcoat and folded it over the back of the chair.

Pope took the envelope of photographs and passed them across the table.

Bloom looked at them, picked one up and looked at it more closely. There were twelve in all. Pope had sent Hannah Kelleher to Marrakech the afternoon following the surveillance of al-Khawari on the way to Le Rosey. She had located the target and put her under close surveillance.

The photographs had been taken with a long lens from positions that would have made it very difficult for the subject to know that she was being observed. Pope recognised the locales from his own visits to Marrakech to see the girl's mother two years ago. There was a picture of the central square, Jemma el-Fnaa, the girl bartering with a local tradesman for a bag of fresh oranges. There was another as she came out of a grocery store with a bag of supplies. Another showed her disappearing into the mouth of a narrow, darkened alleyway, the sort that made close surveillance almost impossible in the city.

The subject of the series of photographs was Isabella Rose. Pope knew that the girl was fifteen, although, as he had confirmed when he had met her on the South Bank on the day of the attacks, she could easily have passed for much older than that. These photos, though, had captured something in her that he hadn't noticed when they had met. The girl had always looked like her mother. She had the same blonde hair, the same blue eyes, the same porcelain skin. But she had grown up. She was taller. Her hair was longer. More fundamental than either of those changes was the severe cast that lay behind her beautifully defined features. Her mother had had the same edge to her appearance, an otherworldly bleakness that Pope had always found unnerving. Isabella had it, too. It was chilling in one so young.

Now, the likeness between mother and daughter was truly striking.

The final shot was in profile. The girl was wearing a sleeveless top and was turned so that her right-hand side was presented to the camera. There were tattoos of two roses on her right shoulder and arm. Beatrix had had the same tattoos, adding another each time she eliminated one of the names on her list. She had never had the chance to add the final rose, the one that would denote her murder of Pope's despicable predecessor as head of Group Fifteen. Her daughter had completed the set for her.

As far as he knew, there were no photographs of Isabella Rose that existed in the information held by Her Majesty's government. There had been an entire file on the girl, but Pope had arranged for Group Two to have that deleted, together with every official reference that she had ever existed. It was a last favour for Beatrix, the request of a dying woman who had been so badly wronged by her country. He had been unable to refuse it.

Bloom dropped the photographs on the table and looked up with a sceptical expression on his face.

'You're serious?'

'I am.'

'How old is she?'

'Fifteen.'

'You want to send a fifteen-year-old girl to spy on al-Khawari?'

'I do.'

'And you know how foolish that sounds, Captain?'

'She's not an ordinary girl. Her mother worked for Group Fifteen. She was Number One before John Milton and before me.'

'What? That's Beatrix Rose's girl?'

'That's right. Isabella.'

'I thought we lost her?'

'No, sir, that's not strictly true. I gave Beatrix my word that I would hide her. We didn't think it would be safe for her after what she was planning for Control. Her mother made some very influential enemies.'

Bloom nodded. Beatrix's quest for revenge had caused ripples around the world. Control and his five rogue agents had been working for Manage Risk, a large and powerful American private military contractor. Beatrix had eliminated them, one after the other, and the fight had concluded on American soil near to The Lodge, Manage Risk's vast headquarters in North Carolina's Great Dismal Swamp. Isabella had murdered Control and two guards in a North Carolina hospital. Pope and Milton had arrived in time to get the girl to safety.

'What are you proposing, Control?'

'Isabella is an unusually talented girl. Her mother trained her thoroughly in the year they had together before she started to work her way through her list. She's had weapons training, she's fit and strong and she's been given the rudiments of surveillance and counter-surveillance. She has no family and no friends that I can find. She won't be missed. I am proposing that we give her a new identity and a cover story, and enrol her into that school with the aim of ingratiating herself with Khalil al-Khawari.'

'The son.'

'Correct.'

'What would that achieve?'

'We've investigated his social media accounts. It's his sixteenth birthday next month, sir. Look at this.'

Pope spread printouts from the boy's Facebook page over the photographs of Isabella. Bloom looked at them. The printouts contained details of Khalil al-Khawari's birthday party. It was to be held at his father's property on the shore of Lake Geneva.

'We would be there with her. Number Nine and Number Twelve would be her parents. I'd be there, too. There might be another way to get inside, but if there isn't, we can run this in the background.'

Eventually, a small smile curled the crinkled edges of Bloom's mouth.

'You know this is madness?'

'A little,' Pope admitted.

'And you know that there is no way I would be able to get it approved?'

'That's an issue for you, sir.'

Bloom steepled his fingers. 'I don't know,' he said.

'With all respect, does anyone have a better idea?'

'No,' Bloom said. 'They don't.'

Chapter Thirty-Six

The house was in Leytonstone, in the East End of London. Queen's Road was a short distance from the Underground station. A Victorian terrace ran along both sides, with gardens between the front of the houses and the road. Most of the gardens had been concreted over to provide parking spaces, and those cars that could not be parked off the road were crammed on both sides, leaving enough room for a single car to pass through. Wheelie bins were left on the pavements, bushes that had never been cut back towered out of overgrown gardens, and Union Jacks and the cross of Saint George were hung against the inside of windows.

Mohammed drove along the terrace, turned and then drove back. He saw nothing to suggest that the house was unsafe, but nevertheless, it paid to be careful. He found a space on the side of the road fifty feet farther along and reversed into it. He waited there for two hours, watching the comings and goings. Elderly women pushed shopping trolleys toward the parade of shops near to the station. Tattooed skinheads walked muscular attack dogs. Kids with nothing better to do smoked cigarettes and drank from bottles wrapped in brown paper bags. It was a poor area, down at heel, with a diverse range of ethnicities and a transient population. The sort of place it was easy to disappear into.

He listened to the radio. There was a discussion about the terrorist atrocity and the steps that needed to be taken to combat it. The usual roll call of suspects was rehashed. Al-Qaeda seemed to be the favourite at this early stage, although there was the suggestion that the Islamic State was a possibility, too. *The usual knee-jerk reaction,* Mohammed thought. *It must be the Islamic bogeyman. How convenient. How easy.* They had much to learn. The discussion moved on to what would happen once the investigation had determined who was to blame. The presenter referred to a snap opinion poll, taken that day, which recorded that the percentage of people who would be prepared to back military action had climbed by 10 per cent. The reluctance to commit British troops to foreign wars seemed to be waning. The thirst for revenge was growing stronger.

Mohammed heard the distinctive *thwup-thwup-thwup* of a Chinook and looked up through the windshield as the big, two-rotored chopper rumbled overhead. There was an airfield at the Honourable Artillery Company in Central London. It must have been headed there. It was an apt underlining of the increasingly martial mood. It wasn't unusual to see the military in or over London these days. That had been anticipated, and he was glad to see it.

Mohammed kept a careful watch on the property throughout the two hours. Nothing struck him as suspicious. Eventually, he concluded that it was safe enough for him to enter.

He approached the property. Mohammed had seen the place advertised on Gumtree and knew that it would be perfect for his purposes. He had paid for a six-month tenancy in cash, the landlord asking him no awkward questions and the paperwork kept to a minimum. The garden had been paved over, and the husk of an old and broken washing machine stood against the wall. The bins had been covered in graffiti and were filled with fetid black bin liners that had been dumped there by neighbours. The front door opened into a small porch with a screen door behind it.

Mohammed took out his key, unlocked the front door, went inside, unlocked the screen door and then stepped into the quiet house. He was in the small sitting room. He had drawn the floral curtains the first time he had visited, and he had kept them closed since. Grey, insipid light leached through the thin fabric, revealing the moth-eaten sofa, the gas fire and the paint that was peeling in leprous folds from the walls. He paused and listened. He could hear the sound of a muffled argument from the street outside, but there was no sound in here. He breathed in, smelling the faintest tang of cordite. Not too strong, but there, and easily identifiable if you knew what it smelled like.

Mohammed knew.

The front room led to a corridor with stairs going up to the first floor. Mohammed had been sleeping up there, but he had other business to attend to today. The kitchen was at the back of the house next to the downstairs toilet. There was a window to the side that was half covered with a dirty roller blind, with enough space beneath it to give a glimpse into an overgrown garden. There was a door beneath the stairs. He opened it and pulled the drawstring to switch on the light. The sixty-watt bulb glowed brightly, casting its light onto the flight of rough concrete steps that led down into the cellar. He had to duck his head as he descended, reaching the foot and then reaching out for the light switch for the strip light that he had fitted to give himself the illumination to do what he needed to do.

The basement was large, filling the footprint of the reception room and kitchen that were above it. He had bought a large decorator's trestle table from B&Q and unfolded it so that he had a large enough surface to work on. The three old artillery shells were on the floor next to the table. They were about two feet in length, reaching up to just below his knee. They were cylindrical, with an ogive-shaped nose that made them look like oversized bullets. They were easy enough to find. Eastern Europe was awash with them, and a contact in Chechnya had sourced six for him. They had been smuggled into the country on the same trawler as the gunmen who had stormed the Palace of Westminster, collected in a rented panel van and driven to London. It had been very, very easy. Mohammed had known that it would be.

He took one of the shells and heaved it up, carefully lowering it onto the table so that he could get at the fat rounded end. The shell was equipped with a percussive fuse that detonated the explosive on impact with the ground. Provided he was careful, it was safe to handle. He used an electric saw to cut away the cartridge case that held the propellant charge, so that he could get to the projectile itself. He opened it up and started to scoop out the explosive inside. He made a pile of it on the table. Each shell contained eight kilograms of plastic bonded explosive. The three bombs that he had prepared for the first attack had been created from the explosive that he had accumulated from the first three shells.

He took a plastic Tupperware container and swept the explosive into it. There were already fifteen full containers on the table. He was planning on twenty-five. The rest of his equipment was on the floor. He had bought twenty bags of galvanised 30 mm nails. He had spread those purchases out across several builders' merchants so as not to arouse suspicion. They would be packed in tight around the explosive to maximise the damage the blast would cause. He had two suitcases; cheap wheeled ones that he had found in a shopping centre near Dalston Kingsland station. And he had two pay-as-you-go mobile phones that he had picked up from the Carphone Warehouse in the same precinct. He'd soldered wires to the speaker output circuits of each phone so that when they rang, current would flow to the trigger of a thyristor that would then send current to the alligator clips that he had fastened to the detonators.

He only had to finish with the explosive, and he would be ready. It was another three or four hours.

He picked up a fresh shell, lowered it to the table and started to work.

PART FOUR

Chapter Thirty-Seven

Isabella slowed at the junction to the road that would approach her new armoury. Her mother had drilled many lessons into her during the year that they had spent together in Morocco, and this exhortation – that she must observe the surroundings before approaching a building containing material that could be compromising – was one that she particularly remembered. She watched the comings and goings – the taxis bearing tourists to the out-of-town shopping mall just off the Route de Safi, the trucks and vans of the local traders – until she was confident that she – and the street – were not observed.

She gunned the engine of the KLX, crossed the road, put down the kickstand and slid off the bike. She stood outside the door to the unit and waited again, listening. She could hear the screech of a buzz saw from one of the other units, but nothing nearer that gave her cause for concern. She took the key from the string she wore around her neck, slid it into the lock and turned it, then heaved the door halfway up.

She took the key for the lockers, pushed it into the lock of the nearest cabinet and opened the door. This one was reserved for her AR-15 semi-automatic. She took the gun, hefted it in her hands and then held the stock against her shoulder. She hadn't fired it for a while. Too long. She grabbed six hundred rounds of 5.56 ammunition and put the boxes into the bag she had brought with her. She broke the rifle into two parts, separating the receiver from the barrel, and slipped them into the bag, too. She shut and locked the locker, pulled down the main door until it clicked shut, and locked that, too. Then, she put the bag on her shoulders, straddled the bike and gunned the 250 cc engine.

She rode away from the row of units, left the shops and outlets behind her, and headed south, out into the desert.

She passed through Mechouar-Kasbah, past the airport and then down on the R203. She went by the lush green of the Argan Golf Resort and continued for another twenty minutes until she was in the desert. The Moroccan Sahara was nearly two hundred miles away, and the arid landscape was a little too green to be called a real desert, but there were sand dunes and displaced rocks and, most important, isolation.

It was six in the evening, and the sun was falling quickly down into the horizon. It would be cold soon, but for now, the earth pulsed out enough heat for Isabella to sweat beneath her helmet.

She passed a Freightliner heading into the city, rode on for another ten minutes and then cut onto the dirt track that she remembered from her previous trips here. It descended into a wadi, the dried-out riverbed hidden from view by steep walls and a grove of thirsty acacia and yucca. She rested the bike against the wall of the wadi, opened the bag and reassembled the AR-15. She pushed a magazine into the well and walked a few extra steps away from the bike.

She practised for an hour. First, she went through a dry-firing exercise. She picked a rock a hundred feet away, and with the weapon cocked and on safety, she assumed the position of a patrol carry and walked forward. She brought the weapon up, aimed and practised the squeeze of the trigger. Then she dropped to the sandy bed and lay prone. She cradled the weapon, carefully placed a coin on the barrel and then squeezed the trigger so carefully that the coin stayed balanced and in place. Her mother had explained that a good steady squeeze on the trigger was the most important thing, assuming that a weapon's sights were aligned, to ensure an accurate shot. She clambered up and went through her reloading drills, both with and without retention of the magazine. She shouldered the weapon, pushed in an empty magazine, dry fired, dropped the magazine and, in the same motion, brought a new magazine up. She guided the second magazine home with her index finger pointed straight up its side. She hit the bolt release and went back to dry firing. It was a smooth and well-practised drill, and although it wasn't easy to time precisely, she felt that she had shaved another fraction of a second from her previous best time.

These exercises took her half an hour. By the time she was done, she was bathed in sweat. The sun was below the level of the horizon now, and she was beginning to get a little cold. She collected a jacket from her bag and then climbed back down to the riverbed again.

Finally, she fired the weapon with live ammunition.

She ended with a misfire routine, and then, two hours after she had arrived and with six hundred rounds down range, she decided that she was done.

She was pleased. Her mother had taught her a saying. Beatrix had said that an amateur practised something until she did it right, but a professional practised until she couldn't do it wrong. Isabella worked to that standard. She felt that she was making progress.

She dropped to her knees and collected the spent rounds, dropping the brass into her bag so as to leave as little trace as possible. She broke down the rifle, stowed it in her bag and got back onto the bike again. She rode along the desiccated watercourse until she found an easier slope to get up and out of it, and then traversed the desert back to the road. She felt the smoother asphalt beneath her wheels, gunned the engine and headed back to the city.

Chapter Thirty-Eight

Isabella decided not to go back to the armoury that evening. It was getting colder, and she was a little clammy from the dried, cold sweat on her skin.

She lit candles as she heard the call to prayer from the nearby mosque. She took the bag through to the storage space that had once been the riad's tiny hammam. She had fitted a gun safe against the wall, and she stored both pieces of the rifle inside, together with the ammunition that she had not fired. She had just closed the safe when she heard the knocking at the front door.

She stayed stock-still, wondering if she had misheard it. She didn't have visitors. She didn't know anyone in Marrakech save Johnny Ink, the guy who had done her tattoo, and he didn't know where she lived. No one did. She had never had a single visitor here.

She heard the knock again.

Rap-rap rap rap.

Jaunty. Brisk. Friendly.

She opened the safe and took out the Springfield EMP that she had stored there. She had plenty of experience with bigger handguns, but this one fit nicely into the palm of her hand. She preferred the stopping power of a .45, but her mother had taught her that using the same calibre ammunition for both her pistols and rifles would lessen the chances of loading the wrong round when she could ill afford a mistake. Isabella had practised with the Springfield extensively and was very accurate with it. She readied it to fire and started across the courtyard to the vestibule.

Rap-rap rap rap.

She had paid for an entry system to be fitted to the front door. It was the only easy way to get into the property, and she wanted to make sure it was as secure as possible. There was a screen fixed to the wall that showed the feed from a camera that was positioned high above the door outside. The security light was activated by a motion sensor, and it had come on now, its harsh glow bleaching the upturned face of the man who was on the other side of the door.

Michael Pope?

What?

What was he doing here?

And how had he found her?

She paused. She could stay here, leave the door unanswered, but what good would that do her? He knew she was here. If he wanted to see her, he'd just come back. Or he'd wait outside, or leave an agent outside and wait for her to come out.

Whatever it was, it was better to find out now. Get it over and done with.

She pulled out the drawer of the table that stood next to the door and dropped the handgun inside.

She took a breath, looked up at the screen again and finally unlocked and opened the door.

The noise and clamour of the souk outside overran the tranquillity of the riad.

Pope smiled at her. 'Isabella,' he said.

'Mr Pope, what are you doing here?'

'I need to talk to you.'

'What about?'

'It's . . .' He paused, looking left and right with awkward unease. 'It's quite sensitive, Isabella. Do you think that I could come inside?'

'Are you alone?'

'Yes,' he said.

She paused, still uncertain. But he had helped her mother. He had rescued her from a very uncertain future, too. And then she thought about the locket that she wore around her neck, and the trouble that he had gone to in order that she might have it. But even as she thought of that, the doubts came. Why had he gone to that trouble? It couldn't be charity or because he was feeling philanthropic. Surely there was an agenda. She suddenly had the thought that perhaps he had found her because of the locket. She wondered, knowing it was ridiculous but wondering it anyway, whether they could miniaturise a tracker so much that it could be concealed in the locket. Or was the locket a tracker?

She was confused, but it was no good standing here, with him on her stoop. He had built up some credit with her. She could spare him a little time. It would give her the opportunity to have her questions answered, too.

'Come in.'

She offered him mint tea partly because she wanted to be hospitable and partly because she wanted to be able to observe him from the iPad in the kitchen that gave access to the CCTV cameras that were arrayed around the house. She boiled the kettle and picked the mint leaves and watched as he wandered around the courtyard, gazing down into the plunge pool and feeling the weight of the fruit that she was growing from a pair of large potted orange and fig trees. He was dressed casually in a loose-fitting suit, a white shirt that was open at the collar and a pair of brown desert boots. She looked for the telltale bulge of a concealed weapon, but she couldn't see one. She would proceed on the basis that he was armed. It was very likely, and besides, it was prudent.

She put the mint leaves in the boiling water and let it steep, collecting two small glasses and a tray and taking the collection back to the table and chairs that were arranged at the edge of the pool.

'This wasn't where you lived before,' he said.

'No.'

'Did your mother leave it to you?'

'No. She left money. I bought it and refurbished it.'

'I didn't ask before. How old are you now, Isabella?'

'Fifteen.'

He shook his head in evident admiration. 'And you did all this. That's very impressive.'

She waved it off impatiently.

'Your mother would have been very proud of you.' He nodded down to her chest. 'You're wearing it. The locket.'

She said nothing, studying him for any sign that might give away his purpose in coming to Marrakech to speak to her. Nothing was obvious.

'Are you wondering how I found you?'

'Not particularly,' she said, although that was the question she wanted answered the most.

'You don't have anything to be ashamed about. I've had a very talented agent looking for you.'

'Where did they find me?'

'In the square.'

She only just managed to arrest the lowering of her brow before it became a frown. She was careful with her counter-surveillance routine. Her mother had drilled it into her. She might not have been able to avoid being seen in the square, and she couldn't very easily ignore being there, but she should have been able to detect someone following her as soon as they got into the streets of the souk. That was lazy.

'Don't worry about it,' he said. 'Like I said, she is very good.'

'Who said I was worrying?'

'Her name is Hannah. She'd like to meet you.'

She could read him. All this forced bonhomie was to mask his awkwardness. He was awkward because whatever he was here to ask her was something that he found difficult to say. That made *her* feel nervous. 'What are you doing here, Mr Pope?'

'Yes,' he said. 'What *am* I doing here?' He stood and went back to the orange tree, running his finger over the skin of a particularly juicy fruit. 'Do you watch the news?'

'A little,' she said. 'The Internet, mostly. Is this about London?'

He nodded. 'It is.'

'I was there.'

'Where?'

'In the station. My train was just pulling out when the bomb went off.'

His mouth dropped open. 'Jesus,' he started. 'Are you – '

She regretted mentioning it as soon as the words left her lips. The last thing she needed was his paternalism. 'It's all right. I was fine. But I saw what happened. I know what it was like. I had to come out through the station right afterwards.'

'Isabella, I didn't—'

'I'm fine,' she said, holding his eye. 'Really. I'm *fine*. But, yes, to answer your question, I know what's been going on.'

'Things are bad at home.'

'Your home, Mr Pope,' she corrected. 'Not mine. This is my home.'

'Of course.' She had put him on the wrong foot. He groped around for a neutral place to start the conversation. 'I'd like to tell you some things that are secret, Isabella. Very delicate things. Do you mind? If I tell you them, you must promise that you'll keep them to yourself.'

'Who am I going to tell?' she said, waving her hand around the riad. 'It's just me here. I haven't got any friends. You're the first person I've spoken to in days.'

'All right.' He let the orange fall free and came and sat back down again. 'You know that I'm in charge of the unit your mother worked for before . . . well, before she was betrayed. You know that?'

She nodded.

'The authorities are investigating the attacks. We have intelligence to suggest that there will be others. It's urgent that we find those responsible before they can strike again.'

'Go on.'

'We have a very strong indication to suggest that one man was responsible for financing the operation. It was complicated to arrange, and it wouldn't have been cheap, but this man is very rich.'

'And you want to talk to him.'

'Very much.'

'So go and arrest him.'

'I'm afraid it's not as easy as that.' He paused. 'The evidence we used to find him couldn't be used in court.'

She gazed at him evenly. 'You tortured someone?'

Her brazen lack of feeling, the matter-of-factness of her response, took him aback again. She could see that the effect she was having on him was slowing the whole conversation down. She resolved to dial it back a little.

'That's one way of putting it,' he said. 'It doesn't really matter. We're confident that the information is correct, but we can't act on it. Legally, I mean.'

'He's in the Middle East?'

'No. Switzerland.'

'So speak to the Swiss.'

'We can't do that. They won't give him to us. And I doubt he'd make himself available for a cosy chat.'

'Who is he?'

'His name is Salim Hasan Mafuz Muslim al-Khawari. He has properties all around the world, but he is currently at a large house on the shores of Lake Geneva. Apart from being rich, he is very cautious. His property is very well defended. He has a team of guards with him at all times.'

'Why is he in Switzerland?'

'There are probably several reasons, but one of them appears to centre on his son, Khalil Muhammad Turki al-Khawari. He's a student at an exclusive boarding school close to Geneva. He is fifteen, nearly sixteen, very rich, very arrogant and quite stupid.'

'This is why you want to talk to me?'

He smiled. 'Yes. We don't think there's a realistic chance that we could get to Salim safely. So we've had to think laterally. We think it might be possible to arrange it so that you are put into the same school as Khalil. We know that his sixteenth birthday is next week. There's a party at his father's house. We would like you to try to befriend the boy so that you are invited to the party.' He paused, looked at her, then added apologetically, 'If you were prepared to do it, of course.'

'What would I have to do?'

'We would give you a very small device that we would like you to leave in the house.'

'A bug?'

'Sort of.'

She paused, considering it.

'You saw what happened in the station,' he started. 'We need to stop that from happening again.'

She almost told him that appealing to her sense of civic duty wouldn't work. She had no sense of civic duty. She was born in the

United Kingdom, but she didn't owe it anything. No, if anything, things were the other way around: *it* owed *her*. She held her tongue. If she was going to allow herself to be involved, it would be for another motive.

'This man – his father – is dangerous?'

'Probably. But you wouldn't be on your own. I would be there, and two of my agents would be posing as your mother and father. Hannah – the agent I mentioned earlier – would be one of them.'

'Sounds very elaborate,' she said. 'You've been planning. Did you think I would say yes?'

'I didn't know what you would say. And if I'm being honest, I wouldn't mind at all if you said no. Really – I mean that. I have no right to be here asking you this. Most people would consider it unethical, and that's only if they're being charitable. But things are very serious. That's the only reason I'm asking.'

'I'm not most people. And I'm not a child. I can look after myself.'

'I know you can. I remember what you did in the hospital.'

And then I was sick, she thought. *And I needed your help to get away. That won't be necessary again.*

She looked around at the riad. She had worked out a nice, regular routine for herself. She had continued the training that her mother had started. She had added to it. The languages she was learning, for example. But no one had come for her. Manage Risk had lost her, or they had forgotten, or they didn't care. No one was coming to avenge the old man and the guards she had shot. And if that was true, then why was she hiding?

She did have a reason to consider his request. Her mother had spent a year training her. She had continued that training. But how would she be able to test herself? She wouldn't.

There had been a thought, playing at the back of her mind ever since she had arrived home again. Now she acknowledged it for the first time: she had an itch and she needed to scratch it.

One day, she would have found that piece of paper with Pope's telephone number, and she would have contacted him. Not to ask for his help. To ask if she could help him. This, she decided, was providence.

Fate.

She was being offered the chance to do what her mother had done.

The chance to test herself.

The chance to make her mother proud.

She stood and collected their empty glasses.

'Isabella?'

'What do I need to do?'

PART FIVE

Chapter Thirty-Nine

Le Rosey is one of the most exclusive and expensive schools in the world.

It is near to the village of Rolle. Thomas Snow drove the BMW along the coast of Lake Geneva, turned to the south among the picturesque vineyards and farms, and after a few miles they came to a driveway so discreet that it would have been easy to miss. The only sign that this was the correct turning was the 'CHATEAU DU ROSEY' that was engraved into the stone pillars.

'Here we go,' Snow said as he slowed the car and turned off the road.

The road snaked through a grove of regal chestnut trees. The car crossed a stream by way of an ancient humpback bridge, and after five minutes, they reached an old chateau that was surrounded by a cluster of newer buildings.

Kelleher was studying the materials that Pope had provided for them. Isabella had looked at them last night. The prospectus was glossy and impressive, and listed the names of alumni who had gone on to become famous international figures. The names spoke of huge wealth. The children who attended the school came from Persian Gulf oil magnates, Greek shipping lords, Italian textile billionaires, Spanish banking families, American tobacco barons, Japanese industrial tycoons and Hong Kong real estate moguls.

'You know how much it costs to send your kid here?' Kelleher said.

'One hundred and twenty grand,' Snow replied. 'I know. I read it.'

'And listen to this: "We do not make a play of 'classical' education, but promise to inculcate a series of attributes in our students which will stand them in good stead for all that life has in store for them. We promise 'physical balance,' oral expression and a sense of solidarity with one another."'

'They mean they'll make sure they understand the differences between the spoiled few and the rest of the world.'

'"Le Rosey seeks neither 'an intellectual elite' nor a set of 'model' students. We promise an education that will avoid academic failure and/or completely deviant behaviour." Basically,' she said, 'it means the spoilt little shits can do whatever they like.'

Isabella listened and said nothing. She had read all of this in advance and then done additional research so that she could play the part she knew she would have to play. She knew, for example, that Le Rosey was known for royalty. The Shah of Iran, the Aga Khan, King Albert II of Belgium and Prince Rainier of Monaco had all gone there. So had the sons and daughters of the royal families of Egypt, Greece, Yugoslavia, Italy and Britain. It had always appealed to the Arabs, and had taught a number of sheikhs, the children of Saudi Arabian arms dealer Adnan Khashoggi, and the son of the owner of Harrods, who had been killed with Lady Diana. There were the children of movie stars, rock stars and innumerable European and American fortunes. She saw names like Rothschild, Botin, Niarchos, Benetton, Duke, du Pont, Rockefeller. When she Googled them, her sense of trepidation increased.

Snow parked the car in the central courtyard and looked out of the tinted window at the buildings that loomed over them. There were other cars in the courtyard: Ferraris, big Porsche SUVs, BMWs, a Bentley.

Kelleher turned in her seat. 'Are you okay?'

'Yes,' Isabella said.

'No need to be nervous.'

'I'm not,' she said, although she was.

'You're going to do fine. What's your name?'

'Daisy McKee.'

'Where are you from?'

'London.'

'What does your father do?'

She nodded at Snow. 'City trader.' Kelleher paused, then gestured with her hand that she wanted the rest of the cover story. Isabella sighed, then continued with it. 'He owns McKee Capital. He trades stocks and shares on the London Exchange.'

'And me?'

'Charlotte McKee. You own an art studio in Chelsea.'

'Brothers and sisters?'

'Two brothers and one sister. Their names are Ethan, Charlie and Abigail. I'm the youngest. Ethan is working with my father, Charlie is at Eton and Abigail is working for Médecins Sans Frontières in Africa.'

'Very good.'

'You don't need to worry,' she said. 'I've memorised it. All of it.'

'Remember' – Snow took over – 'you have a cell phone in your bag. If you need us, send a blank text to the number for Uncle Rupert. And keep the phone charged and with you at all times. We'll be able to track you as long as it's on.'

She nodded that she understood.

'You ready?'

Her attention was drawn to a group of teenage girls passing between the BMW and the Bentley parked ahead of it. They were dressed well, all with bright white smiles and tanned limbs. They practically dripped money. Isabella had inherited a generous estate from her mother, but she did not flaunt it. She had invested most of it in her riad, but the rest she had saved. She was not extravagant in any way. Her mother had taught her that extravagance was a good way to make yourself stand out, and standing out was not something that she wanted to do. Her mother had also taught her that having a good sum of money on standby allowed you the flexibility to move quickly and decisively, should the need arise.

Isabella was wealthy, by the normal standards of a fifteen-year-old girl, but she knew that she would be a pauper in comparison to these girls.

She felt another twitch of unease before she chided herself for her stupidity. What was real and what was false was irrelevant. It was what appeared to be true that mattered, and credibility was all about confidence.

'Daisy?'

'What?'

'Are you ready to go?'

'Yes,' she said. 'I'm ready.'

Chapter Forty

They had a welcome interview with the admissions tutor. His office was enormous, with a similarly spacious waiting area outside. His door opened at three on the dot, and he came out into the waiting area to greet them. His name was Pires, and he was full of so much false bonhomie that Isabella took an immediate dislike to him.

'Mr McKee, a pleasure to meet you at last.'

He offered his hand. Snow put out his and shook it.

'And Mrs McKee, good to put a face to a voice. I hope the admissions procedure was painless enough?'

'It was,' she said. 'You were very helpful. Thank you.'

He waved the compliment away and turned to Isabella. 'And you must be Daisy?'

'Hello,' she said, forcing a bright smile onto her face.

There came a knock at the door, and at Pires's curt 'Come in,' a waiter entered with a tray bearing four bone-china cups, a large carafe of coffee and a plate of petit fours. Pires thanked and dismissed him and then set about pouring the coffee himself.

'Our roll is limited to just four hundred boys and girls,' he explained as he handed the cups around. 'They are aged between eight and eighteen, and they come from sixty-one countries. Instruction is in English, with French as a subsidiary, or in French, with English as a subsidiary. I believe you prefer English, Daisy?'

Isabella spoke good French from her time in Marrakech, but she remembered her cover story. Daisy was conversant, but not proficient. 'Yes,' she said. 'English.'

'I think you'll find the school offers a unique environment. The education here is peerless, and the extracurricular activities are varied. Waterskiing, sailing, scuba diving, flying, riding, shooting and, of course, skiing. You won't be bored.'

'I'm sure I won't.'

The man proceeded to recite what Isabella suspected was a memorised spiel about the benefits of an education at Le Rosey. She listened and answered his questions with a promptness that suggested that she was attentive, but her focus was on the room and the world beyond the broad window. Her thoughts switched back to the preparatory meetings that they had had in London. Michael Pope had explained in greater detail what it was that she was being asked to do. He had shown her the tiny device that they wanted her to fit to Salim al-Khawari's computer, how it was used and the best ways to avoid being seen as she did it. A whole day had been invested in developing Daisy McKee's persona and backstory until she could answer questions fluently and without thinking about them. Pope had left a file on the table of the hotel room that they had used for the training. It had been marked with one word: 'Angel.' When she had asked him what that meant, he had told her – with a smile – that 'Angel' was her codename.

Isabella switched back into the present as Pires asked her a question about what she liked to do in her spare time. She told him that she liked horses and ballet. When he asked her what her favourite ballet was, she answered, with perfect conviction, that it was *Swan Lake*, that her favourite composer was Tchaikovsky and that the first time she had seen it was when her mother had taken her to the London Opera House in 2007. Zenaida Yanowsky had played Odette. It had been wonderful.

'A very good choice,' he said. 'You know we have ballet classes at Le Rosey?'

'I do,' she said with a smile. 'That's one of the things I'm looking forward to the most.'

He stood. 'Well, then. Should we all go and see your room?'

Isabella kept her eyes and ears wide open as Pires guided them from the administration building to the school's accommodation.

The room was simple and not as extravagant as she had expected. There was a bed, a wardrobe, a desk and a set of shelves. The floor was carpeted, the walls painted a neutral beige and a large window offered a view over the impressive campus all the way to the waterfront. Isabella wheeled her suitcase to the wardrobe.

'What do you think?' Pires asked.

'It's lovely,' Kelleher answered. 'Daisy?'

'Lovely,' Isabella agreed.

'Students rise at 7 a.m.,' Pires said. 'You have a shower, then you go downstairs and have breakfast. It's a large buffet, the only informal meal of the day. Between 8 a.m. and midday, there are five periods of class, with a mid-morning "chocolate break."'

'Chocolate?' Snow said.

'This is Switzerland.' He laughed. 'What do you expect? Every Monday at midday there is a school assembly, which brings the whole school together for notices, reflection and sometimes for dialogue. On the other days of the week you are free until lunch. Classes begin again at 1.15 p.m. and finish three periods later at

3 p.m. From 4 p.m. to 6 p.m. you have a choice of sports and arts. After you have showered, you'll do homework and "prep" in the study hall from 6.20 p.m. to 7.20 p.m., or you might be involved in choir, orchestra or drama rehearsals.'

Pires was interrupted by a knock at the open door. Isabella turned. There was a girl there, a little older than her, and very beautiful.

'Ah,' Pires said. 'This is Claudette. She is going to be Daisy's buddy until she's settled in.'

'How lovely,' Kelleher said.

'Hello, Daisy.'

The girl extended her hand. Isabella took it and made the effort to smile. It was returned, although she noticed that her eyes remained cool. 'Hello,' she said.

'Claudette has been at Le Rosey for two years. She's one of our prefects.'

'That's wonderful,' Kelleher said.

'I was just going through the daily schedule,' Pires said to the girl. 'I got up to prep. Do you want to tell her about dinner?'

'Of course, Monsieur Pires. Dinner is served at 7.30 p.m. Students are given a place at a table with other students and a teacher. The food is always excellent. It's the best time of the day.'

'It all sounds wonderful,' Kelleher said.

'Unless you have any other questions, there's nothing else I need to say,' Pires said.

'No,' Snow said. 'I think we're good.'

'Very good. I think we can leave Daisy in Claudette's capable hands.'

Kelleher turned her back to Pires and placed a hand on each of Isabella's shoulders. She looked into her eyes, gave the tiniest of nods and then, right back in character, hugged her and told her with brash confidence that she was sure that she was going to settle in here just fine. Snow was next, kissing her on the cheek and squeezing her hand.

'Goodbye, darling,' Kelleher said.

'Bye, Mother.'

'We'll see you at the end of the term.'

That was six weeks away. Isabella realised that she should probably be showing a little more emotion, but she wasn't a good enough actress to summon tears on demand. Daisy would probably have cried, but it was not something that came easily to Isabella. Instead, she hurried back across the room and hugged Kelleher again, hiding her lack of emotion by pressing her face into Number Nine's neck. She held her there for ten seconds, then allowed her arms to be unpeeled.

'You'll be fine,' Kelleher said.

Isabella nodded, found a brave smile and watched as they thanked Monsieur Pires and left the room. Pires followed. The girl, Claudette, stayed at the door. The friendliness was gone from her face now that she was not on show. Isabella thought she saw something unpleasant in her eyes: a knowingness, perhaps. Had she seen through her already?

'What now?' she said, keen to at least try to make a friend.

'Get your stuff unpacked. Dinner is at seven-thirty. I'll come and get you.'

She turned and walked away down the corridor, leaving the door wide open. Isabella realised that she didn't know where the girl's room was, what she was supposed to wear for dinner, how that would work out . . . anything.

She went to the window as she heard the crunch of a car's tyres on gravel. The BMW pulled away, rolling slowly across the courtyard and then onto the long drive through the trees. Number Nine and Number Twelve were gone. They were staying in a bed and breakfast in Perroy, ten minutes away, but that wasn't much succour.

Isabella realised for the first time just how far out of her comfort zone this really was.

She felt vulnerable and alone.

Chapter Forty-One

Isabella spent the next few hours in her room. She wanted to start to feel the atmosphere of the place, the sounds and noises of the buildings and the girls in the rooms on either side of her own. It was quiet, with just the occasional burst of chatter. She idled over to the window and looked down onto the courtyard below. Students passed between the accommodation blocks and the school buildings, their feet crunching on the gravel.

She put her suitcase on the bed and unpacked it, hanging up the expensive new clothes they had bought in Geneva and then slotting the empty case into the wardrobe beneath them.

She spent an hour going through the notes that she had made on Khalil al-Khawari. Pope had not provided very much information on the boy and had complained that it had been difficult to find anything particularly useful. She had researched him herself and found a little additional material. Between Pope's skimpy dossier and her own, she felt that she had enough to form a preliminary idea of what he might be like.

She had found several pictures of him on his social media profiles. He was a handsome boy who wore a perpetually haughty expression. He had thick black hair that he wore long enough to drape over the bottom edge of his collar, and a wispy attempt at a goatee beard. His eyes looked sleepy, and when he smiled, there was a lasciviousness there that hinted that he was used to getting what he wanted. There were pictures of him shooting grouse, riding horses, skydiving over the Burj al Arab, racing jet skis and bodyboarding. The pictures were advertisements for excess. Isabella preferred a spartan life and found his distasteful.

She had trawled his social media accounts. His Facebook profile listed three thousand friends, and he had twice that number of Twitter followers. Both profiles were repositories for links to his favourite musicians and films. Neither suggested much in the way of taste. He supported Manchester United, and several of the first team were followers of his Twitter account.

He had been a student at Collège Saint Marc before attending Le Rosey. He suggested in one post that he planned to go to Sandhurst once he had finished school.

He was a playboy.

She had nothing in common with him at all.

She waited until seven-thirty, but Claudette didn't return to take her to dinner. She put on her jacket and followed the sound of conversation to the refectory. It was a large conservatory that had been equipped with twenty round tables. There was an excited atmosphere in the room as friends who hadn't seen each other for the summer were reunited.

Isabella could see the cliques forming as the students filed inside. Two tables, adjacent to one another, were reserved for a group of glossy girls, with Claudette's voice ringing out the loudest of all. The remaining tables accommodated other groups of friends, everyone talking loudly and enthusiastically.

It didn't take her long to find Khalil al-Khawari.

He was at a table on the far side of the refectory. She recognised him from the photographs that Pope had shown her. His clothes were understated and obviously expensive, and as he raised his hand to wave at a newcomer who had just entered the room, the light glinted on the face of a chunky wristwatch.

Isabella realised that she had nowhere to sit. She didn't know anyone. She crossed the room self-consciously, made her way to the table where Claudette and her friends were sitting, and smiled down at them.

'Hello,' she said.

Claudette turned to look up at her. 'Yes?'

'I thought you were going to come and get me.'

'Sorry. Forgot.'

'Can I sit here?'

The girl glanced back at her friends, her eyebrow cocked and the corner of her mouth twitching up in a cruel smile. 'I don't think so,' she said.

'There's a spare seat,' Isabella pressed, although she was feeling more and more uncomfortable.

'That's reserved,' Claudette said. 'For a friend.' She shone an insincere smile. 'Sorry. You'll have to go somewhere else.'

There was no point in protesting. Isabella was aware that the girls at the adjacent table were watching Claudette's little display, and she had no desire to make a sideshow of herself on her first day. She returned the smile and left for a table in the middle of the room that had two spare seats. She could see that the three outcasts at the table were in the same position as she was: not connected with the popular girls and left to themselves.

She knew she was being watched as she left Claudette's table. She heard laughter behind her as soon as she turned her head, and others looked at her with amusement that they made no attempt to disguise. She was surprised by her reaction. She had spent so much time alone, she had thought that she would be inured to childish callousness. She knew it shouldn't bother her, but it did. She felt acutely exposed.

She was halfway to the 'outcast' table when she looked up and glanced over at Khalil's table. The other boys were deep in conversation, but he had turned his head to look at her. He saw that she had seen him and his handsome face broke into a wide, welcoming smile. She returned the smile, and as she pulled back the chair to sit down, his grin became even more intense, and he delivered a theatrical wink.

'Hello,' said one of the girls at the table. 'Who are you?'

'Daisy McKee,' she said.

'I'm Eve. First day?'

'That's right.'

'Don't worry about Claudette. She's a bitch – everyone knows it. Don't waste time on her.'

Isabella relaxed into the small talk. She gave enough effort so as not to appear rude, but her attention was elsewhere.

The waiting staff circulated and took their orders. Isabella allowed herself a moment to turn and look across the tables to where Khalil was sitting. All she could see was his glossy head of black hair. He had turned away and was lost in conversation with the other students at his table. She thought of the task that Michael Pope had set for her. Getting to know Khalil was the first, and most important, part of her assignment, and she felt that she had taken a small step toward it today.

Chapter Forty-Two

Isabella awoke at six the next morning, dressed in her running gear and went out for a run. The grounds were expansive. She saw more accommodation blocks, a large canteen, a gymnasium and generous playing fields. She kept running, and after ten minutes she was out in the countryside, with the lake to her right. Her mother had said that running had always been the best way for her to clear her mind, and after Isabella had taken it up herself, she had come to agree. She kept running, cutting a route through the verdant hills and woods, and allowed her thoughts to flit over the task at hand. What did she need to do? She would have to appear natural and at home, comfortable with the atmosphere of the school and the circumstances of the other pupils. She had read in the handbook that had been left in her room that the staff cleaned up the students' rooms. Isabella had taught herself to be entirely self-sufficient, and she found the prospect of being attended to like that to be distasteful. But she would have to pretend that it was not.

She thought about how she would ingratiate herself with the others and, in particular, Khalil al-Khawari. She knew that would be a challenge. The last year had been spent almost entirely alone, apart from the grandmaster at her dojo, and her childhood had been a procession of homes and foster parents, never staying long enough to form connections with anyone. She was self-aware enough to know that she could be seen as distant, even truculent, and she knew that a friendly and open attitude was something that she would have to work hard to project.

She reached a kink in the lake and decided to turn back. By the time she returned to her room it was seven, the sun was up, and she was breathing heavily and lightly bathed in sweat. She undressed and showered, closing her eyes and again running through the cover story that Pope, Snow and Kelleher had concocted for her. She wanted it to be second nature. She had studied it for hours and was confident that she could carry it off.

She wrapped a towel around herself and went to stand in front of the mirror. She knew that she was pretty. She had her mother's icy complexion, her blue eyes and her long blonde hair. She had never had a boyfriend before. There had been boys in some of the homes, and she had fooled around with a few of them, but she would not have described herself as experienced or even particularly confident. She didn't know how hard she would have to work to attract Khalil's attention. In spite of her research, she really knew very little about him, and his behaviour was unpredictable. She would handle that on the fly.

She made an effort to look involved with the day's lessons, but she was distracted and they passed her by. The sessions bore little resemblance to the hours she had endured in cold and leaking classrooms in a succession of sink estate schools, but there were similarities enough for her to remember the boredom and the unpleasantness of being someone apart, with no friends to help ease the monotony. Her experience of formal education had been rudimentary. There had been schools as she was growing up, but her peripatetic existence meant that she was never in one for long enough to feel as if there was any point in taking it seriously. A long line of teachers dismissed her as a lost cause, the kind of girl who would never amount to anything. She helped to reinforce that conclusion; her hair-trigger temper inevitably led her into the fights that had seen her suspended and then expelled.

They had given up completely in the end. A family was chosen who had promised to homeschool her, but that effort lasted a month before the impatient mother threw up her hands. Isabella taught herself to read, and when she finally persuaded the teachers that there was no profit in them trying to force her to cleave to their list of recommended reading, she won herself the opportunity to read whatever she liked. Books became her escape from the grim reality of her daily existence. She devoured Sir Arthur Conan Doyle, then Dickens and Hardy. Mark Twain transported her from the drabness of the English commuter towns through which she was shuttled. She tore through Austen. Asimov and Banks broadened her horizons. Dante and Joyce tested her.

Her mother had continued her education during the year that they spent together, and now that she was gone, Isabella had undertaken to complete it herself. There were the practical lessons in the use and maintenance of weapons, the physical improvement, the language classes that meant that she was fluent in Arabic and French, and passable in Italian, Spanish and several others.

She sat at the back of the classroom and thought about what she was going to do.

Chapter Forty-Three

Isabella enjoyed her dinner that night. The food was excellent. Her diet was basic in Marrakech – a succession of tagines and vegetable dishes – so the succulent fish she ordered was a pleasant change. Her table was joined by a boy who had issues with crippling shyness. The other girls made an effort to include him in the conversation, but the atmosphere was stilted. None of them were particularly comfortable in talking to the others, Isabella included, and although she knew that she should make more of an effort to fit in, she found it difficult to motivate herself. She had no intention of staying in the school any longer than she had to. As soon as she had met Pope's objectives, she intended to return to her riad and the peace and quiet that she had come to realise was of great importance to her. In the end, the others came to the conclusion that she was disinterested, the conversation faltered even more and then continued round her.

She finished her meal, wished them a good night and went back to her room.

She spent half an hour in meditation, preparing herself for class tomorrow, until she was disturbed by loud music from the common area outside. She took a moment to tamp down her irritation, put herself back into character, opened the door and went outside.

Claudette, her friends and the other girls from the corridor were seated around the coffee table. One of the girls was playing music from her phone through a portable Bluetooth speaker. There were bottles of gin and vodka, a two-litre bottle of Diet Coke and a stack of plastic cups that had been taken from the water dispenser at the end of the corridor. The girls were dressed in party clothes and all made up.

Isabella was dressed in tracksuit bottoms and a T-shirt, and felt plain in comparison. She forced a smile onto her face and aimed for a casual impression as she leaned against the wall. 'What's happening?'

No one answered.

'Where are you going?'

Claudette made a show of rolling her eyes. 'First week of term?' she said, phrasing it inquisitorially.

'So?'

'So there's a party in the boys' common room.'

'Can I—'

'Can you what?'

'Come with you?'

The girls laughed.

'Not with us,' Claudette said archly.

'You know any of the boys?' one of the other girls asked.

'No,' Isabella said. 'Only got here yesterday. I don't know anyone.'

'I wouldn't go if I didn't know anyone,' the girl said to the others. 'You'll just look like you're desperate.'

Isabella felt the tension in her hands as she clenched her fists, her nails pressing into the soft flesh of her palms. She looked at Claudette, at her glossy face and lacquered hair, as pretty and fake as the hair on a child's doll, and felt the heat of her testiness begin to rise. A hair-trigger temper was a trait that she had shared with her mother, and it had gotten worse after Beatrix's death. Regular meditation had been helpful in keeping it under control, but there were limits. Her imagination played out how simple it would be to embarrass this girl in front of her friends, to flip her off the sofa and onto her back, to choke her out or mess up that pretty face, but she knew she couldn't possibly do that. She would be expelled, and then how would she do what she had agreed to do?

No.

Isabella smiled at Claudette, said good night to the others, and went back to her room.

She opened the wardrobe and ran her finger across the clothes that had been purchased for her. Some of them were still wrapped in their plastic sheaths, the names of the brands emblazoned across them. She took a dress from the hanger and tore the plastic away from it. It was black, simple and stylish, and she had liked the way that she had looked in it when she had tried it on. Kelleher had said that it made her look good, too. It was more revealing than she was used to, a little *too* short and a little *too* low cut, but that would serve her purpose. She needed to make an impression.

She went into the bathroom, ran the shower and undressed.

She waited for two hours, until eleven, before she locked her room and went outside. It was cold as she walked across the courtyard that separated the boys' accommodation block from the girls' and she drew the woollen wrap around her shoulders, scant consolation against the chill breeze that was blowing in off the lake. She had a tight little nub of anxiety in her stomach, the sense that she was about to give a performance without having had the chance to rehearse. It was a good opportunity, too good to pass up, but she would have preferred to have had a chance to prepare herself.

Her feet crunched over the gravel. A night bird hooted high overhead. She could hear the muffled thud of bass, and it was louder as she opened the door. The sound was coming from above. The configuration of the block looked to be identical to her own, so she climbed the stairs and turned in the direction of the communal space.

The party had spread out from the communal space into the corridors that fed into it. All of the rooms were open, the doors flung wide. Little clutches of students were gathered in the corridor as she approached. Others were in the rooms. There was the strong, sweet smell of dope in the air, and plenty of the kids were drunk. One girl was laid out on the floor, a plastic cup tipped over and a sticky puddle spreading out from it. She stepped over and around them all, looking for Khalil. She guessed that he would be here. His reputation was as something of a playboy, and she would have been surprised if he had missed a chance to party.

She reached the communal space. A sound system had been set up and one of the boys was DJ-ing. The lights had been extinguished and blankets hung over the windows. Lava lamps had been set up, and they cast pools of warm light around the room.

She paused in the doorway and looked. She saw Claudette immediately. She was sitting with her back to the wall, a bottle of expensive vodka stood between her and the boy who was talking to her. She saw Isabella, her face crumpling into an angry frown. She said something to the boy, pushed herself onto unsteady legs and walked across the room to meet her.

'What are you doing here?' Claudette demanded.

'I fancied a drink.'

'I told you, you don't know anyone.' The words came haltingly, through the haze of drink, but the antipathy could not be mistaken. 'You have to know someone. You're not welcome.'

She put her hand on Isabella's elbow and started to pull her towards the corridor. Isabella didn't struggle. She didn't want to make a scene. As they passed one of the open doorways, she glanced inside and saw that the bedroom beyond was empty. She planted her left foot, reached out with her left hand and clasped her fingers around Claudette's wrist. She pressed her thumb and forefinger, penetrating between the bone and tendon, and was rewarded with a little gasp of pain. She used the moment to guide Claudette into the room, advancing with her and flicking the inner door shut with a flick of her leg.

She bent the girl's arm around behind her back and squeezed again.

'You're not very friendly,' she said.

'It . . . hurts . . .'

'I don't really care whether you like me or not. But if you ever try to tell me what I can and can't do, we're going to have a problem.'

'Get . . . off . . .'

'You know why I'm here? At this school?'

The girl grimaced as she shook her head.

'Because I was expelled from my last one. Got in trouble with a bitch like you. We ended up fighting. It didn't go too well for her. Hospital. I messed up her face. Do you understand me?'

'Hurts . . .'

'Do you *understand* me?'

'Yes.'

She released her grip. Claudette drew her arm in, rubbing the back of her wrist with her spare hand.

'Stay away from me,' she said.

Chapter Forty-Four

Khalil was in the common space when Isabella emerged from the room. He was in a corner, passing around a joint with a group of two girls and another boy. Isabella dismissed thoughts of Claudette and made her way to the bottles of booze on the table. She watched Khalil in the corner of her eye. He saw her, smiled and disengaged himself from the group and came over to meet her at the table.

'Hello.'

'Hello.'

'What's your name?'

'Daisy.'

'You're new, right?'

'Yes. The new girl with no friends.'

'I saw what happened at dinner last night. Don't worry about Claudette. She's a bitch. Her friends are, too.'

She saw Claudette emerge from the corridor, still rubbing her wrist. She saw that Isabella was talking to Khalil and glared at her. Isabella held her eye for a moment until Claudette looked away.

Khalil noticed the exchange. 'You and she had an argument?'

'We just set a few things straight. I don't like bullies.'

'Good for you,' he said. He still had the joint in his hand. He put it to his lips and inhaled deeply. He held the smoke in his lungs for a long moment, tipped back his head and then exhaled toward the ceiling.

He offered it to her.

'No, thanks.'

'You don't?'

'I used to. Got into trouble. I try not to now.'

He gave a nod as if to say that he understood, carefully extinguished the joint and slid it behind his ear.

'You know my name?'

'You're Khalil,' she said with what she hoped would be a suitably flirtatious smile.

'How do you know that?'

'I asked.'

'Is that right?'

She disguised her awkwardness by reaching down for a plastic cup.

'Let me,' Khalil said, unscrewing a bottle of Grey Goose and pouring out a very generous measure. She set out a second cup and he filled that, too, collected it and made a show of touching it against hers. *'Santé.'*

'Cheers.' She put the cup to her lips and drank. The vodka was sharp and acrid, and she had to fight the urge not to wince.

He noticed her discomfort. 'You don't drink either?'

'Not for a while.'

'How old are you?'

'Sixteen,' she lied. Her enrolment forms said that she was sixteen. She knew she looked older than fifteen. There was no reason why he would suspect unless she gave him reason. She cursed herself for the gaucheness with the drink and, to compensate, said, 'Fuck it,' and indicated that he should give her the joint.

He did. Isabella put it to her lips; he took a lighter and flicked flame. She puffed hard until the hashish and tobacco caught light, and then inhaled. The smoke tickled her throat, and she thought she was going to cough. She mastered it, taking instruction from his example, and exhaled. She felt woozy almost at once, and then a little nauseous. It made her feel vulnerable.

Khalil put a hand on her shoulder and guided her away from the table to a quiet corner of the room that had been scattered with pillows and cushions. He sat down, his back to the wall, and indicated that she should sit next to him.

'What do you think of the school?'

'Haven't had much of a chance to look around yet.'

'Where were you before?'

'Collège Alpin Beau Soleil.'

'In Villars-sur-Ollon?'

'Yes,' she said.

'Why did you leave?'

She thought of the lie she had told Claudette. She had to double down on it, just in case he spoke to her. 'It wasn't my choice.'

He cocked an eyebrow. 'They threw you out?'

'Something like that.' She shrugged helplessly and then grinned at him. He laughed. She was pleased. She felt that she was doing well.

He pointed at her arm. 'Nice tattoo.'

'Thanks.'

He traced the tip of his finger down her arm, across the tattoo, and she let him. 'Does it mean anything?'

It means I killed a man. It means I pressed a pistol against his chest and pulled the trigger.

'Not really. Just something I liked the look of.'

He started to talk. She found small talk very difficult, so it was a relief that he was evidently so self-obsessed he could keep up the conversation by himself. She found it all so inconsequential. Khalil regaled her with stories about the things that he had done. She learned that he had just been bought a new BMW as a present for his forthcoming birthday. He told her that his father owned a house on the shore of Lake Geneva and that he was planning on buying a jet ski in the summer. He told her about a skiing trip he was planning for the winter, the nightclubs that he preferred in Paris and London, the places he liked to shop. How was she supposed to pretend to be interested in the pointlessness of his rich, cosseted life? He was vain and egotistical, but she realised that he was telling her all of this because he wanted to impress her.

She nodded and made the appropriate noises to show how she was impressed, and as he reached out and looped his arm over her shoulders, she did not demur. He leaned over to close the distance between them and moved to kiss her. His lips brushed against hers. She smelled alcohol and stale weed on his breath. She pulled away, smiling coyly.

'What?' he protested. 'You don't like me?'

'It's not that,' she said. 'I don't know you.'

'Come on.'

'We only met tonight.'

'I thought that was what we were doing. Getting to know each other.'

His hand was still on her shoulder. She reached up and squeezed it. 'We are.'

'You have a boyfriend?'

'No. But I don't like rushing into things, that's all.'

'Fine.' He took his arm away. Isabella could tell that she had hurt his feelings. She guessed that he was not used to anyone saying no to him, and unless she moved adroitly, she would spoil any chance of developing their relationship so that she could further her objectives.

He started to stand. Isabella put her hand on his shoulder and held it there. 'Don't be like that,' she said.

'You don't like me,' he said haughtily. 'Fine. Plenty of other girls do. Claudette does.'

She followed his gaze across the room. Claudette was watching them with a look of displeasure on her glossy face.

'I didn't say that. I just said I prefer to move more slowly. And my parents are coming to see me tomorrow. Early. I wasn't going to stay out as late as this tonight. I need to get to sleep.' He sighed but he relaxed, sitting down again. She reached across and ran a finger down his cheek, feeling his downy hair. 'You've got a birthday party soon, don't you?'

'Who told you about that?'

'People are talking about it,' she lied.

'It's Monday.'

Isabella touched his cheek again and gave him another coquettish smile. 'I haven't been invited yet.'

He turned, saw the way she was looking at him, and found his confidence again. 'You'd come?'

'It's at the house on the lake, right? The others told me. They said it was spectacular.'

He grinned. 'It's pretty cool.'

'I'd love to come.'

'All right.' He nodded. 'It's invitation only. Not everyone is going to be there. But I can get you one.'

She sensed that now was the time to go. She wanted to leave him with the impression that she was a challenge, more difficult than the simpering girls who fawned over him, but a challenge that would be worth the effort. She stood, finished her drink, and then stooped to kiss him on the lips. He arched his back to push his face at her, trying to press his tongue into her mouth, but she withdrew.

'Give me an invitation,' she said. 'And then we'll see.'

And then, knowing that his eyes were on her body, she walked out of the room and out of the building into the frigid cold of the night beyond.

Chapter Forty-Five

She had more lessons the following morning. She took a seat at the back of the room again and made a show of listening, but her thoughts were elsewhere. She had wondered whether she should report her progress to Snow and Kelleher, but she had decided against it. All she had done was make contact with the target. The meeting had been encouraging, but there was still a long way for her to go.

There was a small courtyard between the classrooms, and she was gazing out of the window into it when she saw Khalil arrive there. He sat down on a bench, and when he saw that she was looking at him, he raised his hand in a friendly wave.

He was still waiting for her twenty minutes later as the class spilled outside.

'Good morning,' he said.

'Hello.'

'Did you enjoy the party?'

'It wasn't bad. What time did it finish?'

'I think it's probably still going on.' He grinned. 'My father is coming to see me today, so I had to call it quits.'

'He wouldn't approve?'

He shuffled a little. 'Not really.'

Isabella wondered whether she was trespassing on something he was not comfortable discussing. 'If it's any consolation, my parents would be the same.'

'I don't know, Daisy. Unless you're going to surprise me, I'd be surprised if your parents were well known in the Muslim community.'

She shook her head and made to laugh with him.

'You still want to come to my party?'

'Sure.'

He reached into his bag and took out an envelope. It was made from heavy stock. It felt expensive. She opened it and took out a card, similarly creamy and expensive, with an invitation to the party and directions to get to the house by the lake.

'Keep it to yourself,' he said with a grin. 'Like I said, I haven't invited everyone. Don't want people to get too jealous.'

'No. Don't worry. I will.'

'And I have to keep it quiet. If my parents found out . . .'

'They don't know?'

He laughed. 'No! There's no way they'd let me have a party.'

'They won't stop it?'

He smirked. 'They'll be in Paris. There's nothing I can do about the staff telling them, but it'll be too late by then. I'll get in trouble when they get back, but I'm going to make sure it's worth the aggravation.'

They sat quietly for a moment. She had the feeling that he was a little awkward, and when she turned to him, his cheeks were flushed.

'What are you doing for the rest of the day?' she asked.

'Not much. You?'

'Lessons.'

'Really?'

'What? You're not?'

'Lessons are kind of voluntary. They only care that your parents pay the bills and that you don't do anything too depraved. I'm going into Geneva.' His face lit up as he knew what to say to her. 'You should come.'

She feigned reluctance. 'I don't know—'

'You said you wanted to get to know me.'

'I do,' she said.

'What are you waiting for, then? Let's go and have some fun.'

Isabella knew what she should do. The school didn't matter. The whole purpose of this charade was to win Khalil's trust and get into his father's house.

'Why not?' she said.

'You'll come?'

'Let's go.'

He called a taxi. It arrived in ten minutes, pulling into the wide courtyard. Isabella was aware of people watching them as they got into the car, but no one said anything. She saw a teacher that she recognised from the refectory, but he just watched idly and did nothing. The attitude toward attendance seemed to be relaxed.

'They let us come and go as we please?'

'Not everyone,' he said, grinning. 'Just some of us.'

She pretended to be uncomfortable.

'Relax, Daisy. You're with me. All right?'

'If you say so.'

Khalil told the driver to take them to Geneva and Rue du Mont Blanc and then reclined in the leather seat and looked across the cabin at her. His legs were spread wide and his knee touched up against hers.

'What do your parents do?' he asked her.

It was the first thing that he had said that wasn't all about him. 'My father is a commodities trader. He owns his own brokerage.'

'That's great,' he said, making an effort to appear interested, but not doing a very good job. 'Your mother?'

'She's into art.'

'Really? Wonderful.' There was an awkward silence, and she realised that this was going to be the extent of his efforts to get to know her. He wasn't very good at it, she decided. Probably didn't need to be. A young man in his position, with his father's wealth and reputation behind him, he would be used to other people doing all the running.

'You're not very good at small talk, are you?'

Her good-natured rebuke brought his focus back on her. 'I'm sorry . . .' he began, saw that she was joking and then smiled. His teeth were bright white.

They were coming into the city now.

'Have you been here before?'

'Never. I've only visited the airport.'

'The shops are great. The Swiss love shopping. It's practically a national pastime. You'll have a great time.'

Khalil knew his way around Geneva and seemed keen to show off. They set off walking down the Rue du Mont Blanc to the Pont du Mont Blanc so that they might have a pleasant view of the harbour. They crossed the bridge, and Khalil pointed out the little island on their right.

'It's the Île Rousseau. There's a statue of Jean-Jacques Rousseau. Never seen it, but I think it's there.'

They saw the Jet d'Eau, the famous fountain that shot 140 metres into the air, drawing water from the lake. They crossed the bridge and headed through the Place du Molard to the 'Rues Basses.' They followed Rue de la Confédération, Rue du Marché and Rue de la Croix d'Or, staying parallel to the lakefront. Khalil turned onto a flight of stairs going up to their right, and after ascending, they arrived in the old town. They visited the Cathedral of St Pierre and climbed the tower for a view of the city.

They could see for miles. It was cold at the top, and Khalil took advantage of the moment to put his arm across Isabella's shoulders and draw her closer to him.

'How long have you lived here?' she asked him.

'A year. And just for school. My father has places around the world.'

'Where were you before this term?'

'Qatar. Boring.'

'I've never been.'

'Don't bother. You can't drink, you can't do anything. Everything's so new and sterile. Lots of money, but nothing to do with it. I hate it.'

'Better here?'

'Here's okay, but it's provincial. London, Paris, New York. That's where I'd rather be.'

'What does your father do?'

'Stuff with oil and gas. That's boring, too. It's all boring.' He sighed, as if it were the most tedious subject imaginable. 'We should go and look at the shops. Sound good?'

'Sure.'

Chapter Forty-Six

Khalil ended their tour back on the Rue du Mont Blanc. There was a string of exclusive jewellers on the street, and he made her stop and look into the window of one of them. The display was spare and almost empty, the few pieces on show obviously priced at extortionate amounts.

He put his arm around her shoulders again and pointed at one piece.

'You like it?'

It was a Rolex Lady-Datejust in stainless steel and pink gold, decorated with rubies and sapphires.

'Sure,' Isabella said, unable to completely hide her distaste.

He took it for reticence. 'Want it?'

'Don't be crazy. It's bound to be stupidly expensive.'

Isabella had no time for extravagant trinkets. Even when she had refurbished her riad, she had been very careful to make sure that she wasn't exploited. She had paid for quality, but none of her decisions were made frivolously. There was plenty of money left, but she had husbanded that carefully. She knew that it would not last forever, and she needed to stretch it out for long enough until she had decided what she wanted to do with her life. The thought of squandering money on an ostentatious piece of jewellery was beyond her.

He fluttered his hand at that and went to the counter. Isabella was watching him take out his wallet when her attention drifted out of the window. She gazed over the racks of gold and silver and saw Kelleher on the other side of the street. There was a café there, with tables arranged in a square outside the front, and Pope was sitting there with a cup of coffee. He was wearing a pair of dark glasses and was looking right at her. She felt a burst of relief. She had thought she had been doing well, but she had been riding the adrenaline to help her forget the icy nugget of fear and trepidation that seemed permanently lodged in her gut. Pope had said that they would be watching her. She knew that he could have stayed invisible if he had chosen, and realised that he had revealed himself so that she could be reassured.

And it was reassuring.

She felt a hand on her arm. 'Hey,' Khalil said. He had the watch in his left hand.

'Don't be crazy,' she said.

'What?'

'It's ten thousand, Khalil.'

'Just money. You know how much my father is worth?'

She made as if she was bashful. The watch was hideous, and the fact that it cost so much was obscene. She did not wear jewellery, and even if she had, she would never have chosen something as baroque as this. She glanced up and over his shoulder at Pope. He was staring at her, and as she watched, he gave a tiny inclination of his head.

Khalil started to rub his right hand up and down her arm. 'Take it,' he insisted.

She held out her left arm and pulled back her sleeve so that her slender wrist was bare. He opened the clasp, draped the watch around her wrist, and then fastened it again.

'Beautiful,' he said. He was leering at her. She knew what had just happened; she understood his interpretation of the transaction. He thought he had bought her. She felt the hand on her arm, his fingers tracing patterns through the fabric of her sleeve. It was possessive, and she felt a little ripple of revulsion.

She looked through the window again. Pope was gone.

Isabella let him lead her onto the street. He was searching for a cab to take them back to Le Rosey when a big car slowed down, pulled out of the sluggish traffic and drew up alongside them. It was a Bentley Continental. The paintwork gleamed, and the sun sparked off the chrome grille and the hubs of the wheels. It looked obscenely expensive, even among all the opulence on the street.

'Shit,' Khalil breathed out.

'What is it?'

'My father.'

The driver's door opened, and a uniformed chauffeur stepped out. He went around to the rear and opened the kerbside passenger door. A man got out. He was shorter than average and of slender build. He had a head of white hair and a spatter of tiny dark lesions across his otherwise smooth brown skin. He was dressed well in a three-piece suit that fit him so well that it must surely have been bespoke. Isabella recognised him. It was Salim Hasan Mafuz Muslim al-Khawari, and his face was marked with a furious scowl.

'Get in the car,' he said.

'Father—'

'You make me repeat myself?'

'Father, I—'

'Get in the car, boy.'

Khalil paused for a moment. He looked at Isabella, all the confidence that he thought he could buy with his father's money gone in an instant. She looked back at him, unsure what – if anything – she should do or say. She chose to do nothing.

Salim took a step to Khalil, raised his hand and cuffed him hard around the side of the head.

'Now, Khalil!'

His face flashed with pain, and with his eyes cast to the ground, he hurried across the pavement to the car and got inside.

Salim turned to Isabella. She caught the scent of his perfume and recognised it as attar, a perfume extracted from rose petals that was popular among the well-heeled Arabs in the Marrakech souks.

He smiled at her. 'I am sorry, miss,' he said. 'My son knows he should not be here with you.'

'Why?'

'You are not Muslim.'

'What difference does that make?'

He smiled again. She saw that he had thin lips and hard eyes that glittered like diamonds. 'I am not saying that you and Khalil may not be friends. He has many friends who are not Muslim. All I am saying is that I prefer it if he is not alone with a pretty girl who is not a Muslim.'

She found him patronising, and she was tempted to argue the point with him, but she remembered what she was here to do and that she would do herself no favours if she annoyed him and found her invitation to Khalil's party rescinded.

And so she ducked her head respectfully and told him that she understood.

'What is your name?'

'Daisy.'

He gave a little bow. 'Then it was nice to meet you, Daisy. Perhaps I will see you again.'

He stepped back and got into the car. Isabella watched, saw Khalil staring glumly back at her, and next to him, an extravagantly coiffed woman. She only caught her profile, but recognised her as Khalil's mother. The chauffeur closed the door, walked around to the other side of the car, got in and drove away.

None of them seemed concerned about how she would return to the school.

Chapter Forty-Seven

The weekend passed without difficulties. Isabella kept herself to herself, going out for early morning and late evening runs and then spending the rest of the time reading in her room. She realised that she was apprehensive about the party on Monday and what she had been asked to do.

It was the thought of being in Salim al-Khawari's house. Khalil had said that he wouldn't be there, that he would be in Paris, but the thought was still daunting. She knew little about the older man, just the pieces of information that Pope had given her. She had augmented the intelligence with her own research, just as she had done for Khalil, but all she could find were vague generalities that went no further than the broadest strokes.

He was, the websites and newspaper articles agreed, an aggressive businessman with a sharp temper. He was vain and extravagant, and prone to fly off the handle at the most insignificant perceived slight. One profile, unusual for daring to go deeper than the manicured public image, suggested his chippiness might be because of his humble beginnings. The journalist who had written the profile had been hauled through the courts for her temerity in deviating from the prepared script. It was obvious that al-Khawari did not like it when matters proceeded out of his control.

On Sunday evening, at the end of a long day during which she had wound the tension until it was tight enough to snap, she gave in and took out her cell phone.

She found the number for Uncle Rupert and sent a text.

All going well. I can talk now if you're free?

She hurried outside to take the call, and only had to wait a minute before the phone rang. She picked it up and looked at the screen. The number had been withheld.

'Hello?'

'It's me.' She recognised Pope's voice. 'How are you?'

'I'm fine. I'm outside. There's no one here. I can talk.'

'Well done. It's going well?'

'It is.'

'I was watching in Geneva.'

'I know.'

'Has he invited you to the party?'

'Yes. It's tomorrow night.'

'And you feel ready?'

'Yes.'

She did, but she was nervous.

'What about Salim?'

'Not going to be there.'

'Do you need anything?'

'No . . .' She paused. 'Where are you?'

'Very close. And we will be tomorrow night, too. If you need help, you know what to do.'

'I won't.'

'No. I don't think you will. You're doing well, Isabella. Very well.'

She heard a crunch on the gravel behind her and, turning, saw two boys emerging from the squash court.

'I better go,' she said.

'Good luck.'

She ended the call.

Chapter Forty-Eight

Isabella was distracted all the next day. She paid little attention in the morning's classes, just enough to at least give the impression that she was concentrating, even if her thoughts were a million miles away. She went over how she thought the evening might unfold. It was difficult to be precise when she had no idea of the layout of the house, nor how difficult it would be to find a networked computer and fit the device that Pope had given her. Would there be many people there? How long would she need? Would anyone notice her if she was gone for very long? What if she was found in an area of the house that she was not supposed to be in? What would she do then? She ran these thoughts around and around, coming up with answers and testing them out.

And then she thought of her mother. Beatrix had told her enough about her own work for Isabella to know that what she had agreed to do for Pope was not too distant from the things that her mother would have done. Of course, she reminded herself, Beatrix's activities were more complex than this. She had killed people for the government, and she had been very good at it. Had she felt this way before she went out on an assignment? Kelleher and Snow were in the same unit as Beatrix had been. Isabella assumed that they did the same kind of work. Did they feel this way, too? She wondered whether she should have asked them, whether there was some way to deal with the nerves.

She skipped the afternoon's lessons so that she could go for a run. She didn't really care if that would get her into trouble. It wasn't very likely that she would be in the school beyond today. The charade would be over, one way or another. She ran out to the spot where she normally turned back, but kept going for the same distance again. She passed through the grounds of the school and out into the countryside beyond, running on the slope of a hill that meandered down to the waterfront below. She saw boats on the lake and a pair of jet skis cutting lines of froth across the glassy surface. It was a cold and fresh afternoon, and the air made her lungs burn. She ran on until she had been out for an hour, and then turned back. By the time she returned to the school, she guessed that she had covered fifteen miles.

She showered, standing under the hot water for fifteen minutes until the mud and sweat had been scoured away and her skin was tingling. She wrapped a towel around her torso, ran a hand across the mirror to swipe away the condensation and looked at her reflection. She wasn't accustomed to considering her appearance. She wasn't vain or self-obsessed in the slightest, and had nothing in common with Claudette and the other girls. She had never had the occasion to take advantage of her looks before she met Khalil. It felt duplicitous. She preferred to be honest and open, like her mother had been with her. She realised she was being naïve. Of course her mother would have used her looks if that meant that she could secure an advantage for herself. You worked with the tools that you had at your disposal. Honesty would get her into trouble. She would save that for when it mattered.

She went into the bedroom. She got out the other dress that she had bought with Kelleher and took it from its cellophane wrap.

It was a pink mini, zipped up at the back. Kelleher had suggested a pair of metallic skyscraper heels and clashing red lip gloss. It was the kind of dress that Isabella would never normally have worn. She was most comfortable in jeans and a T-shirt, and this was showy, flirtatious and desperate for attention in ways that she found instinctively uncomfortable. She put it on, applied the lip gloss and mascara, and stood before the mirror and conceded, a little reluctantly, that it was what she needed. She looked older, for a start. That was good. She thought that she looked attractive.

She took the watch that he had bought for her and slipped it on her wrist. She had a small clutch bag, and she put her cell phone and two €50 notes inside. She wished that she had a gun – something small and easy to hide, like the Springfield XDS 9mm she had in her dresser at the riad – but she knew she would never have been able to explain what she was doing with it if it was found. No. She would have to trust that Pope and the others would be able to get to her quickly if she found herself in trouble.

She dragged her suitcase out of the wardrobe and took out her spare pair of running shoes. She pushed her fingers inside and pulled out the insole. The device that Pope had given her was hidden inside, and as she turned the shoe upside down it dropped into her hand. It was wrapped in cellophane and was small. Not much bigger than her thumbnail. She took her clutch, took out her lip gloss and pulled off the lid. There was enough space between the hollow lid and the lip gloss to fit the device and still have room to click it closed.

She checked the time: 6.50.

Khalil had hired a coach that would make runs to and from the house every thirty minutes. The first coach was leaving at seven. She would let the first two go without her and get the third one at eight-thirty. She wanted the party to have started by the time she got there. The more people there, and the more drunken they were, the better her chances of slipping away from the others without being noticed.

The coach was able to accommodate fifty passengers, and it was full. Isabella recognised several of the partygoers from the refectory. There were six boys at the back swigging from a plastic bottle of Coke – laced with vodka – that they passed between them. There were four other quieter boys of Middle Eastern appearance who looked a little discomfited by the rowdy, drunken atmosphere onboard the coach. The rest were girls. Claudette wasn't there – Isabella had seen her through the window of her room as she had gone to catch the previous bus – but there were girls whom she had seen at her dinner table. Isabella was sitting next to one of them; the girl turned around on the seat so that she could join in the lascivious conversation behind her. They were as haughty and supercilious as Claudette, barely sparing her a glance and certainly not interested in including her in their conversation. That was fine. Isabella had no interest in talking to them either. She didn't need the distraction or the investment of energy it would have taken to try to be someone she was not.

She gazed out of the window as the Swiss countryside rolled by. She thought about Pope. He had said that he would be able to track her phone, but it would have been good to know where he was. They might have been following in a car, she thought. Or perhaps they had split up, with someone waiting outside the house. She realised she had no idea how something like this would be organised. It made her feel vulnerable again. She would have liked to know.

She caught sight of her face in the glass. She looked pensive. She clenched her teeth and told herself to get it together. She had to look as if she was supposed to be at the party. Khalil had to think she was happy to be there, that she had no other agenda. No secrets. That she was just there to get drunk and have a good time.

She thought of the little component that she had hidden in her bag.

The bus slowed down, waited for a large pair of automatic iron gates to open and then passed into the grounds of Salim al-Khawari's mansion. The big building was lit up, the illumination from within spreading out of the expansive windows. The driveway was picked out by lights that glowed from little sconces on either side of the gravel, and external lights lit a path down to the boathouse and to the garage block. Isabella looked at the house and felt small and insignificant. It was huge and must have cost millions to purchase. With something as impressive as this, surely there must be sophisticated security inside? Alarms? Motion sensors? She quailed at the prospect of what she had agreed to do. How was she going to manage? They would see right through her. She wouldn't last five minutes.

The bus slowed right down and drew to a halt. She reached into her bag and took out her phone. She opened a message to Rupert and typed out two words.

I'M HERE.

She pressed 'Send.'

The door of the bus opened on wheezing hydraulics, and Isabella waited her turn to step down. It was cold, and the dress did little to keep her warm. Claudette's friends were right behind her, and she heard them make a joke at her expense. She ignored them. The house was at the end of a short path. It loomed up out of the ground, all shimmering glass and cold steel, its light thrown out in rippling shafts across the gentle waves on the lake. She collected herself, ignoring the cold knot of apprehensiveness in her stomach and the dryness in her throat, and followed the others to the big front door.

The party was in full swing. A large reception room had been cleared for the night. Furniture had been pushed to the walls to open up a wide space for dancing. A table was making do as a makeshift bar, the guests helping themselves to drinks.

The atmosphere was drunken. Isabella remembered reading that drinking was un-Islamic; Khalil and his guests were not paying much attention to that. She saw a woman in a maid's uniform standing in an open doorway, her arms folded across her chest and an expression of discomfort on her face. What Khalil had said must have been true: Salim al-Khawari couldn't possibly know what was happening here tonight. She remembered the coldness in his eyes when she had met him in Geneva. The thought that he was somewhere else was reassuring. How long would he be away for? The maid, and presumably the other staff, must have reported to him what was happening. What would he do? Get them to close it down?

A DJ had been provided with a table to set out his laptops and equipment. He was mixing hard, aggressive house music that Isabella had not heard before. She couldn't say that it was to her taste, but it was thunderously loud, and it added to the host of distractions that she knew would prove useful.

She tried to work out where she was in relation to the rest of the house. This big room was on the lower level. There was an elevator in the middle of the room with a spiral staircase wrapped around the shaft. She believed that there were another three floors above her. A door to the outside was open so that smokers could have access to the area around an ornamental pool, where they could enjoy their cigarettes. Some ignored that and smoked inside. Others smoked joints. There was another set of doors opposite her, across the dance floor. They stood open a little and looked promising.

Isabella took it all in.

The atmosphere was rowdy and confused. It felt on the edge of control.

That was good.

She wanted it to be like that.

It would be easier to slip away unnoticed.

She looked for Khalil. He was sitting in the middle of a wide sofa with two girls, one on either side of him. He had his arms around both of them, squeezing them close to him as someone took a picture with a phone. He was a quarter turn away from her, and distracted, and she was able to move around the room so that the elevator and stairs were between them without him noticing that she had arrived. There was a mirror on the wall in front of him, and she was able to observe for a moment. He was the centre of attention. She wondered whether he would even remember that she was coming.

There didn't seem to be any reason why she should wait.

The next bus departed in thirty minutes. If she was lucky, she could fit the device and be back in her room at school within the hour. She could say that she felt ill. It wouldn't matter what she said.

She walked across the room, her eyes on Khalil, until she was two metres away from the doors. She checked again, one more time, turned back to the doors and saw that they had been left ajar, pushed them and stepped through.

Chapter Forty-Nine

There was a corridor on the other side of the door. She followed it deeper into the house. She had decided that if she were questioned, she would say that she was looking for the bathroom and had lost her way. That seemed like it would be a legitimate situation for her to find herself in, especially if she pretended to be a little drunk.

The corridor was long, and as she walked, the noise of the party faded away behind her. Pope had shown her the architect's plans for the property, and she had studied the satellite images from Google Maps as she was preparing for her visit. She knew that it was comprised of two large four-storey wings that were joined by the single-storey span that she was passing through. The corridor, which was more like a hallway, was glassed on both sides. The first door she passed had been marked with a sign that indicated it was the bathroom. That was annoying. It would be difficult to argue that she had missed it. She passed a cream sofa, a low glass table and a selection of vases and standard lamps. The open windows showed out onto a rock garden on the left and a view to the lake on the right. They were uncovered and made her feel particularly vulnerable.

She reached the end of the hallway. There were two large glass doors, and beyond them, a second vast living room. She saw a huge circular sofa, pieces of confusing modern art, an enormous television fixed to the wall and another spiral staircase in the centre that wound around a second clear glass lift shaft. There was a table with a fruit bowl. A bottle of wine and a corkscrew had been left on the table next to the bowl.

There was no one inside the room.

She opened the door and went inside.

It really was vast. She hadn't been able to see quite how big from the other side of the doors, but now that she was inside, she saw that the ceiling reached up to the third floor, thirty feet above the ground. There was a pool outside, the water lit from beneath with a series of twinkling lights. She paused, listening. She could hear the muffled bass from the party, but nothing more.

She went further inside.

There was a door to the north.

She crossed the room, paused at the door and then, when she was satisfied that the room beyond was empty, opened it.

There was a noisy clatter from inside as something toppled over.

She clenched her teeth, her stomach tight with tension, and waited. Nothing. The noise from the party would be helpful to her now. She waited a little longer, then went inside.

It was a smaller room, but still big. There was enough space for a large desk, a roller chair and several large bookcases. There was an overturned lamp on the floor. She had knocked it over when she opened the door. It looked like the room was used as a study. She found what she was looking for on the desk: a PC tower.

She crossed the room and was at the desk, ready to move the PC, when she heard someone behind her.

'Excuse me?'

She froze. She turned and saw a well-dressed middle-aged woman.

What?

She recognised her: it was Jasmin al-Khawari, Khalil's mother. The woman was wearing an abaya cinched by a belt featuring an oversized buckle and studded with Swarovski crystals. Her face, immaculately made up and bearing the signs of surgical intervention, was haughty and unfriendly.

What was she doing here?

She was supposed to be in Paris.

Khalil must have been mistaken, or his mother had changed her plans without telling him.

She guessed that he was about to find himself in a world of trouble.

That would be true for her, too, unless she was quick on her feet.

'I thought I heard something,' the woman said with no attempt to mask her distaste for her. 'You little *kafirs* running amok in my house.'

'I'm here for the party,' she said.

The woman's eyes narrowed. 'What are you doing in here, then?'

Isabella twisted her mouth into an awkward smile. 'I'm sorry. I'm a bit lost.'

'What are you looking for?'

'The bathroom.'

'Well, this *obviously* isn't the bathroom.'

'No, I can see that. I'm really very sorry. If you could show me where it is . . .'

Isabella took a step towards the door, but Jasmin stepped across to the side so that she was blocking it. Her lip curled with distaste as she asked, 'Do you think I'm an idiot?'

'No, I—'

Recognition bloomed on her face. 'I remember you,' she said. 'You were the little bitch who was with Khalil.'

'You're overreacting, Mrs al-Khawari. You—'

The woman lunged forward and gripped Isabella around the bicep. 'I'm not.'

'Let go! You're hurting me.'

'No, I won't let go. You know what I think? I think you came in here to steal something. That's what you are, isn't it? A thief? A nasty, ungrateful little *kafir* thief.'

Isabella jerked her arm and managed to free it from Jasmin's grip. The woman lost her balance and stumbled against the wall. Her face became clouded with fury, and before Isabella could raise her hands to defend herself, she slapped her hard in the face. The blow was sharp and stinging, and as Isabella put her hand to her cheek, she could feel the hot blood rushing to the surface.

They paused there for a moment, staring at each other. The woman's eyes were hot with anger.

'You little *bitch*!'

Jasmin came at her, reaching for her arm again.

Isabella reacted. It wasn't a question of panic; her training was much better than that. It was a hard-wired response, a reaction rendered automatic by hours of repetition. Her mother had taught her that in moments like this, instances of threat, there could be no equivocation. No second-guessing. The most effective self-defence requires an expression of force that either incapacitates the antagonist or makes it very clear that further aggression will be more trouble than it is worth. Her Krav Maga instructor had reinforced the message.

You didn't stop until the threat was neutralised, knocked out, disarmed or dead.

Isabella didn't consider any of that, at least not consciously.

She just reacted.

She dropped her right foot a half pace backward, closed her fist and delivered a straight right-handed jab. Jasmin wasn't expecting her to strike her; her guard was down, her avid hands clutching for her, and as Isabella transferred her weight through her core, leaning from back to front, the punch landed heavily on her chin.

It knocked the woman out instantly.

Her eyes rolled back into her head and her knees buckled. She toppled forward.

Isabella caught her and lowered her the rest of the way to the floor.

She looked back to the door. Nothing. No sound, save the thud of the bass.

She had to move quickly.

Pope had taken position on the same vantage point from where he had originally scouted the big lakeside property. The place was lit up tonight, the lights blazing and the reflection glittering far out into the dark waters of the lake. He held his binoculars to his eyes and scanned the estate, left to right, looking for anything that might suggest difficulties. He saw nothing. The last coach bearing guests to the party had arrived twenty minutes ago, waiting for the gates to open and then rolling down the driveway to the courtyard area. He watched as a handful of boys and girls, wearing not very much at all, stepped outside and disappeared into the house.

The property itself offered no additional information. Most of the windows were dark and others were covered. He could see oblongs of light that were cast by the picture windows that faced the lake, but those were angled away from him, and he couldn't see inside from this position. He would have to go up onto the wall, maybe even get into the grounds themselves, before he could get the angle to see inside them.

Something caught his attention, and as he turned his head and looked out to the south-west, he saw a glow of light as a car from the direction of Geneva negotiated the turn of the lake. The car continued towards them and then, turning the bend so that they, too, were visible, came more cars. Pope counted ten. The road was usually quiet. He had only seen three cars since he had been up here. He brought the binoculars to his eyes, found the cars and tried to identify them. It was too dark, and the glare of the headlights was too bright.

'Control, Nine,' he said into his microphone. 'I've got a convoy of vehicles approaching your position from the south-west. Be aware.'

'Copy that.'

Chapter Fifty

Jasmin al-Khawari was breathing, in and out, her eyes closed.

Isabella hadn't planned for this. She felt a flutter of panic. No, she said to herself. She had done the right thing. There was no other choice, not if she wanted to carry out Pope's orders. But now? She had to do something. She couldn't just leave Jasmin here. If she awoke and sounded the alarm before she had boarded the next bus out of the estate, she would be compromised. She started to breathe a little faster. Her pulse began to run. She concentrated on maintaining her calm.

Think, Isabella. Think.

There was a long electrical flex that connected the printer to the power. She pulled the jack from the socket at the back of the device, and removed the plug from the wall. Another flex supplied power to a standard lamp; she unplugged that, too. She took the two lengths of flex and made two loops. She took off Jasmin's shoes and secured the first one around her ankles. Then, arranging her arms so that they were behind her back, she fastened the second noose around her wrists. She cinched it tight between her wrists so that the knot was below her thumb joint, too far away for her to reach with her fingers. She pulled until both were tight and then fastened the loops together with the woman's belt. The windows were covered by thin curtains. She yanked on one of them, hard, and tore it down from the rail. She stuffed as much of the gauzy material into the woman's mouth as she could, unplugged the mouse and knotted the cable around her head so that it held the fabric in place.

That would have to do.

She returned to the desk and carefully turned the tower around so that she could get to the cables behind it. She remembered Pope's instructions and, working carefully, extracted the cable for the keyboard from the USB port. She opened her clutch and took out the lip gloss. She removed the small component and fitted it over the cable's USB jack. It was the same utilitarian beige, and when it was fitted, only the seam between the original jack and the extension suggested that there was anything there. It was hidden behind the tower, too, and would have been difficult to spot even if it was visible.

She pushed the tower back against the wall, put the lip gloss back in her clutch and went outside.

Khalil was there.

She felt a sudden emptiness inside her stomach.

'Khalil!' she said. It wasn't difficult to pretend to be surprised, but she played on it. 'You surprised me.'

'What are you doing?'

She would have to try it again and hope for a better outcome: 'Looking for the bathroom.'

'Really? You walked right by them. At the start of the corridor.'

'I didn't see them.'

'That's my father's study.'

And your mother is tied up inside it.

She faked a laugh. 'I can see that. Embarrassing.'

He looked at her for a long moment, and she couldn't tell whether he believed her or not.

What if Jasmin woke up and made a noise?

What would she do then?

Khalil shook his head, and a sly smile passed across his face. 'Never mind,' he said. 'I don't care where you go. At least you're on your own.'

She felt a stir of unease. She didn't like the way he was looking at her. 'The bathroom is back here? Could you show me?'

He didn't answer. Instead, he sauntered forward. 'I saw you come in,' he said. He pointed down to her wrist. 'Saw you had my watch on, too. You like it?'

She started to glance around, assessing her position in the room. 'Yes. Very much. I really need the bathroom – '

'It was expensive,' he said. 'You know that, right?'

She scanned for something that she could use as a weapon. 'I didn't ask you for it.'

He reached out with his left hand and grabbed her elbow. He pulled her arm up on the pretext of looking at the watch. 'Didn't say no, though, did you?'

'Khalil, you're hurting me.'

'Don't tell me you're like the others. They all think they can take what they want from me, no need to do anything in return. But it's not like that, is it, Daisy? Not like that at all. Nothing's for free. Everything has a price. You know that, right?'

He took her by surprise, taking her by the shoulders and pushing her backwards against the wall. He moved with her, pressing his body onto hers, his head dipping so that he could nuzzle her ear and the side of her neck. She wriggled, trying to slide away from him, but he took her wrists in his hands and pinned them above her head. He ground his groin against her pelvis, his breath coming in ragged pants. Isabella reacted instinctively, before she had time to think. She brought her knee up, the point crashing into his crotch. His mouth fell open, and he gasped. Isabella tingled with anger. He was doubled over.

He got to his feet, gasping for breath. He sobbed.

She hesitated.

He charged her, his shoulder catching her in the midriff and sending her back into the wall with a heavy thud. The back of her head cracked against something solid and her vision was cowled for a moment, long enough for Khalil to throw a right-handed punch that landed flush on her chin. The impact forced her jaw to close and her teeth sliced down into her tongue. She felt coppery blood in her mouth. She stumbled away even as Khalil closed, his fist raised again. She backed against an armchair, slid to the side and then, as he lumbered at her, tried to hop out of the way.

She was too dazed.

He wrapped his arms around her and, taking advantage of the momentum, brought her down onto a huge sofa and fell atop her.

He straddled her, pinning her waist. She tried to slap him, but he caught her right wrist in his right hand. She tried to strike him with her weaker left, but she couldn't reach. He brushed her blow aside and slapped her, hard, across the face.

'Who do you think you are?' he spat at her. 'You know how lucky you are to even be invited here?'

'Get . . . off . . . me . . .' she said.

'I don't think so.' He managed to catch her flailing left hand and pinned it, and her right, on either side of her head. 'You need to learn some respect.'

He leaned down toward her face. She yanked her head to the side, his tongue sliding down across her cheek. She struggled again, but he had all the leverage, and she couldn't move him. She felt warm blood in her mouth.

Pope was blind and frustrated. 'Snow, report.'

The agent was hiding in the undergrowth diagonally opposite the gates to the al-Khawari estate. *'I see them,'* he radioed. *'Ten vehicles. They're stopping. Shit.'*

'What's going on?'

'They're police. Repeat, it's the police. They're opening the gate. It's some sort of bust.'

'Are you compromised?'

'No, but I will be if I stay here much longer. I'm pulling back.'

Pope acknowledged the message, lowered his binoculars and took his cell phone from his pocket. He dialled and put it to his ear.

'Bloom here.'

Pope had briefed the spook earlier that evening that the operation would go ahead tonight. He had asked to be kept fully briefed.

'It's Control.'

'Go ahead.'

'Do you have any intelligence on a police raid on al-Khawari's house?'

'No,' he said. 'Not a thing. Why?'

'There are ten police cars outside his front gate right now. And Angel is inside.'

'I have no idea, Control. What police?'

'Swiss.'

'I'll make some calls.'

Pope heard Snow's voice in his other ear. 'Hold the line, sir.' He muted the phone. 'Control, Nine. What is it?'

'They're taking the gates down. And it gets more interesting. A man and a woman just got out of the car at the back of the line. They're both wearing FBI windbreakers.'

'Are you sure?'

'Positive. Clear as day.'

'Where are you?'

'Further back. I think I'm okay here.'

'Keep watching.' He took the phone off mute. 'Sir, the FBI are here too. You need to find out what's happening. I am badly unsighted here. Repeat, Angel is inside the property.'

'I understand,' Bloom said. 'I'll make a call and get back to you. Stay in position.'

Pope put the phone back into his pocket and brought the binoculars to his eyes again.

Snow spoke. *'They're through the gate.'*

He was right. Pope watched as the first car turned off the road and onto the driveway. The other cars edged forward. Blue and red lights flashed from the police cars as they raced to the house. The car at the rear of the line was a dark sedan with tinted windows.

The FBI? What was going on?

Isabella.

There was nothing he could do to help her until Bloom got back with details of what was going on.

Until he did, she was on her own.

Chapter Fifty-One

Khalil was too heavy for her. She couldn't plant her feet on the soft cushions, and when she tried, he let go of her left hand and slapped her again. She felt the searing heat of her anger flaring out of control.

She was angry with him, and more, angry with herself for putting herself in a position where this was even possible.

She heard her mother's voice in her head, reminding her to be careful, never to leave herself vulnerable, and still she had ended up like this.

Was he going to try to rape her? It didn't matter what he intended. As soon as she freed herself, she was going to kill him. Fuck Pope and fuck what he needed. She would kill him. She had seen the corkscrew next to the bottle of wine. She would take it and stab him in the eye.

'Stop struggling,' he gasped at her. 'I know this is what you want. I saw how you looked at me.'

He leaned down again and, with her wrists pinioned, managed to kiss her on the mouth. He left his head just a little too close, and she butted him, hard, crashing her forehead into his nose.

He yelled and pulled away.

She saw stars, shook her head to clear them and rolled off the sofa. She saw him, on the floor, blood running through the fingers that he had pressed to his face.

Her options were narrowing. She found herself back in the hospital room in North Carolina, the man who had persecuted her mother helpless in the bed before her, a gun in her hand pressed down over his heart.

'You butted me!' Khalil stammered.

Isabella felt the same way then as she felt now. No options. No choices. Only one way ahead.

She had known then that she would have to kill.

And she was going to have to kill again.

The corkscrew was close.

'My nose . . . you broke my nose!'

It was on the table.

Ten steps and she would have it.

'My *fucking* nose . . .'

She hadn't taken the first step when the doors to the room were flung wide.

Salim al-Khawari was standing in the doorway. His face was tight with tension. She remembered his temper and the things he was reputed to do during his rages. He left the doors open, and two of the security guards followed him inside. They were both toting submachine guns and wearing ballistic vests.

Salim looked at her and then at his son. 'What is going on?'

'Nothing,' Khalil said, his voice muffled through the hands that were still pressed to his face.

Isabella looked at the corkscrew, then at the men with the guns. She had a moment, she thought. She was just a girl as far as they were concerned. Not a threat.

Too dangerous. She dismissed it.

The anger tamped down to be replaced with coiled energy.

Salim crossed the room to Khalil and spoke with him. Isabella was too far away to hear what he was saying, but she could see from the way that he was gesticulating that, whatever it was, it had made him very agitated. She stepped over to the sideboard and reached for the corkscrew.

She watched as Khalil's expression morphed from shame and embarrassment that his father had crashed his party to something that looked very much like fear.

There was a loud crash from the study.

'What is that?' al-Khawari said.

The crash came again, and then the sound of a muffled voice.

One of the guards hurried across the room.

He tried the door.

'It's locked.'

The crashing came again, louder.

'Break it down.'

The man stepped back and kicked the door just below the handle. The bolt splintered through the frame and the door flew inwards.

'It is your wife.'

The second guard put his hand on Isabella's shoulder as the first man went inside the room and released Jasmin. He helped her up; she was unsteady on her feet and had to lean on him for support. There was a purpling contusion on the lower part of her face where Isabella had struck her.

Salim went to her. 'What happened?'

The woman pointed her finger at Isabella. 'She did this!'

'What do you mean, *ghazal*?' he said.

'She is a *thief*,' she spat. 'I found the little bitch in there. She was looking for something to steal. She hit me. She tied me up.'

Salim regarded her. There was something in his eyes, something more than anger and suspicion.

It was shrewdness.

'Maybe,' he said. 'Maybe not.'

'What do you mean, Salim?'

Isabella shrugged the man's hand from her shoulder. 'I'm not a thief.'

'I saw her, too,' Khalil said. 'I tried to stop her and she attacked me.'

Isabella knew: he was taking the chance to absolve himself, to neutralise the questions his father might have had for him.

The guard stepped to her. Isabella stared at his MP5.

'Is that right?' Salim said. 'Are you a thief?'

'No.'

'Liar!' Jasmin said.

Salim regarded her. His anger was still there, but now, Isabella thought, there was an inscrutability. A cunning. 'A thief? Perhaps. But perhaps you are something more?'

The first guard turned. 'Sir – we must go now.'

Salim nodded and gestured to Isabella. 'She comes, too.'

Isabella stepped back. 'What? Where?'

'Move,' the guard said.

'No. I'm not going anywhere.'

The man turned the gun on her. 'Don't be a silly little girl. Don't give me a reason to use this.'

Isabella felt that she was being sucked under.

Deeper and deeper.

She palmed the corkscrew so that the sharp end was hidden between her fingers and the shaft was obscured behind her arm.

And then she did as she was told.

Pope watched as a helicopter swooped down to the mansion from the east. He recognised it: an executive bird, an AgustaWestland

AW119 Koala. The helicopter swung around and touched down behind the sprawling buildings.

'Are you seeing this?' Snow radioed.

'Affirmative.'

'What do we do?'

'Hold position.'

He took out the cell phone again. The line to Bloom was still open.

'A helicopter has just landed, sir.'

'What about the FBI?'

'They're inside the property.'

'Where are you?'

'Outside the property. We haven't been seen.'

'Very good, Pope. Get out of there. The job's done.'

'You've got his computers, sir?'

'We do. Got access ten minutes ago. Your girl did well, Pope. It's done. Come home.'

'I need to be sure she's safe, sir.'

'The FBI will bring her out. She was just another girl at the party.'

Something about it all didn't strike Pope quite right. He had made a successful career listening to his gut. Success in this context meant that he wasn't dead, and there had been plenty of opportunities for him to have bought the farm.

'Control?'

'Yes, sir. I'm sure you're right. Please tell me when you know she is accounted for.'

'I will. Well done, Control. See you in London.'

Chapter Fifty-Two

Isabella moved to the door, the man pushing her between the shoulder blades as she went by him. He pressed a button on the wall, and electric blinds hummed as they lowered down the windows in the hallway, gradually hiding the view outside.

The second guard was behind her. She angled her wrist to hide the corkscrew from him.

She was pushed along the corridor that led out of the lounge and into a part of the house. They passed a flight of stairs that led up to a darkened landing, shorter corridors that branched off this one and several sealed doors. Isabella tried to get her bearings. They were heading away from the front of the house, away from the room that had hosted the party. She heard a new noise in the distance, muffled by the walls of the house, but obviously loud. Behind them, the sound of the music and the chatter of the guests faded away and then became inaudible as a door was opened and they were shoved outside into the darkness beyond. The noise crashed over them. A powerful, deafening roar. Wind whipped around them and debris stung her skin.

They were on the lawns that led down to the water. There was a helicopter, its blades slicing through the air, the downdraft flattening the grass and flinging tiny pieces of debris all around. She didn't know what sort of helicopter it was, but it was around twelve metres from end to end, and its fuselage door was open. The guard who had been behind Isabella hurried ahead, standing post near to the nose of the chopper, his weapon aimed towards the driveway and the gate. He was facing away from her now.

She felt the buzz of adrenaline. She wasn't going to get onto that helicopter.

A chance was coming. She had to take it.

The three al-Khawaris climbed into the back of the chopper, and Isabella saw an opening. The guard was preoccupied. He had turned away from her to help Mrs al-Khawari climb aboard. The quarter turn revealed a Beretta M9 in a holster that was clipped to his belt. Isabella had fired the M9 before. She was familiar with it.

She let the corkscrew drop down a little, revealing two inches of the sharp point and squeezing its spread arms in her fist. The woman was still unsteady on her feet. The guard boosted her up into the cabin.

Isabella darted ahead and plunged the screw between the man's shoulder blades.

In and out, in and out, in and out.

Quick strikes: one, two, three.

His body arched back and stiffened.

Blood speckled each time she pulled the point out of his flesh.

She released her hold on the handle after the third impact. It stayed there, buried up to the shank.

He reached both hands up to his back, showing the pistol.

She reached down and yanked it out of the holster.

He yelled out.

The noise of the rotors and the engine drowned it out.

Isabella centred the handgun in the web of her hand. Her thumb started up high, bumped the safety forward with the first joint, and finished in a down and forward motion. It was ready to fire.

The guard fumbled for the corkscrew that was still stuck in his back.

She drew a bead on the second guard.

Her finger tightened on the trigger.

Something crashed into the side of her head.

Isabella fell to the side, the gun falling from her grip.

Blackness fell over her, a moment's worth, and when consciousness returned, she was facing the house again. The lights were blurred, spinning kaleidoscopically, and she couldn't remember where she was or why she was lying on the ground. She felt hands beneath her shoulders and the ground fell away from her as she was hoisted up. She remembered – the helicopter – and bucked against the grip of the person who was trying to shove her inside the open door.

Arms wrapped around her torso, and she was manhandled inside. Salim and Khalil took an arm each and dragged. She was too dazed to resist.

The cabin had two facing rows of three leather seats. The al-Khawaris were next to each other in the row that faced aft. The second row of seats was empty. A third guard jumped up. Isabella hadn't seen him. It must have been him who had cold-cocked her. He pushed her into the seat farthest from the door, sat down next to her, and buckled her into her harness. He was big, and the seats had only a little space between them. She felt the bunched muscles in his arms and legs, the shoulder mass of his torso. She was woozy, but it wouldn't matter. There would be no getting across him to reach the door.

The first guard came in next. He slid the door shut, fastened his belt, put on a pair of headphones and spoke into a microphone that would connect him to the pilot. Isabella couldn't hear what he said, but almost instantly afterwards, the engines shrieked and the helicopter began to ascend.

She saw the man she had stabbed with the corkscrew. He was walking slowly back to the house.

They cleared the line of the buildings, and then the trees, and then the nose dipped down, and the helicopter began to speed ahead.

Isabella felt weak and nauseous. She blinked and, remembering what her mother had taught her, reached for the soft flesh beneath her arm and tweaked it as hard as she could. The pain flared and she focused on it, using it as an anchor until the disorientation had passed.

She looked through the window to her left. There was a blaze of flashing blue and red as a convoy of police vehicles raced down the drive to the house. She counted eight of them. Two came to a sudden stop in the courtyard next to the showroom where the sports cars were garaged, and eight men spilled out. The helicopter was gaining height all the time now, but even this high up, she could see that the men were armed. The other cars stopped, and more uniformed policemen, similarly armed, disembarked. She watched as they funnelled to the main door. The helicopter began to bank. One of the men was hefting a heavy battering ram, and the last thing she was able to see as they slid over the lawns to the east was the ram crashing into the door.

She looked at Salim. He was gazing out of the window, his jaw clenching and unclenching angrily. Jasmin was staring at her, contempt in her eyes. Khalil was looking out of the other window. Dried blood had crusted around his mouth, and he wouldn't look at her. The guard next to her was checking his weapon, and the other was talking to the pilot.

She turned to the window and watched as the glassy surface of Lake Geneva slipped beneath them.

Chapter Fifty-Three

The helicopter started ahead quickly and, as soon as it was clear of the line of the roof, rushed overhead and then out onto the water, heading back to the east.

Pope toggled the pressel on his radio. 'Control, Nine, Twelve. Report.'

'Twelve, copy.'

'Nine, copy. Orders, Control?'

'Pick me up on the road half a mile east of the house.'

Snow reported, *'On my way.'*

They picked him up five minutes later.

Kelleher swivelled around in her seat. 'Follow the chopper?'

'Yes.'

There was a road atlas in the back pocket of the driver's seat. Pope opened it and looked for the nearest airport.

'They're going to Sion,' he said. 'Commercial airport. Eighty, ninety kilometres east.'

'You worried about Isabella?'

'I don't know,' he said. 'Probably not. It's just . . . I don't know, I just want to be sure.'

'I can live with that,' Snow said.

'They'll get there a long time before we will. You think he has a private plane there?'

'I have no idea. But we have to find out.'

'You know what this is all about?'

'No.'

'The FBI?'

'London doesn't know. It could be a jurisdictional fuck-up. Wouldn't be the first time.'

The lake stood between them and the airport. The fastest route was to follow the E25 around the water in a clockwise direction, passing through or around Lausanne, Montreux, Aigle and Martigny. The satnav reported that it was a distance of 156 km and that it would take them ninety minutes. But it was late, the roads were clear, and Snow was a fast driver. Pope thought they might be able to make it in seventy-five.

Pope thought about Isabella. The girl had done well, as he had suspected she would. She was resourceful and confident. Her mother had trained her well. He would be much happier when she was safely back in Marrakech, though. She bore herself well, and she had had the kind of difficult childhood that would lead to an accelerated maturity, but she was still just a child. An unusual child, certainly – a prodigy – but a child nonetheless.

He was still thinking about her when Snow hit the brakes.

'Roadblock.'

Pope looked through the windshield. There was a car parked across the road two hundred yards away, a flashing blue light fixed to the roof.

'Police?'

Pope tried to think. It might have been fallout from the FBI raid on al-Khawari's estate. The Swiss police were involved. It was possible that they were stopping traffic to and from the area. The helicopter suggested that they had already missed their main target.

Perhaps they were being cautious to make sure they rounded everyone else up.

'Do I stop?'

'Yes. There's nothing to worry about. If they ask, we're driving to Lausanne.'

Snow braked harder and slowed the car to ten miles an hour.

Pope counted three men. One stayed by the car. The other walked toward them down the middle of the road, his hand held up, palm out, ordering them to stop. The other approached from the verge to their left.

'I don't like this,' Kelleher said in a tight, nervous voice.

It was dark, and visibility was limited, but something was off. The two men approaching them wore black fatigues with 'POLIZEI' stencilled over their breasts. Pistols in holsters were clipped to their belts. They wore balaclavas, but that wasn't unusual for armed police. The third man, the one by the car, was standing in a ready position. The rear door was open.

They all *looked* authentic, but there was something amiss that Pope couldn't quite define.

Snow slowed the car to a dead stop.

'Keep the engine running,' Pope murmured.

The cop indicated that Snow should wind down the window.

He did.

The two men drew nearer.

Oh *shit*.

He knew what it was.

The Swiss police were usually armed with Sig P225s, Glock 19s or H&K USPs, but these men were toting something very different. Now they were close, Pope recognised the weapons immediately. They were armed with FN Five-sevens, handguns that were infamous for their ability to penetrate certain types of body armour when they were equipped with the right load. The gun was controversial in the United States, and could only be used by civilian shooters with sporting ammunition.

Whatever they were, these men weren't Swiss police.

The man at the car idled across and stooped at the open rear door. When he emerged, he was cradling a C8 SFW Carbine.

The man on the road reached down to his holster, his hand resting on the butt of his pistol.

'Drive!'

Snow floored the accelerator.

The car leapt ahead, the engine screaming.

He drove at the man in the road, but he had seen them coming and was able to roll out of the way.

The second man pulled his pistol and fired three times in rapid succession.

The windscreen shattered.

Pope felt a splash of something warm and viscous on his face. He looked up and saw Snow lolling at the wheel, his head hanging at an unnatural angle. His foot must still have been on the gas because the car raced ahead, slammed into the rear wing of the blocking car, and careened off the road and down the slope that led to the water.

He heard the rapid crack-crack-crack of the C8 and the rear windshield detonated into the cabin. The car bounced over the uneven ground, a copse of trees fast approaching. Kelleher reached over for the wheel and yanked it, swerving the car to the right. They crashed through a patch of heavy brush, the front wheels launching off a slab of rock and the car twisting through the air. It landed on its left-hand side, throwing Pope against the window, the shattered glass flying all around him. It skidded for what seemed like an age, eventually slaloming through more trees and coming to a halt in a depression.

The engine was still running, screaming as the upturned wheels span impotently.

Pope was on his side, pressed up against the chassis, grass and small ferns poking into the cabin. He tested his arms and legs. He was uninjured. He reached for the seat-belt mechanism, released himself, and clambered out of the shattered rear window.

He looked up the slope. He could see the lip of the road. They had travelled three hundred yards, with parts of the descent steeper than forty-five degrees.

The lights of two torches bounced down the slope, coming closer.

Two hundred and fifty yards.

The terrain would slow them a little, but he didn't have long.

The car was ten feet from the water's edge. It was wedged against an outcrop of rock, on its flank, the passenger side highest. He clambered onto the rocks and then slid across the dented and scratched bodywork until he was over the window of the passenger door. It was still intact. He looked down and saw Kelleher's body slumped toward the ground. Snow was dead; he knew that. But she was unmoving, too.

He looked back up the slope.

The torches were closer.

Two hundred yards.

He pulled himself to a crouching position where he could stomp down against the window. He put the glass through with his second blow, knelt at the window and reached down for Kelleher.

'Kelleher!'

His fingers snagged the lapel of her jacket and he pulled. Her body was limp and fell back as soon as he released the tension.

'Hannah!'

Her head drooped, turning enough so that the moonlight fell on it and exposed the exit wound in her forehead. One of the rounds fired into the back of the car had found its mark. A lucky shot, but it didn't make her any less dead.

Pope felt a white-hot flash of anger, but he was professional enough to extinguish it almost as soon as it flared. He needed to make a quick assessment. He turned and looked back up the slope. The two men with the flashlights had negotiated the steepest part of the descent. They would be able to move more quickly now.

Pope wished he was armed.

He slid down from the car.

A bullet thrummed through the air.

He crouched as a second streaked at him, sparking into the underside of the car. The fuel tank was ruptured. A jet of diesel gushed out.

Pope ran. He had a good start on the two men, and he had to take advantage of it. He manoeuvred around the car, putting it between himself and his pursuers so that he might buy himself a moment of cover. The terrain was gently inclined now, a lazy slope that led down to the water. He saw the Dents du Midi Mountains on the other side of the lake and steeply terraced vineyards down to the lakeside. There was the dark water of the lake itself, and rising up from the north, the mountains of the Chablais Alps.

There was a fringe of aspen and fir between him and the water, and he sprinted for it, vaulting over an exposed shoulder of granite and crashing through knee-high undergrowth.

Another volley of gunfire passed overhead. They were too far behind him to do anything other than spray and pray. As long as he kept moving, he had a good chance.

Thoughts rushed through his mind in a headlong blur. Who were they? Why had they attacked them? They were masquerading as police – that much was obvious – but it was impossible to know anything more than that. Were they with al-Khawari? Someone else?

Pope reached the trees and turned to the north-east, following the shoreline. He stopped for a moment and checked. A large bank of cloud had rolled in and obscured the moon. There was some light pollution from the habitations on the other side of the lake and the lights of the second car up above, but that aside, the dark was deep and welcoming. It might have been Pope's only break. The torches had been put out, but he could see the dim shape of one man standing by the wrecked car. He heard the report of two gunshots. The man was making sure that Kelleher and Snow were dead. His eye was drawn to the lip of the incline. He saw the lights of another stationary car, this one turned towards the lake so that the beams cast out a golden arc fifty feet above him. Reinforcements?

He tried to assess what his pursuers would do. He assumed that they were professional, so the best way was to work from what *he* would have done. He would have sent one man into the tree line to follow him and kept the other one up high, boxing him in. The man in the trees would have to move more carefully in case he was lying in wait for him, but not too slowly; his lack of return fire would have been a good indication that he was unarmed.

He set off at a steady jog. It was bitterly cold, and the wind blasting in off the lake iced the chill into his bones. He moved in a north-easterly direction, keeping to the tree line. There were the occasional cleared spaces. He approached these with caution, waiting in cover before sprinting through them with his head down. The men were quiet. He didn't hear the sound of pursuit. There were no calls or shouts. It was too dark for hand signals, so he guessed they were operating with radios or phones.

He had been on the move for fifty minutes and had covered four kilometres when he saw a jetty with a boat tied to it. There was a boathouse at the start of the jetty. His path around the lake had taken him above several boathouses, but none of those had a boat on the water, and he didn't have time to break in and put one afloat. This was different.

He approached the boathouse. The jetty was made of wood and was a little the worse for wear. There was a boat tethered at the far end. It was a rowing boat with a small outboard motor. He knew that he would be taking a chance if he tried to use it. The jetty was exposed, and he had to assume that they would have seen the boat, too. It was an obvious means of escape. If he couldn't start the engine, he would be trapped and would, most likely, have to swim. The water looked icy. He doubted that he would get very far if it came to that.

The alternative was not much more appealing. Was it possible that there were more than just the three who were pursuing him? Could they call on reinforcements? Dogs? He was confident that he would be able to stay ahead of the men he knew about, but if they could summon more to cut him off to the north-east, he could very easily find himself boxed in. And then he would have to try to swim.

He had to try the boat.

He descended the last few feet to the shore, vaulted a wire-mesh fence and crept toward the jetty. The door to the boathouse was ajar, and light spilled out through the gap. He guessed that the owner of the boat was a fisherman who had been out on the lake for a spot of late night sport. Now he was making preparations to secure his boat for the night.

The jetty extended into the lake for twenty feet. He hurried along it. The boat and the motor both looked old, but he had made his choice now. He climbed aboard and unknotted the mooring rope from the cleat on the gunwale. He made sure the shift lever was straight up in the neutral position then pulled out the choke. He turned the handgrip until the arrow aligned with the start position, pulled the starter rope until he felt resistance from the starter gear and then pulled more forcefully. The engine started. He pushed the choke back in until the engine was running smoothly, turned the throttle control arm until the arrow lined up with the shift mark, and steered away from the jetty.

The first shots rang out almost as soon as he was clear of the structure. A series of crisp, sudden reports, and then little geysers of water thrown up just short of the boat. Pope flattened himself against the thwart, beneath the line of the gunwale, one hand keeping the tiller straight. He prayed the motor held up. If it stopped, or they shot it . . . More shots fired and two rounds found their mark, crashing into the transom and sending out two little showers of splinters. Another fusillade rang across the water, but the reports were more distant, and none of the rounds struck the boat.

He risked a glance.

He was five hundred feet away from the shore. He could see six figures by the jetty. Four of them had handguns, and the other two had carbines. The C8 had an effective range of one hundred and fifty yards, but it could reach three hundred or four hundred with a degree of accuracy if the shooter was any good. Five hundred yards meant he should be safe here. The figures were too distant to make out any details. As he watched, he saw one of them turn to the door of the boathouse and raise his arm. Pope saw another figure silhouetted in the light of the doorway, saw the flash of the gun and watched the figure fall back inside.

It was unfortunate, but there was nothing he could do about that. He turned to the east and assessed the way ahead. The lake was around two and a half kilometres wide at this narrowest point. He thought he would be able to make the crossing in fifteen minutes. He could see the lights of towns and villages all the way along the opposite shore. He would aim to make land again at Collonge-Bellerive.

He checked the time.

Ten.

He had a moment to breathe.

Snow and Kelleher were dead.

He couldn't allow himself the luxury of anger. He tried to work out the angles, any reason at all that might explain how they had been compromised.

He squeezed his eyes shut. He needed to know that Isabella was safe. If something had happened to her, he knew he would never be able to forgive himself. The doubts about his decision to involve her reasserted themselves, crowding over him. It was foolhardy, arrogant and dangerous to put a fifteen-year-old girl into a position like that.

What had he been thinking?

He reached for his cell phone, but stopped. Could he call her? What if she was in trouble? He shook his head. He had no choice. He had to know she was okay. He took out the phone, saw that he had a bar of service, and selected her number.

He pressed dial, listened to the ringtone, and waited for the call to connect.

The man climbed back up the incline. One of his associates had backed their car out of the way while the others began the pursuit. An eighteen-wheeler rumbled along the road, its engine roaring as it sped by. The man looked down the slope as the other member of the three-man unit clambered back up the slope. This man gave a shake of his head. He allowed himself a tight little curse and then erased the emotion. What was done was done. Very well. They would adapt.

He was still a little wary as he took out his cell phone and dialled the number for his handler. The call connected, and with a clipped precision that had come to be his hallmark, he reported that two of the targets had been eliminated, but the third, one of the two males, had evaded them. He absorbed the abuse that he had known would be due to him – he thought it was fair, given that he had failed to accomplish all of his objectives – and then asked for his orders. Once they had been delivered, he ended the call and passed on the information to the others.

He took out his torch and surveyed the road and the verge. The shell casings were scattered around, little copper nuggets that glittered dully in the light. He was uncomfortable leaving them behind, but there was no point in trying to find them all. There were too many to be sure that none were left, and leaving one was as bad as leaving them all. His plan had been to eliminate the targets in a more controlled fashion. If they had stopped, as he had hoped that they would, they would have been able to take them out with a minimum of shots, and in those circumstances, they would have collected all of the evidence before leaving the scene.

He would not normally have been so profligate. He was a man who had always believed that if a job was worth doing, it was worth doing properly, and this felt unprofessional.

He got into the car, his men sliding in behind him, and put it into gear and set off for Geneva.

Chapter Fifty-Four

They were in the air for twenty minutes before the pilot started to descend. Isabella used the time to come around from the blow that had knocked her out. She looked out through the window at the sparkling lights that flashed along both sides of a runway two or three kilometres to the north. They drew nearer, and she could see that it was a commercial airport. There were large jets pressed up against a terminal building, and as she watched, a 737 lumbered down the runway and blasted up into the night sky.

She tried to remember the maps that she had studied. Her focus had been on the immediate vicinity of Le Rosey and Geneva, but she remembered that there was another international airport to the east. She remembered the name: Sion.

The helicopter slowed over a private apron and started to descend. The guards stowed their weapons in two identical black tote bags and unfastened their seat belts. The wheels bounced a little as the helicopter landed, but the guards wasted no time. The man nearest to the fuselage opened the door and jumped down. He unclasped Jasmin's belt and dragged her out, looping a beefy arm beneath her shoulders to hold her upright. Salim and then

Khalil al-Khawari came next, then the second guard. He reached back up and took Isabella's hand, tugging her to the exit. She stumbled down into the vortex of downdraft, her hair whipping around her head.

The first guard led the way across the apron. Isabella could see an aircraft fifty feet away from them, its nose pointed towards the taxiway and the runway beyond. It was a smaller jet, sleek and aggressive looking. A private jet, she guessed. A Gulfstream or a Learjet or something similar, she didn't know which.

She tried to stop.

'Move,' the man said, taking her arm and dragging her forward.

'Where are we going?'

'Somewhere a long way away from here.'

She tried to shake off his hand, but he was too strong. A retractable flight of steps had been unfolded at the front of the jet, and he led her to it. They climbed aboard. The cabin was plush, with eight leather seats, racks of china and crystal and LCD screens fitted fore and aft.

The man slung her into one of the seats. 'Sit down and shut up.'

Khalil took the seat next to her. He fastened his belt, reached across her and raised the blind over the window.

She still had her clutch bag. Her cell phone started to ring.

Khalil heard it. He yanked the bag out of her hand, took the phone and looked at the screen.

'Who's Rupert?'

'My uncle,' she said.

One of the guards indicated that Khalil should throw the phone across to him. He did. The man removed the back of the phone and pried out the battery. He opened the door and tossed the pieces outside.

'Where are we going?'

He ignored her.

The second guard boarded and pulled the steps up behind him. The door was shut and locked, and moments later the engines whined.

'Khalil,' she insisted, 'talk to me.'

'It's too late now.'

'I don't understand. What's happening? Where are we going?'

He turned his attention to her. His eyes shone with anger. 'Home,' he said.

Epilogue
Chapter Fifty-Five

Aqil and Yasin Malik waited in line at immigration. The queue was long and served by a bored woman in a single kiosk. She ushered travellers forward, took their papers, compared them to their photographs and, always satisfied, sent them inside with a desultory wave of her hand.

Yasin fidgeted next to him. 'Come on,' he said.

The flight had been straightforward. Aqil had been unable to read the magazine he had found in the departures lounge. He couldn't concentrate on it, and the words wouldn't go in. Instead, he gazed out of the window at the clouds below them as they flew over Germany, Hungary, Romania and Bulgaria. They passed over the Black Sea and then over Turkey itself. Antalya was on the southern coast. After six hours, the jet started its descent. He watched as the landscape resolved into finer detail. He saw the terminal building, the buildings of the town spread across the coastline and, beyond, the deep blue of the Mediterranean Sea. There were palm trees, the lush greens tempered by bright yellow sand dunes, white-capped waves rolling in to shore. It looked beautiful.

'It's taking forever,' Yasin said. 'We need to get going.'

He was nervous. He had been that way ever since they had set off. Aqil had believed that it was the prospect of being stopped before they could leave the country, but the more he observed his brother, the more he realised that it was something more fundamental than that. For all his brash certainty that this was the correct path for them to take, he still doubted his decision. He was worried about their family and what they would think. There was fear, too: a fear of the unknown, of the things that they might be asked to do when they reached the caliphate. They had seen the YouTube videos and read the literature about what they could expect. It was easy enough for him to pronounce Allah's will from the security of their home. It was more difficult to find certainty when the prospect became less of an abstract idea and more of a likely reality.

They had a long day of travel ahead of them tomorrow. They would check into the five-star resort that they had booked with the travel agency in Manchester. It was important that they did that in order to minimise suspicion. It was more difficult to make passage through Turkey than it had been, and there was a suggestion that travellers who arrived on a package holiday and then did not arrive at their accommodation would be reported to the authorities. They would avoid that. ISIS had produced a glossy document that explained how best to make their way into Syria, and they were going to follow it to the letter.

'Come on! Why can't they open the other kiosks? This is ridiculous.'

It took another thirty minutes for them to pass through immigration. They had no luggage save their carry-on bags, and so they passed quickly through the arrivals hall.

The heat washed over them as soon as they stepped out of the air-conditioned arrivals hall.

Aqil stopped and tried to take it all in. It was a crazy, bustling place. Taxis bullied their way to the kerb as potential fares were shepherded by angry touts. Buses departed for the city. Families struggled with trolleys laden down with luggage. The air was full of the sound of arguments, crying children, the blare of car horns and the roar of jet engines. The sun pressed down on him, woozily hot, baking the asphalt. He was thirsty and hungry.

Yasin looked over the bedlam with bewilderment. 'We need a taxi.'

Aqil's attention was drawn to a blacked-out Mercedes Viano people carrier. It came out of a sealed-off area at the side of the main terminal building and nosed into the queue of traffic, the driver leaning on his horn as a taxi tried to cut in front of him. The taxi driver was persistent, and as the horn sounded again, the Viano nudged up against the car's rear wing. Both vehicles stopped. The taxi driver – a broad-shouldered, deeply tanned man with shoulder-length hair and a prodigious moustache – flung his door open, walked around so that he blocked the Mercedes' onward progress and then started to curse out the driver at the top of his lungs.

Aqil watched as two things happened at once. First, the driver of the Viano opened his door and went around to confront the driver of the taxi. He was big and mean looking, but the taxi driver did not back away. Rather than doing that, he spat at the man's feet. It might have been a mistake. The other man drilled him with a sudden punch, knocking his head back and dropping him to the surface of the road.

Second, and simultaneously, the rear door on Aqil's side of the Mercedes opened. He heard a shout from the cabin and then a flash of movement as a young, blonde girl stepped down onto the sill. He saw her, and behind her, a man and woman of dark complexion, a teenage boy – maybe the same age as the girl – and another, larger man wearing a dark suit. The girl was stopped as the woman wrapped her arms around her waist and started to haul her back. Aqil watched as the girl butted the back of her head into the woman's face, hard enough to loosen her grip. She was just about to break free completely when the man in the dark suit reached out a hand and grabbed the girl by the top of her arm. Aqil saw the effort on her face as she tried to break his grip, but he was too strong. He yanked her back so that she bumped up against the seat and yanked again so that she fell onto it. The teenage boy reached for the handle and pulled the door until it slid closed again.

It had happened in a matter of seconds, and it was so incongruous that, once the door had closed, Aqil almost doubted that he had seen anything at all.

The driver, who had made his way back to the car, now revved the engine. A space had opened up into the outside lane that promised a faster route to the road away from the airport, and he released the brakes and surged into it.

'You see that?' Aqil asked his brother.

'See what?'

'The girl—'

'Taxi!' Yasin shouted, interrupting him. 'Come on, it's stopping. Hurry, Aqil.'

They wheeled their carry-on suitcases across the sidewalk. The taxi driver opened the trunk and put them inside.

'Royal City Hotel, please,' Yasin said.

The driver pulled into the queue, and they crawled out to the main road. Aqil distracted himself by going over their plan again. They would start early tomorrow morning. They would leave the hotel, take a taxi to the railway station and then a train to Iskenderun in eastern Turkey. The journey traced the coastline and passed towns with names that Aqil did not recognise: Alanya,

Anamur, Icel, Ceyhan. From Iskenderun, they would take a taxi to Reyhanli. That would be where they crossed the border.

The short trip over the wire was known as the Gateway to Jihad. With a shiver of trepidation, Aqil couldn't help but feel he was teetering on the edge of something momentous, something that would almost certainly change him forever. He felt his stomach dip, but then he realised the unexpected feeling he was experiencing wasn't excitement. It was fear.

About the Author

Photo © 2014 Tom Nicholson

Mark Dawson has worked as a lawyer and currently works in the London film industry. His first books, *The Art of Falling Apart* and *Subpoena Colada*, have been published in multiple languages. He is currently writing three series. The John Milton series features a disgruntled assassin who aims to help people make amends for the things that he has done. The Beatrix Rose series features the headlong fight for justice of a wronged mother – who happens to be an assassin – against the six names on her Kill List. Soho Noir is set in the West End of London between 1940 and 1970. The first book in the series, *The Black Mile*, deals with the (real-life but little-known) serial killer who operated in the area during the Blitz. *The Imposter* traces the journey of a criminal family through the period; it has been compared to *The Sopranos* in austerity London. Mark lives in Wiltshire with his family.

Made in the USA
Columbia, SC
01 May 2018